Threads of Treason

To Bill, Ted and Rosie.

Threads of Treason

Mary Bale

Mary Bale
2015

CLAYMORE PRESS

First published in Great Britain in 2013 by
CLAYMORE PRESS
An imprint of
Pen & Sword Books Ltd
47 Church Street
Barnsley
South Yorkshire
S70 2AS

Copyright © Mary Bale, 2013

9781781591000

The right of Mary Bale to be identified as Author of this work has been asserted by her in accordance with the Copyright, Designs and Patents Act 1988.

A CIP catalogue record for this book is
available from the British Library

All rights reserved. No part of this book may be reproduced or transmitted in any form or by any means, electronic or mechanical including photocopying, recording or by any information storage and retrieval system, without permission from the Publisher in writing.

Printed and bound in England
By CPI Group (UK) Ltd, Croydon, CR0 4YY

Pen & Sword Books Ltd incorporates the Imprints of Claymore Press, Pen & Sword Aviation, Pen & Sword Family History, Pen & Sword Maritime, Pen & Sword Military, Wharncliffe Local History, Pen & Sword Select, Pen & Sword Military Classics, Leo Cooper, Remember When, Seaforth Publishing and Frontline Publishing

For a complete list of Pen & Sword titles please contact
PEN & SWORD BOOKS LIMITED
47 Church Street, Barnsley, South Yorkshire, S70 2AS, England
E-mail: enquiries@pen-and-sword.co.uk
Website: www.pen-and-sword.co.uk

Prologue

England 1081

The Impostor was not used to convent ways or a nun's habit. The clothes were harsh and the duties and prayers numerous here at the Priory of St Thomas the Apostle. But feigning deafness to avoid speaking had not been difficult – it was almost like a childhood game – and already the others seemed to hardly notice her. However, she'd only been allowed to clean the sewing room with Sister Gertrude and her patience was wearing thin. Waiting had made her nearly lose her mind and now she had her chance, she would take it, whatever the outcome.

The nuns were singing as they sewed; she could hear them from here. The corridor outside the chapter house, where she stood, was empty. Looking down at her white knuckles she examined the inkpot in her grasp – how long it had taken her to gather this dark liquid little by little and place it in this pottery vessel. Her fingers wrapped about its curved body and closed around its narrow neck.

This would be easy, she thought, speed was the answer. She mounted the winding wooden steps that led to the rooms above the south side of the cloister. Her walk betrayed the distinctive grace of an aristocrat as she made her way along the floorboards of the corridor. Even though the nuns needed every chink of light for their work, the door to the sewing room was shut for security. She went past it and slid into the stairway that connected a viewing area above her and, below her, the back yard access to the kitchens. This would be her escape route to her waiting lover, using the wood-pile to climb over the yard wall. But she would not put him at risk in any way.

Waiting for the nuns to take a break made every nerve in her body twitch. Any moment they were due to leave the sewing room and take a short exercise in the completed part of the cloisters. Although it was only moments before she was rewarded, it had seemed so much longer to her. She heard the door being unlocked and the nuns walking along the corridor and down the steps she'd just climbed. The click and clank of the door being shut and locked reached her, as did the shuffle of more nuns taking their leave. She heard Sisters Leofgyth, Winifred and Ethelburga among them. She slipped out of the tower entrance and felt along to the nearest of the row of stones under the windows that overlooked the cloister. There it was. Just as her lover had said it would be. One of the nuns had left it for her, it didn't matter to her who it was. Her fingers scrabbled for the key.

The door, her last obstacle. The heavy, imposing wooden impediment faced her. Her lover had asked her to do this. This was for him, for her love of him. Just one last check round – the sound of nuns walking and talking in the cloisters whispered up to her in the air. Snow was on its way, surely? It so often snowed between the feasts of Saint Valentine and Easter. Lent had seemed so long this year. The Priory observed the fast much more closely than she was used to at home.

She smiled as the key turned. She was in.

The Impostor found herself close to the panel the nuns were working on. She wanted to look at the work, but stopped herself: if it was too beautiful or so intricately worked she might falter in her task. The stopper on the ink eased loose with a twist of her fingers. The sour smell caught her nostrils.

'Don't do it, Sister.'

She swung round. Prioress Ursula was standing behind the door. She froze for a moment. Ursula was not tall but she matched her height. Age had broadened the Prioress's physique.

'So you are not deaf,' said Ursula.

The Impostor thought she could overcome her; though to be sure of success she had to act now. She went to throw the pot, but Ursula was there, gripping her wrist, forcing her hand up above them both, pouring the ink over them. Ursula's strength was considerable. Some of the ink caught the Impostor's mouth; she spat and spluttered to rid herself of the noxious fluid. She snatched her arm down, twisted it, and was free. The inkpot rolled away and she took to the corridor. Already the nuns were returning from their break, so she turned towards the tower steps, the kitchen and escape.

Below her on the tower steps, Sister Agnes was talking to a

kitchen servant in her steady tone. So the Impostor's only escape was upwards. She started to climb the stone steps, already fearing that there was no way out. Prioress Ursula was behind her. Her extra years might slow her down, but not by enough. Ursula had not had the pampered life style of the Impostor which made her breath short and her legs weak. She gasped in the freezing air and light above her. Cold, dry flakes of snow were falling steadily, chilling her. The viewing platform was already covered in a slippery layer of it. Ursula was only steps behind her. A castellated parapet wall was but an arm's length from her. Her body rocked against it as it stopped her forward movement. There had to be a means of escape from here. Snatching glances across the rooftops she hoped to see where the masons had been working on the Priory. Perhaps they had left a ladder she could reach? But there were no steps or roofs near enough to climb to, let alone ladders.

Beyond the wood she knew her lover would be waiting for her. He would not show himself, and she would not call him. After his allotted time he would leave. That was what had been arranged and that is what would happen. She would not betray him.

Ursula came up, out into the daylight. The Impostor leapt on her, but Ursula seemed to expand underneath her, pushing her off. The Impostor found herself bending backwards over the low part of the castellated parapet and looking down, straight down, through the swirling snow, at the ground. To contemplate jumping to her death was to contemplate suicide – a sin. To be forever damned. If she did not do so, then her lover may be compromised, and had she not already sinned for his love? Her condemnation would be his salvation.

'Don't be a fool, little one,' said Ursula. The endearment was typical of Ursula, always kind – and trusting. Ursula stood with her arms slightly out from her sides, the palms of her hands open, like a welcoming angel.

The Impostor looked at her.

'Who is behind this? This was not your idea, was it?' wheedled Ursula. She moved forward half a step.

The Impostor frowned.

'Was it an Anglo-Saxon?' asked Ursula.

Even a small movement of her head could put her lover at risk. The Impostor stepped onto the parapet.

'No,' said Ursula moving towards her.

There was also the nun who'd left her the key to the sewing room to protect. By protecting her, she would hide the path to her lover. Only Ursula had seen her in there; she too would have to die. She would take her with her. The Impostor grabbed at Ursula and jumped. The calm of knowing she was going to die was replaced by the fear that wracked her body from the rush of air and the endless fall. She screamed until the scream was killed by the harsh ground.

Chapter One

The masons had been asked to stop work as the morning shadows from the pillars touched the darker shadow of the grave.

Just outside the chapel, Bishop Odon de Bayeux was introduced to the first two nuns in the procession of mourners by the surveyor monk, Richard of Caen. The surveyor's plump hand gestured towards the front of the convoy of nuns, tracing a path from the priory. There stood two women who were tall and about forty years of age. One of them held herself tightly and, although handsome, with intelligent blue eyes, she had the appearance of an eagle watching its prey. She was Sister Ethelburga. The other nun was Sister Winifred, whose face was kinder and softer. She also had blue eyes but these were of a warmer hue. Sister Winifred had a dainty elegance that was unforced. She greeted him with a smile. Bishop Odon held out his hand to them and they bobbed down in turn to kiss his ring of office.

He also recognised Sister Agnes who was openly weeping at the back of the eleven women. He knew her to be a friend of the Prioress. No one comforted her.

The mourners were to walk from the unfinished Priory of St Thomas through the gatehouse to the back of the chapel where the builders were working on the next phase of the building. They had already laid the foundations and built up the inner wall to seal off the priory from the outside world. The rest of the construction was barely started. Structural timbers and stones were arranged about the building site. The hole in the floor created here was to be the late Prioress's grave. The late February snow had been piled up on each side of the path from the gatehouse to the grave for the funeral procession. At the grave the snow had been scraped to the side and then the earth from the hole had been mounded on top of it. The builders had dressed all with planks of wood. A small area of ground had also been cleared for the mourners to stand on.

Bishop Odon led the troop of mourners from the gate-house. Stopping by the grave, he adjusted his bear-skin lined cloak about his shoulders, and noticed Alfred, Prioress Ursula's brother. There was a certain measured lack of expression on Alfred's evenly featured square-shaped face. He looked up and then bowed in acknowledgement of the high-ranked clergyman. The body had already been laid in the bottom of the grave, which the mason had lined with five pieces of stone to make a coffin. A stone slab stood ready to cover it on completion of the service.

Odon looked down at the wrapped body. How small people looked in death. And he started praying. The words were so important to him. When the words stopped he took a moment to reflect; winter took so many victims. But how could such a thing have happened when he was only a few miles away in Rochester? Prioress Ursula was a good woman, had been a good woman, he corrected himself. A pillar of this small community of nuns, surely she had been innocent? He tried to ignore the rumours as he looked round at them. He knew they were all Anglo-Saxons, or English as his half-brother, King William of England and Duke of Normandy, called them, but their religious conviction was without fault. He had to accept, though, that at least one had already proved to be a traitor and her burial was to be without ceremony or attendance, conducted on unsanctified ground.

He glanced up at the congregation. Next to Sister Agnes was a wide nun who was very short and of ruddy complexion. The rest were just young women who could sew. He had to, at least, show them respect for the work they undertook at his direction. The words of parting to the next life completed, he raised his large pale hands to bless the cold group of eleven nuns and Prioress Ursula's brother, Alfred. He had stood throughout the ceremony like a carved rock wrapped in his cloak, but bare headed in the freezing wind exposing his fair, weathered skin and silvered hair. Odon remembered when it was corn yellow.

He wanted to speak to the East Anglian after the service, but Alfred was already leaving. A groom had brought out a black cob which he mounted. Before Odon could call or move, Alfred had turned his horse and was heading towards the builders' encampment in the valley.

Who was behind this outrage, Odon wondered. The last panel of the embroidery was almost destroyed, but the nuns involved were dead. He looked again at those before him. A couple of the young women were clearly twins with matching light brown hair and dull eyes. They had large, big fingered hands and he considered the cleanliness of their clothing inadequate for the occasion. They were clearly not involved in the sewing. They stood with their bodies slightly turned towards each other as if an invisible piece of string was trying to pull them together. Two or three of the girls could be described as beautiful. Of those, two were clearly Anglo-Saxon in build and colouring and the third was a dark haired girl possibly a Britain from the west of the island. The wide one wiped her nose on the back of her hand and coughed while Sister Agnes lent her a small clean square of cloth. Sister Agnes was a friend of Prioress Ursula. He could trust no one in England anymore. There was so much more at stake than the embroidery.

'Bishop Odo,' said Sister Ethelburga, suddenly beside him. He noted her expectant voice using the English version of his name. He would have to choose a successor for Prioress Ursula in the absence of Abbess Eleanor. No doubt this was why she was here. He tried to avoid her cool, azure stare. 'Yes, Sister,' he replied.

'I want to talk to you before you leave for Normandy.'

'I will meet you in the chapter house in a few moments,' said Odon. He wanted to collect his thoughts. Having removed his vestments he took himself up to the first floor rooms on the south side of the cloister and used the Prioress's keys to gain entry. Lifting the protective sheet, he gazed upon the last panel of embroidery being worked; all the threads were neatly finished, all the stitches small and full coloured. These women were truly skilled. The panel was, at least, undamaged. Not a drop of ink had reached it. He gazed at the wooden screen at the end with the threads arranged in order of their colours. Everything looked in general good order but his frown deepened. When he commissioned this great work he'd wanted it finished in time for the completion of the Bayeux Cathedral. But, with the warring in Normandy at that time, it did not seem to matter that the embroidery was progressing so slowly. It seemed like a blessing. Now, with this terrible incident occurring in the Priory, he regretted not getting the work completed sooner. Still, the Royal

Court would be in Bayeux for Christmas and he was determined that the embroidery would be there too. At present he couldn't risk the work continuing. He was short of time so he left the sewing room and locked the door. Outside, instead of turning right to go down the steps towards the chapter house he went left and up the stone tower steps.

Looking over the white blanket of snow across to the coppiced woods, he wondered whether he ought to move the embroidery, but that may be more dangerous than leaving it here, if the Anglo-Saxons were keen to attack it. And if he spoke of this to King William there would be yet more deaths. Odon himself had been a man in his prime when he'd fought alongside his half-brother to take this land, but he knew God did not want him to waste life. He sighed and ran his fingers through his greying red hair. Secrecy was best, as always. He needed to talk to Abbess Eleanor. This priory was, after all, under her jurisdiction. He would arrange for her to investigate this matter herself, and at that time the work could continue.

Odon's gaze was attracted by activity below. People were setting out from the infirmary with a handcart. The servants and a nun he took to be the one of the Infirmaries toiled through the snow down the hill and along the edge of the coppiced wood in the valley. A burley man was pulling the shafts while the others pushed when needed. This was the other body being taken out to its resting place. He turned away. Now it was time to see Ethelburga and give her due authority. Under the circumstances she seemed the right person for the job. He could no longer delay his trip across the small expanse of ocean to Normandy.

Normandy, France

'Sister Therese, wake now,' said Sister Miriam. 'The Abbess is asking for you.'

'It is not time. Go away.' She'd lived in this abbey all her life, but still the place felt foreign to her. 'There are hours before our next prayers, Sister Miriam.' Therese lowered her blanket and gazed at her fellow novice. There were rules for every part of their day, mostly of silence. She'd never heard Miriam so excited. Her friend's round face was beaming like the midday sun and her eyes were like polished walnuts. Miriam was almost bouncing in front of her.

'Bishop Odon has been here all night talking to our Abbess.'

Therese threw her blanket on the floor and Miriam helped her on with her habit.

'Why is she asking for you, Sister Therese?'

'I don't know, Sister Miriam.' Therese straightened her novice's veil. It was so dull and insignificant compared with the full veil she would get when she finished her noviciate.

'You look fine, Sister Therese. All soft blue eyes and rosy cheeks, you could look innocent of the most heinous crime without any effort. Just watch that pointy stubborn chin; and those eyes don't always look straight ahead and slightly down as they should.' Miriam adjusted the position of Therese's head.

'Do you think I'm in trouble?' asked Therese.

'Who can say? We are young, foolish and brave. We are expected to get into trouble.'

'If I listened to you I would always be in trouble,' Therese admonished her friend and tried to tie her rope girdle.

'Quick, they are in the visitor's hall.' Miriam set off through the door and along the passage so quickly Therese had to run, despite her naturally long strides. Running along corridors, she knew, was forbidden. She tried to walk a few paces, but could not. Sister Miriam stopped by a wall hanging.

'What have you stopped for?' asked Therese.

Miriam pulled back the wall hanging and revealed a door. 'It leads into the visitor's hall.' She opened it so a crack of fading firelight fell on them.

'I never knew that was there,' said Therese.

'Hush, I can hear voices. I can hear Bishop Odon and Abbess Eleanor talking,' whispered Miriam.

The Novices leaned their heads towards the stonework. They heard a man's voice. It was gravelled like a voice that had been worn down by much use and deep from age and his authority clipped a little at the words. 'Abbess Eleanor, I need you to leave here and go to England. A guard of my knights will escort you.'

'Sister Miriam, we should not be listening,' scolded Therese quietly.

'Wait, Sister Therese.' Miriam caught her arm. 'Listen.'

Abbess Eleanor could be heard saying in her level tones, 'I can't believe Prioress Ursula is dead.'

A curl of dark hair came loose as Miriam nodded at Therese. 'You are right. We should not be listening,' she said. Miriam pushed back the unruly strands of hair, closed the door and set off up a stone stairway.

Therese pointed to the door. 'Where are you going?' she asked. 'Why can't we go through this door to the visitor's hall?'

'Because the Abbess will know we heard them from here. This door is not meant to be in use. There is nothing that woman cannot work out. I cannot afford the penance for such a sin.'

'A sin is still a sin, whether you're caught or not. The truth is always the truth,' said Therese following her.

Miriam turned, straightened Therese's veil, divided the fair hair falling in front of her face evenly and tucked each piece neatly into the edges of the veil. She stood back to examine her work. 'There, that's better,' she said.

A few more strides took them to the main entrance door to the visitor's hall. Therese was in front. She looked around to tell Miriam how nervous she was and found herself alone. After a moment she pulled herself straight and opened the door.

Bishop Odon and Abbess Eleanor were sitting opposite each other by the fire. The glowing embers cast shadows across their faces and picked out the reds and golden colours of the brightly painted walls.

'Come in, Sister Therese,' said the Bishop.

Therese rushed towards him and nearly fell at his feet, eager to show her deference, her obedient respect. He stretched out his hand and she kissed his ring of office.

'You may sit,' he said. Abbess Eleanor beckoned her to a stool close to the dying fire. The facets of her black rosary beads caught the flickering light.

Therese glanced up from her position to look at the Bishop. His beady eyes shone out from his pale skin; they were enquiring but gentle. 'Abbess,' he continued, 'Sister Therese is already a young woman. Does she speak the language of the Anglo-Saxons?'

Therese looked up at Abbess Eleanor and noticed a hint of hazel in her eyes, reflecting the gold of the embers. The Abbess's serene face was slightly etched by the responsibilities of her office, but she also looked well cared for considering her half-century could only be a few years away.

'Indeed, Your Grace. We have taught her as best we can, she knows Latin, and she reads and writes.'

'I have arranged a grand token of the Church's esteem for my half-brother, William Duke of Normandy. It is an embroidery showing him claiming his rightful lands of England. It will be exhibited at Christmas in Bayeux Cathedral.' The Bishop's greying hair formed an evenly trimmed frame to his rounded face.

'Your Grace,' said the Abbess. 'She does not need to know all. The less she knows the safer she will be, surely?'

'You are probably right,' said the Bishop taking a poker and rattling the embers with it, 'but this is already common knowledge. It is also common knowledge that some would like it destroyed.' Therese noted the Abbess give the Bishop a warning look. The Bishop gave in to her pressure. 'You, Sister Therese,' he continued, 'are to accompany your Abbess to Canterbury in England. You will be useful to her with your skills. Now go and ready yourself. You leave before dawn for the coast. At last the weather has improved. You really must cross the channel before it deteriorates again.'

'But…' said Therese.

'We have taught you better than to question our decisions, Sister Therese,' said Abbess Eleanor. 'England is our destination.'

'It is a foreign land,' said Therese.

The Bishop smiled indulgently at her and rested the poker in the hearth.

The Abbess patted her hand. 'A difficult time awaits us there, without doubt, Sister Therese. We will trust in God. The Bishop has instructed us and we have his protection. Two of his own knights will guard us.' The Abbess frowned at her. 'But you have never shown fear before, Sister?'

'I am not scared. I would just like to know if Sister Miriam will be coming with us.'

'Just you and I, Sister Therese, will be travelling to England. Sister Miriam will remain at Bayeux and pray for our success.'

Therese sat on a bench next to Abbess Eleanor as the wind fuelled the boat's momentum, pulling them away from the Normandy coast. They were positioned in the body of the vessel, just before the mast.

Suddenly the world seemed so large. She licked her lips; they were salty. Surely God had truly worked to make this wondrous place with the movement of the water and the vastness of the sky above it. Among the complement of guards were the two knights promised by Bishop Odon. They took up their positions: one at the bow, the other at the rudder. Both wore chain mail tunics and helmets with nose-guards; they carried heavy swords and shields shaped like birds wings. Norman knights, Sir Gilbert and Sir Brian, both with the height and strength of their Viking ancestors. Their very presence made Therese feel safer, but her Abbess seemed uneasy. She caught the odd glimpse under the Abbess's sleeve of the golden cross she used sometimes. Abbess Eleanor clasped it in her right hand and touched it with her left index finger. Therese had never seen her so preoccupied.

The boat turned in to the open sea, towards England's coast. Cold spray found their faces. As the hours turned the sun from east to west so the movement of the water beneath them became rougher.

'I'll fetch us something to eat,' said Abbess Eleanor. The cross had been secreted in one of her pockets but her rosary beads still hung by her side from her girdle.

'I'll go,' said Therese. If the Abbess required food, it was surely her job to fetch it for her.

But Abbess Eleanor shook her head and laid a hand on her shoulder as she rose. Therese had noticed the care she'd taken in stowing the casket she'd brought on board containing their food. It had been placed with that of the boatmen, alongside the supplies for the guards and knights. But when Abbess Eleanor came back she brought nothing with her.

'Are you hungry?' she asked Therese.

'My stomach could not take anything, Abbess, with the boat rising and falling like this.'

'That is just as well,' said Abbess Eleanor, taking back her seat on the bench.

The boatman cast a cover over them. 'That will keep the spray off you,' he said, so they sat under it, as in a makeshift tent.

'You may never see your home again, Sister Therese,' said the Abbess.

'No, Abbess?'

'No, Sister. Nor may we see Normandy or France again.'

'The sea will not take us, Abbess.'

'It may not be the sea that takes us, child.'

Therese searched the eyes of her Abbess. She'd never called her 'child' before, even though she'd lived all her life in the convent with her. She could not fathom the Abbess's thoughts.

'We have someone on board we cannot trust. I packed the food myself and it has been tampered with.' Her frown deeply furrowed her brow.

'Perhaps they were just hungry?'

'Nothing has been eaten,' said Abbess Eleanor. 'I placed wax seals on the pots myself, and they have been broken.'

'We must tell our guards.'

'I fear it was one of them that did it, child.'

'But if we do not they could be…' Therese daren't say the word, "poisoned".

Before either of them could say anything a blast of wind caught their cover and a wave tossed the boat up. It came crashing down the other side. Therese and the Abbess were thrown off their bench. The boatman shouted at them to move as the crew needed to bring down the sail. They braced themselves against a strut running across the boat while the work was hastily undertaken. Just after the Abbess and Therese were re-installed into their position, with their tent over them, a shout went up, 'Man overboard!'

The corner of their sheet flipped over revealing a group of men stooped over the stern of the boat, but the knight who was stationed there was not among them. The men were looking out into the black sea.

'We have no hope of finding Sir Brian in this storm,' the boatman told Abbess Eleanor. 'It is set to get worse. We must make haste for the English coast. It is not far now.'

Therese pulled at Abbess Eleanor's sleeve; the meticulous woman's clothes were dishevelled. Therese said to her, 'Do you think Sir Brian ate anything?' All sense of safety was draining away with the loss of one of their protectors.

The Abbess nodded in acceptance of the idea, but said, 'I doubt if he had, but I will ask. In addition, I will instruct the food to be put overboard. If any of it is left. We must take every precaution.' She made her way slowly over to the remaining knight and the boatman at the rudder. Abbess Eleanor held what she could to keep her purchase with the rolling sea beneath her. Therese heard the boatman's voice raised against the wind and sea in reply; he would carry out her instructions. She saw his head dip towards the Abbess and say more in a way others would not be able to hear. She replied in a like fashion. They spoke thus for some moments before he returned to his duties.

Watching her return, Therese pondered the possibility that the missing knight could have been pushed overboard by a traitor still on the boat. These thoughts spilled out into words as the Abbess sat back next to Therese and pulled the cover over them.

'I have already asked, Sister Therese. The sea is rough, no one saw anything. They are sure it was an accident and that is almost as bad, because the boatmen think such a thing is a bad omen. So, I have set them to praying as they work. It will keep their minds off such nonsense.'

Having settled the makeshift tent, Abbess Eleanor turned to Therese in the darkness cast by their covering and said, 'I am going to tell you a story. This is a true story and it may protect you in England if anything happens to me. Now listen, child.'

Therese reached out and touched Abbess Eleanor's hand, 'I'm not afraid,' she said. The Abbess gripped her hand in turn, her long sleeve slipped back, showing a heavy ring. Therese recognised it as belonging to Bishop Odon. It was not his ring of office but a small red jewel she'd seen on the smallest finger of his left hand. The

Abbess wore it on the middle finger of the same.

'You ought to be scared,' said the Abbess tilting her head so she spoke directly into her ear. 'You were born into a land of fire and death. You are an Anglo-Saxon. You were born in the summer of 1066.'

Therese frowned and said nothing. To argue the nature of her Norman heritage with her superior would be impudent. To cry would be weak and to exclaim that she always knew she was different and belonged elsewhere would be ungrateful.

'When,' continued Abbess Eleanor, 'William Duke of Normandy crossed the channel to conquer that usurper of England's crown, Harold, one of the ships landed at Romney away from William's fleet at Pevensey Bay. The people of Romney killed all our brave men aboard that vessel. When the Battle of Hastings took place Bishop Odon fought alongside his half-brother, William. The Pope himself had sent his backing for the enterprise.'

'Our Duke defeated Harold and became King of England,' said Therese proudly.

'Please listen, my dear. The people of Romney had to pay for what they'd done to the ship that landed there. King William laid waste to the village.' The Abbess stopped.

'Go on, please,' said Therese. She sensed some difficulty for the older woman in what she had to say. 'I want to hear the truth.'

'At Romney, Bishop Odon found a baby girl hidden when all else was dead and burnt. A blonde baby. The baby was you, Sister Therese. He hid you inside his robes and sent you back to me in Normandy for safekeeping. I have brought you up as he asked and now he is returning you to your homeland.'

The story was so strange. Therese hardly attached it to herself. 'But that is not why we are going to England, Abbess. I do not need an escort of knights, I am just a simple novice. Bishop Odon said something about looking after a great embroidery for his brother.'

'The reality of your story will take time to settle on you. And you must understand that we cannot look after the embroidery, Sister. Two nuns and a few guards would not be enough to protect it, even without a traitor among us. No, I have been sent to find out who is behind the difficulties at the priory where the last panel is being made. If we can uncover any problems we do not need to confront them ourselves, we can inform Bishop Odon and he will find a remedy for the situation. I only tell you this so you know what you are up against if anything happens to me.'

Therese gripped Abbess Eleanor's hands. 'Do not fear, Abbess. I will finish your work if you are unable to do so yourself.'

'No, you must not, Sister. I am telling you this so you will leave well alone and, if you fall into danger and you cannot reach Archbishop Odon, declare your Saxon blood. Now, the sea is getting rough again. You will need to hang on. With God's help we should not be far from the English shore.'

Therese partly accepted the words of advice from her senior, but her heart refused to accept them. She suddenly realised how soaked and cold she was. The sea water had penetrated to her skin and every time the tent moved a blast of wind took away more of her body heat.

She wanted to consider her new history, but could not as it took all her energies to hang on to the boat. The sea heaved and the boat was kicked by the waves; sometimes it gave to them, other times it rode them and sometimes it seemed to fight them. The boatmen yelled at each other and Therese felt her thrill of life shift to wanting to live just a while longer. God, she thought, would not mind waiting for her. She curled up in the bottom of the boat until the movement and shouting subsided. She wasn't sure if they'd reached safety even when she felt the boat scrape on sand. In the dark she could not tell if she'd reached the land of her birth.

Abbess Eleanor was holding her shoulders and pulling her upright. The Abbess had already straightened her clothes. 'We are here,' she said. 'Tidy yourself. I have spoken to our remaining knight, Sir Gilbert. He will be coming with us to Canterbury. I will dismiss the others. I cannot trust them.'

'But we need more than one knight to guard us, Abbess?'

'I cannot take the risk, Sister Therese. We have our own investigations to make, and we must not be prevented from completing them. It is the only way I can be sure we will not have a traitor with us.' With the sea behind her the Abbess seemed to have regained her authority.

'Yes, Abbess.' Therese tried to sound as if she understood, but she remembered clearly the Bishop's instructions to help the Abbess. And this woman was her superior in every way.

'We will go on to Canterbury through the night. I am told Lympne Castle is not far from here. They will provide us with dry clothes and a cart, and a wagoner to drive us.'

Therese didn't doubt Abbess Eleanor's ability to do as she said and she soon found herself in dry clothes with her wet habit bundled into a roll placed in the back of the cart. The simple garments she'd been loaned were not dissimilar to those she'd removed. Abbess Eleanor had insisted on wearing her own clothes but had been heard to compromise. She wore her own over tunic, a fresh, dry borrowed chemise and a borrowed cape lined with lamb-skin. Therese was seated next to her on the front seat of the cart headed for Canterbury. A wagoner had been engaged to drive the vehicle and Sir Gilbert rode next to them.

Therese greeted the wagoner, who grunted in reply and pulled his hood down further over his head like a man wanting his bed. She fell to praying. It comforted her to pass the beads of her rosary through her fingers as she recited her Ave Marias. The Abbess did not seem to be praying. She sat upright, staring at the stars in the clearing sky.

'I feared this, Sister Therese,' she said. 'I begged Bishop Odon to leave you in Normandy. You would have been safe there.'

'But only half-alive,' said Therese forgetting to grip the bead she was up to firmly. Her fingers slipped. She looked down at her rosary. She would have to start that set of ten again.

'I may have brought you to your death, child.'

'I will say an extra rosary for good measure.' Therese smiled to herself. She was beginning to sound like Sister Miriam.

'To be sure,' agreed the Abbess and she returned her attention to the sky.

Chapter Two

Normandy, France

Odon de Bayeux came out of the chapel. He was energised and comforted by his prayers. Today would be a better day. The rising sun brightened the host of painted angels on the wall. The birds captured by the artist flew among the heavenly creatures and Odon fancied they sang with the voices of the birds outside.

Feet fell on the stone corridor beyond the turning ahead of him. They took him back to his youth, when his mother's other, elder son was already Duke of Normandy. The young Duke William would run with the same step as that which approached him now. The owner of the steps came around the bend and halted in front of him. Robert. None of the males of the family were tall, but Robert had always been the shortest. Queen Mathilde had always held out hope that as a boy he would catch up with his recently departed elder brother, but he was soon overtaken by his younger brother, William Rufus, and the Queen let the matter drop. Odon could see the likeness to his father in his steady eyes and strong limbs, but there was a gentleness about him that was not like his father and a laugh which could only have been inherited from his mother, Queen Mathilde.

'Uncle, you will risk my father's ire coming here,' Robert said with a frown. 'I am already virtually an outcast.'

'I have risked King William's anger more than once, Robert. But it is always a pleasure to see my nephew.'

'Being my father's half-brother does not make you untouchable, Uncle, nor will being a member of the clergy bother the King of England. He is just as likely to throw you into prison as a plundering Dane.'

'You have fought him yourself, Robert.'

'Only because he gave me the Dukedom of Normandy but will not let me rule in my own right.' Robert looked out of the window. 'You have always fought alongside him.' He turned to face him. 'So how many sons have struck their own fathers in battle?'

'He has learnt to give you some distance,' said Odon.

'Yes, but I have tried to do as he has asked. I even fought for him in the North of England putting down the uprisings against us in that area – as you well know.'

'Yes, I too was involved with that and a lot besides,' said Odon.

'And still he will not let me rule Normandy,' Robert protested.

'You will. He has promised.' Odon could see that Robert was turning to his old grievances.

'I might as well not be the eldest son. He will not name me as his successor to the English throne. He is saving that for Rufus. He is always with my father, but I have to spend most of my time here, powerless. Even Henry gets all that he asks for.'

'Stay your hand, Robert. Your brother Henry is barely more than a child. He is no challenge to you. And you are not at war with your father now. Let this amnesty breathe awhile so peace may have a life.'

'I've not come for your advice, Uncle. I have come to advise you. You know my father expects you to be in England.'

'Protecting the South coast from the Danes. I know, I know. Like you I am a caretaker King for a King that makes endless war. And, like you, I grow weary of the demands. I have been a warrior for him, but he also appointed me Bishop and that is where I see my future now.'

'He will not appoint you Archbishop of Canterbury. The monk Lanfranc holds that post.' There was a teasing glint in Robert's eye.

'I do not want it, Robert, no matter how much that old Italian monk vexes me. Bishop of Bayeux is status enough for me. Once I have completed my present task I will settle in to the holy life.'

'You have not settled to it before,' said Robert with a grin.

'Robert, that is no way to address a Bishop,' smiled Odon.

'The only person who can speak to you thus is my father, the King,' conceded Robert.

'One day you may have that right, Robert, but not now.' Odon watched the young man. His muscles were like his father's. He was at his prime as a warrior with experience and skill but with none of his strength lost to age.

Robert looked back out of the window and Odon could not

fathom the young man's thoughts. But he was already more than a young man at twenty-seven. Uncles can so easily forget such things. Odon scolded himself and set to take his leave when Robert caught his arm. There was a sudden loss of loneliness in his hold, as if the same blood coursed through their bodies.

'Edgar the Aethling has aligned himself to me,' said Robert.

'To have the backing of an Anglo-Saxon with his own rights to the English throne is very dangerous,' warned Odon. 'He has grown into a fine warrior but his allegiance, although sworn to King William, has previously been with whoever fitted his purpose and that has most recently been his brother in law, Malcolm III of Scotland – a most dangerous alliance.'

'You have your own enemies Uncle. I will not tell the King you are here, but you can be sure there will be both Normans and clergy as well as Anglo-Saxons ready to betray you.'

'I will be careful, Robert. You know my loyalties rest with you, but for now trust me, as I trust you to do what is right.'

'There was one last thing, Uncle,' said Robert. A smile robbed his face of its concern. 'Mother wants to see you before you leave.'

Queen Mathilde sat at her embroidery caught in the light from her window. Odon saw a shadow of sadness before she disguised it with a welcoming smile.

'I must stitch in the good light, Bishop,' she said A silk veil concealed her hair but Odon remembered the auburn tresses that she wore as a girl and wondered if they were greying like his own. 'My eyes are not what they were. My ageing has been worth it though for I have a strong King, fine sons, beautiful daughters and I am Queen of England. How does that sound to you?' She asked him with a nod. The sun caught the gold thread that ran through the trims that edged her iridescent blue tunic and gold jewellery that adorned her neck.

'The Archbishop of Canterbury would caution you against pride, Your Majesty.' Odon spotted her short beaver fur lined cape abandoned on a seat by the fire grate where a fierce fire was keeping the last of the winter chills at bay.

'Archbishop Lanfranc is a holy man,' said the Queen. 'And you, brother-in-law, what would you caution me against? The power of my men folk? Do you think my husband too hard on the rabble of England, Odon?'

'I am always in the fullest recognition of King William's greatness.' Odon bowed.

'There may be a time, Odon, when rulers will not need to be hard on their enemies to command respect, but that time has not come yet.' She leaned towards him. 'Can you imagine being a Duke from the age of eight with everyone trying to take your Dukedom from you? It has made King William a strong and ruthless man.' Her voice trembled with admiration. 'Do you think he would still be King if he was not?'

'No, Your Majesty.' The Bishop bowed to her; he knew that she was right.

She waved her hand as if dismissing all that had just been said. 'Bishop,' she said softly, 'you are concerned about a vast wall-hanging you have commissioned to honour our King, I understand.'

'With respect, Your Majesty, I am surprised you have come to learn of the reasons for my visit.' Odon felt a shiver of worry cross his shoulders. Secrecy, it was his code, and yet still the Queen could find out so much. If she could find out about his problems, who else might know?

'My nuns hear whispers, how can they not?'

Odon wrestled with the thought that his own people could gossip so loosely.

'Don't look like that, it was not your Abbess Eleanor who told me.'

He straightened his face, but still he could not hide his concern.

'Nor was it your little Therese. You dispatched them both to England so quickly no-one could have got a word out of them.'

'What do you know of Therese?'

'Enough.'

'You will not tell the King about her, will you?'

'Your secret is safe with me. He might think you weak for saving a baby, especially one that should have been slain.'

'No-one in England would call me weak, Your Majesty.'

'Even the mighty Odon cannot guarantee her safety in England.'

'I know that, but I will soon be there myself to protect her.'

'You should have gone with her yourself.' The Queen was looking at him keenly searching for a chink in his mask.

Odon made further efforts to hide his inner thoughts from her scrutiny, but he was obliged to justify his actions. 'England is such hard work. I needed time away.' Odon helped himself to a seat away from the fire and sank down in it. She did not make him move.

'I have not called you here to squabble, my husband's brother.' And she smiled; a little light caught her eye, and his temper and tiredness melted. 'I have also come here,' she continued, 'to see Robert. The King need not know that either of us has visited his wayward son.' She raised her eyebrows at him, indicating the trust they now shared. 'I have a little ruse in mind to protect your embroidery, your great English work.'

'What is that, Your Majesty?'

'You may put it about that I am making it here in Normandy.' The Queen's smile broadened to embrace her whole face. Odon smiled in reply, wondering how much she knew of the enterprise.

'Stop fussing, Odon. I do not know where it is and if I did, why would I want any harm to come to this wonderful tribute to my King?'

Odon was alarmed, as he always was, at how well she read him despite his efforts to thwart her. Her face beamed, then a chuckle started somewhere deep inside her and rocked her until she openly laughed.

Odon laughed with her. Recovering slightly, he managed to say, 'I will start the rumour immediately.'

'And so shall I,' said Queen Mathilde, and then laughter overtook them both.

Eastern Normandy, France

Edgar Aethling put down the letter from his sister, Christina, running both of his hands through his dark hair. This news meant he could not avoid a visit to England. It would, however, be pleasant to visit Christina in her convent in England, beyond

Winchester at Wilton. He could then travel around the coast and go on to Dunfermline to see Margaret, the Queen of Scotland. He found her husband, Malcolm, easy company. Although now he had to be more careful about his friendships for they might be considered allegiances by the Normans.

He was delighted with his elder sister's brood but, for himself, marriage and children at the present time would be too great a risk; their safety could not be assured. Any legitimate offspring would have too strong a right to the English throne for King William to leave them in peace, but his bloodline could still sit on the throne of England with some tact and cunning. He would leave his small eastern corner of Normandy very quietly and take just two trusted guards with him; Sir Guy, a mountain of a man, and the athletic Sir Alun. England was a very dangerous place for him to be.

Kent, England

Therese was amazed at the change in the weather. The storm had passed and now the air was cool and still. Her breath looked like smoke. She mused that the mules looked as if they were breathing fire.

The Abbess strained her neck as she stood on the wagon seat to view the countryside around her. She addressed the wagoner. 'We are not taking the right road, Thorkell. I said I wanted to go the most direct route and that is across country, not by way of the coast.'

Therese knew Abbess Eleanor spoke English, but it was strange to hear her speak it outside the abbey, where she had learnt the language from her.

'That is not the safest way,' said Thorkell in a strong local accent. 'We are better to go along to Dover and then up Watling Street. It was the King's own route when he arrived in England. There are more folk that way.'

'There is a Roman road through the woods to Canterbury. It is part of the Abbey's land. We will take it.'

'It is more dangerous, Abbess,' said Thorkell.

'It is a shorter distance. Sir Gilbert will be with us, we need not fear. Speed is essential.'

Thorkell shook his hooded head and drove his pair of mules on up the hill, away from the coast and the moonlight playing on the sea. Therese turned away from the sea too. The knight set off ahead of the cart to check that the way was clear, but Sir Gilbert's horse was used to a faster pace and he was soon lost from view. He turned back to check on them from time to time, but he was often out of sight. The wagoner muttered endlessly about the loneliness of the route, how much better a surface the coast road had and how many more places there were that way for gaining refreshment. Therese heard him mutter, 'Fools,' as he stopped the cart at the junction to the Roman road.

'What are you doing?' asked the Abbess.

'Protecting myself,' replied Thorkell, cutting a branch from an oak tree there. Thorkell pushed back his hood. He revealed a shock of untidy dark hair and a ragged dirty beard. Therese definitely preferred the clean shaven and short haircut of Norman knights.

'Sir Gilbert does not know we have stopped. We must move on immediately,' said the Abbess.

He nodded in acceptance of her demand but gave one last longing look back towards the coast and trimmed his branch to make a club.

'Quick!' demanded Abbess Eleanor.

'I need it. It is not safe down there.' Tucking the club down beside him, Thorkell urged the mules on.

The road made a sharp turn and Therese saw, by the light of the moon, the down-lands below her. The roman road cut straight into woodland and was lost among the trees. Wings rushed by her face; it was an owl flying up beside her. She looked again at the woodland but the moon was hidden by cloud and the view was in darkness.

'Take some rest,' the Abbess told her, and she settled down among the sheaves of hay and straw left from the wagon's former loads.

Sleep came, but from time to time something would wake her, although she didn't know what. She would reach out as if something should be there above her, but there was nothing, not even the memory of anything. Perhaps she was dreaming of owls.

When she awoke she would notice how rough the road was and wondered if the noises she heard in the forest were really the spirits of Romans marching beside her and if her dreams were of Roman eagles. She liked this image, it was one of protection. Thorkell was clearly less happy with the night's noises and looked round like a man expecting his death. He urged his mules on.

Hooves clattered on the stony path ahead. Therese reached out to the Abbess. Surely she could not be sleeping? No; when she touched her, she heard the mutter of prayer and the sound of her black rosary drawn onto her lap. She withdrew her hand. Ahead, Sir Gilbert and his grey horse stood across the road. On seeing them Sir Gilbert swung his horse around and came up beside the Abbess. She continued to pray.

'I think there are people in the wood,' he said in English. His rich voice broke the still night air. 'Animals are stirring that should be asleep and the night animals are restless.'

'There are plenty of people making their living on this land,' said Thorkell. Therese wondered how he could say such a thing now when just moments ago the same noises had clearly worried him, but she could sense he was masking his fears in front of the knight.

'Only poachers make a living at this time of night,' said Sir Gilbert briskly.

Thorkell considered this for a moment. 'The noises are coming from the front and from the north of us, m'Lord,' he said.

'You are mistaken, wagoner,' said Therese without thinking that it was not her place to speak. 'There are rustlings to the south and behind us.'

Sir Gilbert leaned on the pommel of his saddle and brought his helmeted ear closer to the nuns. Therese looked directly at him. The helmet with its nose guard made his face difficult to see. His light blue eyes were vexed with concern and his helmet was seated with a felt inner which fitted neatly about his pale face. He wore his chain mail vest but had no mail neck cover, leaving his square chin and strong leather-covered neck exposed to blades.

At last the Abbess opened her eyes and broke from her prayers letting the rosary fall back to her side.

'Sister,' said the wagoner, 'You are not experienced in these things.' He turned back to the knight and said, 'I tell you I am right.'

'Silence,' said the Abbess to Thorkell. 'You talk too loudly.'

'I have not heard any people only the disturbances of the animals from in front, but I will search to the north. Then I shall come back here and check with you before looking to the south. Keep travelling as fast as you can, Thorkell,' ordered Sir Gilbert. He turned his horse away.

Flashes of grey horse appeared and disappeared among the trees to the north. Sir Gilbert was checking Thorkell's description of the noises. The rustle and muffled thudding of the horse's hooves so close to Therese drowned out any other sounds.

Sir Gilbert came back. Thorkell beckoned him over. The knight rode up and reined in beside him. He leaned towards the wagoner to catch what he said. In reply Thorkell, in one swift movement, lifted his oak-branch-club with one hand, dropped his reins, and swung at the knight's head. With the horseman unbalanced he leapt on him and pulled him to the ground. Therese rose from the back of the cart and fell upon the wagoner but he thrust her small frame aside as he continued to beat the fallen man. She pulled herself upright ready for another onslaught when the edge of the woods to the south erupted with rugged men. They teemed across the open space formed by the road holding clubs and knives. At that moment a hand grabbed her clothing and pulled her to the back of the cart. She turned to see who held her and saw Abbess Eleanor.

'Sir Gilbert,' protested Therese.

'Hush, we must hide! We will see to him later.' She gestured towards the back of the cart as a place to hide. Therese shook her head and pointed to the woods to the north. The Abbess nodded and they slipped away, their dark clothing melting into the shadows.

Therese ran past about a half dozen trees. The Abbess followed her. There was little undergrowth after the winter and the pigs had also done their work to keep the ground clear. The ground was frosty and radiating cold through her shoes. Her feet stuttered on the ground as she slid behind a large spreading beech tree. Abbess Eleanor joined her and they tried to quietly recover their breath. Squatting behind the tree they listened to the conversation between Thorkell and the men from the woods.

'You were supposed to go by the coast road,' said one with a gruff, heavy voice.

'I couldn't. They insisted on coming this way. I left you a marker; I left a sign cut in the tree I took this branch from.'

'You are lucky we saw it', said the gruff one. 'Or I would have slit your throat. I hope this was not a wasted raid, or I may do it anyway.'

'Look at what this knight has for us, Tancred,' pleaded the wagoner. 'I knocked him senseless before he could use his sword. It is magnificent, and there is so much silver on it. It is worth a fortune in itself. Then there is his armour, his horse, and his cloak is half-lined with wolf skin.'

'Yes, the knight is a good prize,' came the reply. 'I will have that cloak.'

Therese felt anger well up inside her. She went to fight them but the Abbess caught her arm and held her back.

'They are only thieves,' she told her in a whisper. 'They are not after us; no one over here knew we were coming, let alone the reason for our visit. If we let them go with their prize they will not risk killing us, but if we fight now we might be killed in the heat of the moment. Our lives are more important than any amount of silver.'

Therese settled back on the bark of the tree.

'What about the others?' asked Tancred.

'They were only two nuns.'

'Were they carrying any jewellery: crosses, rosaries?'

'The young one only had wooden beads, but the older one carried a jewelled cross and her rosary was beautiful. It looked like jet but different.' Thorkell paused. 'You cannot take holy things.' There was fear in his voice; a greater fear than even he had shown Tancred.

'Alright,' said the gruff voice of Tancred. 'They must have had something else.'

Thorkell paused, then said, 'Come to think of it, I thought I saw a ring on the finger of the older one, hidden under her sleeves. Gold with a red stone on her middle finger and she had a cloak lined with lambskin. I would like that.'

'You get nothing, Thorkell,' said Tancred. 'You have led me a merry dance.' He turned to his men and shouted. 'I want that nun.'

Behind the beech tree Therese turned to her right and looked at the Abbess. She was looking at her with the same alarm she felt coursing through her body. They knew to run would be the quickest way to get themselves caught, so they slid down further. The roots of the tree reached out across the woodland floor like gnarled, knotted fingers gripping the ground. They fanned out, forming segments of hollow ground between them. The two women slunk down into the hollows, trying to look like part of the ground. The tree's roots gripped at the earth for dear life and so did Therese.

A group of men were soon working their way through the woodland. One man came close, but tripped on one of the roots and went away blaspheming. They heard them regroup and discuss further whether pursuing the nuns was worthwhile. Just as Therese began to relax her grip on the earth Tancred growled, 'I want that ring.' Thorkell and Tancred stayed by the wagon. Therese could hear them talking. Then the search started again, in the same area as before.

'Listen,' whispered the Abbess, 'I can hear horses.'

Beyond the noise of the thieves searching in the wood came the thud of hooves. They held a quick steady rhythm, more like ponies than war-horses. Therese did not know whether to be pleased or not. The people approaching would not be warriors, and perhaps not even Norman. She wondered for a moment whether she and Abbess Eleanor could pass themselves off as Anglo-Saxon. The thought made her uncomfortable. 'Because I am,' she said out loud.

'Shush,' said the Abbess.

The blaspheming thief was almost upon them.

"Because I am Anglo-Saxon," she repeated, completing the thought in her head.

Chapter Three

The blaspheming thief went to lean up against the beech tree in an attempt to hide himself from the approaching ponies and their riders. Therese saw him slither round to the right of the tree. He stumbled backwards and his foot caught Abbess Eleanor's fingers. Therese jumped at her stifled cry and looked up to see the thief already had the older woman, with her arms gripped against him and a hand over her mouth. In the dark, Therese knew he hadn't seen her down in the next nest of beech tree roots, so she sprang on to the man's back and wrenched at his arms. Surprised at first, he staggered back and then he called for help. The other thieves ran towards them including Thorkell and Tancred. Tancred gave gruff voiced instructions to his men.

Just as they reached Therese and Abbess Eleanor, the pony riders arrived at the wagon. Attracted by the commotion in the woods, the riders jumped from their animals, slung their reins at the small boy they had brought with them as accompaniment, and ran towards the rowdy thieves. From her position on the thief's shoulders, Therese saw them coming. No matter how she tried she could not make out any more than their rough shapes in the dark. The man in front carried a short sword in one hand and a dagger in the other; they caught the moonlight as he ran into the woods. A great shout boomed from his chest. It struck Therese that he was shouting to her in English and she hadn't caught a word, but she shouted back anyway. The only words she had breath for were, 'Here,' and 'Hurry!'

The thieves turned on the pony men. The two groups whacked and beat each other with such force that Therese shut her eyes, but she still pulled and kicked at Abbess Eleanor's captor. His swaying, swinging body made her giddy, so she opened her eyes to see a dozen or so thieves about her, struck down by the riders. Beyond the pile of wounded a few of the raiders fought on against the riders. She could not see the wagoner or Tancred. While most of the rescuers stood before her watching the spectacle of a nun riding on the back of a thief with her arms and legs flailing like corn beaters.

She looked at the man at the front of the riders and noticed that the Abbess was standing with him.

'You can let go of him now,' said Abbess Eleanor.

Therese slid off his shoulders and he pelted off into the woods, zigzagging around the trees. She was pleased that the dark hid the redness of her face.

'I am Michael from Montgomery,' said the leader of the rescuers, in English. He beckoned to them to follow him out of the trees while his followers dealt with the last of any remaining thieves.

'Your voice is Welsh,' said Abbess Eleanor to the thickset, black-haired rider.

'And I can hear that your English is that of a Norman,' he returned.

'It is indeed, Sir. Would that knowledge have changed your actions in helping us just now?' asked the Abbess.

He thought for a moment. 'The Anglo-Saxons have a word for slave, which means Welshman. I find their present predicament almost acceptable. I have nothing against the Normans as long as they leave Wales alone, and I myself travel with clergy.' He nodded to the boy holding the ponies. A man dressed as a priest stood beside him.

Therese could not see Sir Gilbert so she started to run towards the wagon dreading that he would be lying dead inside. As she approached the cart, the priest stopped her with, 'The knight is not dead. He has stirred, so we've got him into the back of the wagon.' She silently thanked God while the Abbess went over to Sir Gilbert and spoke with him. Therese didn't hear what was said but she noticed that the knight's sword, helmet, shield, chain mail and cape were no longer with him. Therese went over to Sir Gilbert herself and saw him for the first time without his helmet and his nose-guard. Sir Gilbert's short fair hair was bloodied and his face was cut and bruised. His nose was swollen and a foot print indicated where someone had stood on his square chin. She didn't investigate his injuries further.

She looked at Abbess Eleanor who said, 'Come,' and drew her away. Back by the mules, she said, 'We will go on to Canterbury.

Sir Gilbert can rest there. He assures me he is strong enough to make the journey.'

'I am going to Canterbury myself,' said Michael. 'We can see you safe to the city, if you will allow us?'

The Abbess nodded her head. 'We would be grateful for your consideration, Welshman. You have, after all, the name of an Archangel.'

As he helped them onto the driving bench Therese looked across at Sir Gilbert, their Norman protector bereft of strength, and wondered at the wisdom of placing their trust in such a wild man, someone they knew nothing about.

Abbess Eleanor took the reins, ignoring Michael's offer of a driver from one of his own men. Sir Gilbert's horse was hitched to the back and they set off. Therese watched the rider up ahead. Michael was clearly used to his pony and his pony used to him by the casual way he rode him with loose reins and dangling legs. As time passed the mules became lazy about lifting their feet and the Abbess went to urge them on, but her sleeves flapped and caught around her fingers. She tutted and pulled up her sleeves out of the way. Therese noticed her hands were bare. Bishop Odon's ring was missing from her finger.

'Mother,' she said without realising that she'd slipped from formally addressing her superior, 'The ring – it is missing.'

'It was supposed to give us safe passage, but it nearly got us killed. I do not wholly trust our Welsh friend so I have given it to Sir Gilbert for safekeeping. We will need it again in Canterbury.'

As if someone had called his name, Michael came back and set his pony level with Therese. She kept looking at her knees, cloaked in her brown habit and braced against the movement of the cart under her. He rode thus for some distance before he said, 'Your Duke William has a mighty strength?'

'Our Duke of Normandy is now your King,' corrected the Abbess.

'Harold should never have been England's King,' said Michael.

'What do you mean?' asked Therese. She thought everyone in England supported King Harold. She'd begun to wonder if she too ought to feel this way.

'Edgar should have been the King of England, Sister. By birth he was closest in line,' said Michael.

'Everyone knows King Edward gave the throne to Duke William,' said Therese.

'Everyone knows,' said Michael, squaring his shoulders and looking at her steadily, 'Harold kept Edgar's father away from King Edward so he would think that he did not care for the throne of England. When Edgar's father died, Harold manipulated the situation until he too was given the rule of England. It was King Edward's weakness that has given this land such strife. You cannot promise two strong men, such as Harold and William, the same thing.'

'Harold should have handed the throne to Duke William. He had vowed his allegiance to the Duke long before King Edward's death,' said the Abbess.

'That was a trick set up by Bishop Odo of Bayeux,' explained Michael with a hint of disgust in his voice.

Therese and the Abbess gasped as one and stared into the darkness at Michael, their rescuer and yet also teller of such wickedness that their ears burned. Therese could not bring herself to speak. Her dearest Bishop would not trick anyone. She was here, after all, because of him; this insult insulted her almost as much as the absent Bishop.

'You, you..,' stammered the Abbess.

'I'm sorry if I've offended your Norman sensibilities. I only tell it as I see it. Depending on where we sit, we see things differently.'

'Edgar has given his allegiance to King William,' said the Abbess. 'He does not look for the throne of England.'

'But he did battle for the English throne for many years, alongside Malcolm King of Scotland,' said Michael.

'Even Malcolm has settled with King William now,' said the Abbess. 'And Edgar has been given Norman lands.'

Therese felt caught between them as they argued across her, and yet the stories of the land of her birth held a new intensity for her.

'Many rebels have given lip-service to the King. Such bought peace cannot last,' said Michael. 'Malcolm married Edgar's sister. When a Scottish King becomes King of England, then you will have a truly English King.' Michael leaned back in his saddle.

'That will not happen in my life time,' said the Abbess. 'Welshman,' she added curtly, 'we would be more comfortable if you rode at a distance.' She shook her reins at the mules and turned away from the rider.

Having ridden just ahead of them Michael turned back and said: 'The Welsh have not rolled over for William the Conqueror of England with his border Earls fighting our Welsh Kings. He will have to fight for every grain of Welsh soil.'

'We shall see,' said the Abbess. She yelled at the mules in her native tongue and Therese had to grip the edge of the cart as the wheels lifted and fell over the rutted track.

Michael and his men did not approach Therese and the Abbess again. At the church of St Martin, well outside the gates of Canterbury, Michael's strong voice reached Therese, just as the sun rose, 'Good journey.'

She looked round. The low sun glanced across the riders, the boy and the priest as they trotted past them. Michael raised his hand in salute. Therese tried to take in the details of his face, as she hadn't seen it properly during the night. She noted his dark eyes, quick smile and broad nose. Abbess Eleanor barely looked in his direction, only giving a slight nod in recognition of their services. Their saviours, just like that, were gone.

'Are we not going to do anything about the Welshman?' asked Therese. 'He has surely spoken treason to us.'

'Much is said in the dark of the night, you cannot pay it too much attention once the sun has risen,' Abbess Eleanor replied.

The wagon continued on its way to Canterbury and Therese looked about her. The road was already busy with people hurrying about their business. Some were travellers on the road to London, most were on foot but some carried their luggage or wares strapped to a donkey, small pony or on an ox-cart.

As they came closer to St Augustine's Abbey Therese thought they would stop and get help for Sir Gilbert. Therese mentioned her concerns to the Abbess who replied with: 'I understand the Infirmarer at Christ Church Priory is very good. We will soon be there. The two priories are very close to each other.'

Therese looked at Sir Gilbert in the back of the wagon. He seemed to be sleeping so she relaxed a little and returned to the street scene. She soon realised a large number of the people were builders carrying their tools wrapped in cloths, secured with shiny buckles.

'King William has commanded all of this grand building work, Sister Therese.'

'Is this where we will find the Archbishop of Canterbury?' asked Therese.

'No, Sister,' said the Abbess leaning across her to point out the gateway. 'St Augustine's Abbey is being rebuilt as you can see but a vast cathedral is also being constructed within the walls of Canterbury. Christ Church Abbey is the abode of our great Archbishop Lanfranc, while the Abbot here at St Augustine's is called Scotland.' The Abbess settled back on the driving bench. 'King William has been good to the Church. He has the greatest respect for men and women of God.' She smiled at Therese and Therese looked out at the endless throng of stone masons and carpenters about them. 'I have seen much work done at our abbey in Normandy,' continued the older nun. 'They make a wooden structure to build a stone arch.'

'But I cannot see anything much from here,' said Therese, almost standing in her seat, 'except rubble.'

'Sit down, Sister. You will look like one of these mules braying if you stretch yourself like that. Don't worry, you might get a chance later. There will be grand pillars and decorated arches to see. Some parts may even have reached the stage of being plastered and painted by the decorators.'

Therese sat up straight, remembering her dignity, which she'd lost for a while in the woodlands of Kent. 'It will be just like home,' she said.

'More so each day,' agreed the Abbess.

The wagon swung through the gates of Canterbury and through the bustle to the gatehouse of Christ Church. In the courtyard the Abbess checked on the health of Sir Gilbert and found someone to take him to the infirmary.

The Infirmarer came out to direct the removal of his new patient and brought two servants to transport the injured knight on a pallet to the infirmary. He was so engrossed in his patient he did not look up. Therese couldn't help noticing his large knobbly sandaled feet. She wanted to remark on it as she would have done to Miriam but she stopped herself saying anything to the Abbess who was giving instructions to another servant, a groom, to care for the mules and Sir Gilbert's horse. The Abbess told Therese to get down from the cart and follow her.

'Where are we going?' asked Therese.

'I am going directly to obtain an audience with the Archbishop of Canterbury. We need his help.' The Abbess pulled up her sleeve to reveal Bishop Odon's ring back on her finger. 'This will give me the power to open many doors.'

'With the greatest respect, Abbess, why do we need to ask him?' Therese hopped and skipped to keep up with her superior, who'd suddenly started to stride away.

'To get into St Thomas's.'

'But you are the Abbess of St Thomas's Priory, you can enter there any time you please.'

'I am indeed the Abbess, but it is not as simple as that.' She said it in a way that meant she would answer no more questions.

So Therese hastened to follow the Abbess to the visitors' hall, where they were allowed in. The Abbess spoke with the servant who fetched another; she spoke to him and he fetched a monk. Therese flicked her gaze over him and away before he thought her impudent. He was grey-haired and grey-eyed, his stoop was the sort worn by people who'd worked with books for many years, and she thought she could smell recently drunk wine on his breath. He told them his name was Brother David. Abbess Eleanor gave him Odon's ring and explained the urgency of her mission without mentioning too many details. He left by a door at the far end. Some time passed until yet another monk arrived bringing food and drink. This one informed them that there was an unavoidable wait for the great Archbishop Lanfranc and that they might as well take sustenance. 'The water is from a good source here, but you may have ale if you wish,' he added.

The plain bread and water looked good beyond belief to Therese. They had not eaten since leaving Lympne Castle.

Abbess Eleanor thanked him for the provisions and Therese was eating before the blessing had been given.

'Sorry,' mumbled Therese through the crumbs and the Abbess tilted her head, accepting her apology. The older woman only picked at the food and sipped a little of the drink. Therese was concerned by her lack of appetite, but said nothing.

The door at the far end opened. They looked up at the shadow in the doorway hoping and yet dreading to see the great Lanfranc but it was only the grey, stooped monk, Brother David. He came over and held out the ring that had been given to him. The Abbess took it.

'Archbishop Lanfranc is unable to see you today,' he said.

'Did you show him the ring?' asked the Abbess.

'Of course I showed him the ring.'

'What did he do?'

'Abbess, I cannot divulge the words or actions of the Archbishop outside of his chamber, unless he has specifically allowed me to do so.'

'This is a matter of urgency. People have already died,' blurted out Therese.

'People die all the time,' said the monk, with a little condescending bow.

Abbess Eleanor took her arm saying, 'We will return.' She bowed slightly to the monk – who returned the gesture – and took Therese outside. In a hushed whisper she said to her, frowning: 'You say too much, Sister Therese, and you will endanger us all. I think you already know more than you should. What do you know of people dying?'

'There was the knight, who fell from the boat,' said Therese, but she felt a wobble of guilt in her voice.

'That could well have been an accident in the storm, you know that.'

'There was Sir Gilbert?'

'Sir Gilbert is not dead yet and with God's help he will be fully restored in time. Thieves attacked him, nothing more. No sister, I think you know more than the Bishop or I have told you. I can tell you meant something else in there, Sister Therese. Do you know anything I have not told you?' Abbess Eleanor's voice rose in anger as she said, 'You must tell me, Sister Therese, such knowledge can put us all at risk if you let it slip out in the way you did just now.'

'But we were talking to the Archbishop of Canterbury's clerk,' pleaded Therese.

Abbess Eleanor stood close to Therese and said in a sharp voice, 'we must be totally discreet in these matters, and that means we do not divulge anything.'

Therese slumped down on the ground and started to cry.

'Oh child, I'm sorry. You are exhausted I should not have been so harsh on you. Two tired people are not a happy combination.'

The girl sniffed and wiped her face on her habit. 'I know Sister Ursula is dead.'

'And how do you know that?'

'I overheard you and Bishop Odon de Bayeux speaking to each other before I came in that night at home, in Normandy.'

'The old door.' The Abbess shook her head. 'I thought I heard something. Sister Miriam was with you, I think?'

Therese said nothing.

'There is no point in trying to protect her with silence now. What can I do to her here, in England?'

Therese tilted her head and looked at Abbess Eleanor's hands spread over her knees as she crouched next to her. It was an apology as well as an admission. The words were hard to say, after a moment Therese managed a very quiet, 'I'm sorry, Abbess.'

'I forgive you,' said Abbess Eleanor, 'if you forgive me.' She smiled at Therese. 'Now, did you hear anything else?' asked the Abbess.

'No, Abbess.'

'Are you sure?'

'Certain.'

'Ursula was a Prioress, not just a Sister,' corrected the Abbess.

Therese sensed a loneliness in her companion as she spoke, and she touched her sleeve.

The Abbess laid her hand on Therese's and said, 'We need a

little walk to calm ourselves I think. Let us go and watch the masons.'

Therese moved the dust about with her sandaled toe. The masons had not let them anywhere near the works and now she found herself in an area of the Anglo-Saxon abbey, which had already been demolished.

'Why was this place pulled down?' asked Therese, it seemed as if it had been grand enough from the remains.

'There was a fire,' said the Abbess sadly and then added, 'the best stones will have been picked over and used,' as if she were trying to point out the good things so as to push aside their tiredness. 'All conquerors make the land their own, Sister Therese. You feel your Anglo-Saxon blood, I fear?'

Therese wanted the unspoken comfort the Mother Abbess offered with her soft, kind tones but she felt as if she was slowly being pressed into a different shape. The Norman girl was being squeezed out of her and she didn't know if there was anything to replace her. She searched her mind for reason while pawing the ground with her foot. 'It is not just that Abbess. I cannot deny that I am influenced by the story you told me when we were at sea, but I have come here to serve you as Bishop Odon asked me. Yet how can I hold my counsel, if I do not know what it is all about.'

'You are right, Sister Therese. I thought your lack of knowledge would protect you. I have forgotten the ways of the young; the endless curiosity, the sudden movement, the desire to please and the impetuous enthusiasm. It can be a delightful, if dangerous mix.'

Looking at her intently Therese asked, 'How did Prioress Ursula die? And you asked me if I knew any more than that Prioress Ursula was dead. So how much more is there to know?'

'Oh child,' said the Abbess with a sigh. She took her hand and led her to a group of flat stones, which had once been the base of a pillar, and sat down. She patted the stone beside her and Therese sat next to her. The grief in the older woman pulled at her. 'Prioress Ursula was a dear friend,' continued the Abbess. 'She taught me English, so I could teach you. In turn I taught her our language. I came over here to learn, so I could teach you the right accent and intonation. Bishop Odon wanted you to speak your own language well.'

Therese thought she saw a movement among the remains of an archway, by the original entrance. She dismissed it as a dog ratting among the fallen stones.

'They say Prioress Ursula was a traitor,' continued the Abbess. 'That is what I cannot bear. She was Anglo-Saxon, but all the nuns at St Thomas's are. They have been chosen for their abilities in needlework. Prioress Ursula was a craftswoman and a woman of integrity. But even Bishop Odon will not believe me.'

'Believe what?' asked Therese. She was trying to concentrate but was distracted because she was sure that she saw another movement among the ruins, this time some distance from the first in an area where the altar might once have stood. Therese looked from the first place to the second, she and the Abbess were seated between them.

'Believe me, Prioress Ursula would not have tried to destroy the great embroidery,' continued Abbess Eleanor.

'Why should they think that she would?'

'Because she was there when another woman tried to ink the work, I will call her the Impostor.'

'What happened?' Therese spotted, as she spoke, a movement in the same direction as the first one, by the entrance, but further down the aisle and much closer.

'The Prioress and the Impostor fell together from a tower close to the embroidery room. They were covered in ink, which was clearly meant for the embroidery.'

'Prioress Ursula might have been trying to stop her,' said Therese. Now there was another movement close to her second observation, by the altar. Still she could not catch the substance of it. She was feeling jumpy. She wondered if she should get up and chase the dog, if that was what it was, away.

'The Prioress carries the key to the embroidery room,' explained the Abbess. She slumped forwards and put her face in her hands. 'The room was open, so you see she had to be involved.'

'Surely there was an ink bottle, some ink stains in the room, something to show what had happened?' asked Therese.

'I have only heard that the conspirators squabbled and that is how they fell.'

Therese put her arm about the Abbess and looked around for inspiration. She was at a loss as to what to say to her superior in such a state. Again a shadow moved in the corner of her vision. This time the movement in the aisle had substance. She thought at first it was a builder come for stone, as the Abbess had said. But his movements were darting and he kept looking at them from behind clumps of staggered stones.

'Bishop Odon would not have sent us if there was nothing to find out,' said Therese a little hopefully.

'We are not here to clear Prioress Ursula, we are here to uncover the conspirators!'

'That may be the same thing,' said Therese keeping watch on the little man, who was getting closer all the time. 'Abbess, I think we ought to go.'

The Abbess looked up. 'What do you mean?'

'Look.' Therese pointed him out with a nod. Now she could see he was little more than a beggar from his dirty, ragged clothes. His nosiness was a rude and possibly treacherous interruption to their conversation.

Standing up the Abbess raised her hand and called out, 'Halt, man.'

The man halted. Therese saw that he wore a filthy bandage about his head.

'Come here,' said the Abbess.

Therese wanted to slide behind the older woman, but resisted the urge to do so.

'Stand still, Sister Therese,' snapped Abbess Eleanor.

The man came over. Folds of empty skin shook against his bones telling of the number of lean times he'd survived.

'Are you spying on us, little man?' asked the Abbess.

'I am,' he said without remorse. His small dark eyes shifted about as if he were used to being hunted.

'What do you want to know?' asked Abbess Eleanor.

'If you are from Archbishop Lanfranc or Bishop Odo?'

'Who wants to know?' asked the Abbess, her gaze rising and

turning to a disturbance of rubble behind them.

Therese turned too, recalling the second set of movements she'd observed moments earlier. Her failure to warn the Abbess of such a danger struck her like a blow from a whip.

'I want to know who is your Lord,' said another man in clear English. He walked towards them from an outcrop of ruins. He was barely any younger than the Abbess yet he was as straight in the back as she and built with the strength of a knight.

If the shadows in the ruins, so impossible to follow, were those of two men, could there be more? These men spoke English in the manner of natives, so could they be another Anglo-Saxon gang? From their words they were not thieves, but they could easily be traitors to King William's crown. Already she and the Abbess were flanked on either side. Therese looked around for others. Suddenly, she felt very Norman.

Chapter Four

Abbess Eleanor's face brightened at the sight of her tall inquisitor, but this reaction was quickly followed by a hardening of her expression. Therese wondered why she should hide her liking for this man with his silver hair and cornflower coloured eyes.

'Alfred,' said the Abbess.

'Abbess,' said the man, dropping his head in recognition of her status.

His cloak was of good quality wool cloth with a felted lining, although his leggings and shirt were plain and of a serviceable nature. The brooch holding the cloak was ornate with a dragon formed into a silver roundel. There were no jewels or gold on it. Therese placed his occupation as that of reeve or merchant – he was certainly not Norman. His hands were broad but not rough enough for him to be presently involved in agriculture.

'You spy on us as if you do not trust us, Alfred,' said Abbess Eleanor. 'You even use this little man as your agent.'

'I do not trust your master,' said Alfred.

'But you do not know who that is,' countered the Abbess.

'I trust you, Abbess. So I checked that you were alone with your novice before I approached you. But still I need to know who you answer to.'

Abbess Eleanor's face softened. 'We all only have one true master, Alfred. I answer to Him.'

'My sister, Ursula…'

'I know about your sister, Alfred. I pray for her constantly.'

'You don't know about her. You only know what has been said about her. None of it is true.' Alfred frowned and caught Abbess Eleanor's hand up in his. He looked at her ring and kissed it.

'That is not my ring of office,' said the Abbess. Therese was amazed that her superior did not tell him the ring belonged to Bishop Odon. The older woman just gently lifted his hands from hers and asked him, 'Can you explain what has been going on at Saint Thomas's?'

'Agid,' he addressed the bent old man with the bandage about his head, 'guard us from the rear.' Agid scuffled off to do as he was told. He was barely in place when Alfred had a change of mind and said to the Abbess, 'I can take you to someone who can explain everything.' Before any consent could be given to this, he turned and set off across the rubble. Abbess Eleanor followed.

'Is this not dangerous?' Therese asked her.

'Extremely,' said the Abbess producing one of her little shrugs, as if such things could be shrugged off. She whispered to Therese, 'This is, at present, our only offer of information.'

Agid followed in Abbess Eleanor's footsteps.

The Kitchener at St Augustine's Abbey was arguing with the Cellarer about the number of chickens needed for a feast, so he waved Therese, Abbess Eleanor and Alfred through to the great hall. Agid though was too filthy even for his distracted eye. He barred the door with his burly body and sent him out with, 'I've seen cleaner things come out of a midden.'

The Abbess accused Alfred with, 'The gate keeper let you through with a nod and now you gain access to this place without question?'

'The abbey here has no notion that I am connected in any way to the scandal at St Thomas's, most of which has been hushed up to protect the embroidery. The secrecy surrounding it is as great as any wall a mason could build.'

'You seem to know about it,' accused Abbess Eleanor sharply. 'And these people show you exceptional trust.' She looked directly into his eyes. Therese knew this look. The Abbess was testing his soul, as if she had an invisible probe that could check its purity. This look always made Therese uncomfortable but Alfred did not flinch.

'Much has changed since you saw me last. I was just a young man then. I am a freeman now, Abbess. You know I hail from East Anglia, but I have already given my lands to the monastery at St Edmundsbury, in turn they will look after me in my old age. In the mean time I make my living by the wool trade. I buy Abbot Scotland's fleeces and sell them on for carding and spinning.'

Therese was bursting with questions but she glanced at the

Abbess and knew she must hold her counsel.

They took seats at an oak table and broth was brought to them in wooden bowls. Therese barely glanced at the woman stooped over her burden of hot liquid, but she noticed that Abbess Eleanor could barely keep her eyes averted in the manner required by her position.

The servant sat down and pulled back the curtain of shawl she'd used to cover most of her face to reveal a woman well into middle age with pink translucent skin and deep, laughing blue eyes.

'Prioress Ursula!' exclaimed Abbess Eleanor with surprise and pleasure. 'My eyes were telling me the truth.'

'You are meant to be dead,' said Therese. This lady wore a jolly countenance with laughter lines creasing her skin into almost permanent merriment around her eyes. Therese could see that she was her brother's sister by the determined line of her jaw and brow.

'Hush,' said Ursula. She tucked strands of silvery blonde hair into her pristine linen cap. 'And do not call me Prioress, for I no longer hold that position.' They all hunched down and pulled closer to each other. Ursula supported her sturdy frame with her forearms on the table and she kept her voice low as she said, 'There is treachery in every thread of that embroidery. I have had to hide myself against my accusers, here, among those that are never noticed.'

'They say you are a traitor,' said Abbess Eleanor as she looked about the room for any corners that might conceal snoopers, but they were alone and the doors were shut. These words did not sound like an accusation to Therese, it was more a statement of fact mixed with a question of validity. But she thought she knew the answer.

'You tried to stop the Impostor, didn't you?' she asked more loudly than she expected.

'I am not one of the treacherous ones. I have hidden away with the protection of my dear brother because I can trust no one.' Ursula looked carefully at Therese. 'You are right, Sister, I did try and stop her.' Then she turned to Abbess Eleanor and asked, 'Is she?'

'Yes,' the Abbess replied. She said it with pride, but her pride was tinged with sadness when she added, 'She's the baby from Romney.'

'You've told her? Were you not forbidden to tell her?' asked Ursula frowning.

'I have made a decision based on the changes in our circumstances. It became necessary to tell her for her own safety.'

'You too have come across danger?' Ursula's frown was full of concern.

Abbess Eleanor clearly decided she'd said too much to her old friend and looked down at the broth. Therese used the pause in conversation to drink the broth before her, again forgetting to wait for the blessing.

'Only Sister Agnes knows I am alive,' said Ursula. 'You have to believe me; I did try to stop the girl with the ink. I don't know how she got the key to the room. I chased her up the little tower at the end of the corridor and the silly girl threw herself off the top, pulling me after her.' Ursula shook her head. 'The snow and the poor girl broke my fall, but I was as conscious of this world as a stone. Agnes told them all I was quite dead and had me sent to the infirmary. It was a blessing that one of our other Sisters had recently gone to her Maker, under natural circumstances, and my body was swapped for hers, while Agnes called for my brother. She is the only one there who knows I am alive. As you can see I am much recovered.' Ursula turned to Therese and added, 'Your ward has grown into a beauty.'

'You do her no favours by flattering her,' said the Abbess with a flash of temper. 'Her face is but a shell, it is her heart and soul that count.'

'I only say what I see,' returned Ursula.

The two women held each other's gaze for a moment trying each to sum up the other's honesty and integrity. Their faces broke into smiles and they hugged each other.

'Now tell me,' said Ursula. 'You must be here because of what happened at St Thomas's?'

'I am,' said Abbess Eleanor. 'I have come to find out the truth about who is behind this act.'

'I have come to trust no one,' Ursula repeated her earlier

statement. 'Not even Bishop Odo of Bayeux, nor Archbishop Lanfranc of Canterbury. I do not know which way to turn, or what to do. But I will help you any way I can.'

'Why do you not trust the Bishops?' asked Abbess Eleanor.

'The Impostor was put in place seamlessly. I do not even trust our own clergy.'

Abbess Eleanor frowned but let the statement go. 'Have you learnt anything from the kitchen gossip?' she asked.

'I have been listening to all that, and watching the travellers as they come and go, but I have seen no hint nor heard anything that could benefit you. I do not know who has been trying to destroy the work. No one has even come by looking for the dead girl. And to show how much is seen and heard, it was gossip in the kitchen here that told me you were up at Christ Church. What is more, I know you had difficulties there.'

Abbess Eleanor's mouth dropped noticeably. 'What do you know?' she asked.

'I know that the Archbishop Lanfranc would not see you.'

'We were sent away,' said Therese.

The Abbess straightened her back and spoke with authority, 'I have to tell you Bishop Odon de Bayeux sent me.'

Therese noticed both Alfred and Ursula shudder.

'Please do not tell him I'm here,' said Ursula. 'I hoped you were here under your own volition. My brother insisted you would have your orders.'

'I have my orders, Ursula, but they are to investigate this matter. If you are innocent of wrong doing you have nothing to fear, for God sees us and will judge us. I will keep your secret.'

'You are alarmed at how much someone can learn by watching and listening, Abbess?' queried Ursula. 'But that is the way to find out what you want to know. Let me guess why you went to Archbishop Lanfranc instead of going straight to St Thomas's.'

Abbess Eleanor challenged her with her gaze.

'You,' said Ursula slowly, 'wanted to place a spy inside the priory without them knowing you were behind the new person.'

'You know me too well,' complained Abbess Eleanor.

'It is what I would have done if I were you and if I could have trusted the Bishops.'

'But why,' asked the Abbess, 'do you not trust our two mightiest Bishops?'

'Archbishop Lanfranc sees Bishop Odo as a challenge to his authority. Bishop Odo is Earl of Kent, while the Archbishop's bishopric is also part of the same area. Two powerful men, both men of the church, but they are so different in their views.'

Therese could see Abbess Eleanor becoming defensive as she gathered herself in. She said, 'Bishop Odon was appointed as a young man in Normandy by his Duke long before William became your King. He is not a monk like Archbishop Lanfranc. He is a man of the secular world, but he is no worse for that.'

'I agree, of course. But power struggles can have many innocent victims.' Ursula looked down at the bowls.

'Do you consider,' asked Abbess Eleanor, 'that the events at St Thomas's are connected to such a struggle.'

Ursula shook her head. 'The embroidery is nearly finished. We were working on the last panel when the girl struck. I saved it, but look at the slant that has been put on what I did. I am being called a traitor.'

'You know it is just gossip.'

'But Bishop Odo believes the gossip, doesn't he?'

The Abbess looked at her bowl in confirmation.

'Of course he should condemn me but not for the attempt on the embroidery,' said Ursula. 'I should have stopped that young woman from taking her own life. Her soul will always be in purgatory.'

'I am sure God does not blame you,' said Abbess Eleanor.

While Therese felt the gloom covering their group a worm of an idea wriggled into her head. 'I can be your spy,' she said without any further thought. 'They don't know me at St Thomas's. They obviously know you, Ursula, and the Abbess.'

The two older women shook their heads in unison.

'No, that is quite out of the question,' said Abbess Eleanor. 'Without the help of Archbishop Lanfranc I had in mind Sister Agnes. She is already there, she is in Ursula's confidence. She would be ideal.'

'That is not as good an idea as it sounds,' said Ursula.

Abbess Eleanor raised a questioning eyebrow.

'She,' continued Ursula, 'is the kitchener. That was why she was the first to reach me when I fell. She is not involved in the embroidery at all.'

Alfred sighed, got up from the table and walked across the stone floor.

Ursula nodded at him. 'He doesn't like the thought of any of us endangering ourselves. I tell him life is dangerous. He accepts that I will do what I have to, whatever he says.'

Therese leaned across the table to Ursula realising too late that this was an over-familiar gesture towards a woman who was formerly a Prioress. 'I am a novice,' she said, 'no one will notice me.'

'No, Sister Therese,' said Abbess Eleanor, 'you will remain here.'

'Bishop Odon commanded me to use my skills to help you,' said Therese. 'My youth is my way into the Priory.'

'She is right,' said Ursula. 'She is a brave girl. Bishop Odo was wise to send her with you and not just so she could come back to the land of her birth.' She touched her white hands. Ursula's hands were warm against hers.

Therese wanted to pull them away. They were cold with fear. Her blood and her flesh seemed to be working against each other. Her blood seemed to be boiling with determination and excitement yet her flesh was almost trembling with chill. Ursula smiled at her, Therese was sure she understood how she felt.

'I fear for you, Therese,' said the Abbess. It was a long time since she'd called her simply by her name, Therese realised. It almost made her cry. She bit her lip. The Abbess Eleanor continued, 'But I know you are right. It is the simplest solution. We must not tangle ourselves up in any difficulties between our two bishops, and acting on our own not only ensures this is the case, it also reduces the number of people who know what we are about.'

'Alfred will take her,' said Ursula. 'You will need to write her a letter saying that she is a novice from Normandy you are placing in the care of St Thomas's. You need not travel with her. That may look as if you are giving too much importance to the matter.'

'I will travel with her, and you have given me the perfect excuse.'

Ursula looked at her with a puzzled expression.

'By dying, Ursula. I,' said the Abbess, pulling herself up to her fullest height, 'will be going to visit your grave.'

Ursula blushed and started to rise. 'Pray for Sister Anna, who lies there. I pray for her daily for the wrong we have done her and her family.' Abbess Eleanor checked her progress by placing her hand on her forearm. 'I will, of course' she said, 'but we will have to wait until this is resolved before we can tell her loved ones of her passing.'

'We have already lost one of our knights sent to protect us. He went overboard while we were at sea. The other one I have left injured and lying in Christ Church's infirmary.'

Ursula smiled, but her eyes remained serious. 'Alfred will stay near St Thomas's.' She turned to Therese. 'Sister Agnes will always help you, but if you should need Alfred you need only run to the other side of the wood at the bottom of the hill. He will camp there and wait for your news.'

Alfred looked around and nodded in agreement. His face was grave.

'Now eat up, Abbess Eleanor,' said Ursula, 'or the Kitchener will be cross with me.'

The Abbess obeyed.

Chapter Five

Therese strained her eyes open against the sun. Despite her exhaustion, naps were difficult when taken in the back of a jolting wagon. But at least the morning sun warmed her as they headed northwards. Low wooded hills rolled out in front of them. Woodmen were felling trees. Therese suspected that they were destined for the construction works in Canterbury. Alfred seemed to be driving a fresh set of mules over the lumps and dips in the road. They passed a junction and Alfred told the Abbess that it was a shorter route from Canterbury, but it involved a ferry and he'd wanted to avoid the ferry man's gossip.

Therese was lulled back into a stupor by the sun, only to be stirred by a little knot of excitement caught between her heart and her liver. When she looked out she saw a flatter landscape and then willow and hazel brush lined the roadway obscuring her view. It was beyond noon when she sat up and saw the building of St Thomas the Apostle. Their wagon was atop a hill looking into a valley completely surrounded by low hills. The Priory was in the centre of the square shaped valley on its own hill, but it was too far away to see properly. The road took them along the western edge of the valley and past the Priory.

The stone walls were surrounded and topped by wooden scaffolding and lifting gear. Therese caught the salty smell of the sea, but could not see it, as the mules were reined off to the right onto a track, which approached the priory from the north. The wagon went along the valley. To the east there was an encampment.

'Builders,' explained Alfred with a catch of exasperation in his voice. That sound people made when ants got in the honey pot. 'I will make my camp on the south side, beyond the woodland,' he reminded them. 'You cannot see it from here. I will be out of the way of all the traffic.'

Therese wondered briefly if the whole of England was a building site. All these people and yet she would be alone with her secret inside the priory. Contact with Sister Agnes would be difficult, and probably inadvisable with so many prying eyes and ears.

At the bottom of the hill they turned and started to drive up towards the priory. The incomplete building dedicated to St Thomas the Apostle seemed to be under construction on the site of an old fort, being on a hill with rising ground all around the valley like a protective embankment. The chapel, she noted, was foreshortened. The front end had been created for the use of the nuns, but the nave was a skeleton of piled stones and partly built walls. The gatehouse on the northwest corner was complete, and as they went under it Therese felt chilled from the sun being cut out by the stonework above her.

She smiled at Abbess Eleanor whom she realised was now driving. Alfred was no longer with them. The Abbess smiled back reassuringly and drove the mules into the courtyard.

'Wait here in silence,' she said climbing down from the driving seat. 'I will tell them I am here on a private visit as they will be suspicious of my arrival being unattended by the usual retinue. However, this is less likely to make tongues wag than turning up with Norman knights.' Her mouth twitched with a little smile.

Panic started to rise inside Therese's ribs and clutch at her throat. She wanted to run. Instead she steadied herself and picked up her rosary. She would pray not to be so jumpy. After a while she felt her mind start to relax. The only way to serve Bishop Odon in this matter was to be a free agent; to be able to observe without concern for others. She had to become self-reliant.

She still had her eyes tight shut when Abbess Eleanor touched her elbow.

'You have been accepted,' whispered the older nun.

Therese opened her eyes. A movement attracted her and she looked up at a window overlooking the courtyard. They were being observed by a nun whom she took to be Prioress Ethelburga. At this distance she could not make out her features, just her watchful stance. Therese hid her face with her veil as she asked Abbess Eleanor, 'How?' She wondered if her boldness at coming here to spy on the nuns had only been bravado after all. She found that part of her had hoped that Prioress Ethelburga would not take her in.

'I told them that you were one of the best needle-women in Normandy.'

'But I'm not that good,' protested Therese. England was renowned across Europe for its standard of needlework, she knew she could not match that.

'Don't worry,' said the Abbess. 'They won't want you to stitch the embroidery straight away and you can thread needles for the sewers. By the time they let you touch it, hopefully, your work will be done. Prioress Ethelburga thinks you will be an ideal person to clean the embroidery room each day after work is over. It could not have gone better, Sister.'

'So why is she watching us?' asked Therese. She looked up at the window, but the figure had gone.

'Perhaps she is relieved that they can restart the work on the embroidery. Bishop Odon had them stop until I arrived.'

'You did not say this to Ursula?' Therese looked at her quizzically.

'Hush, Sister. For your safety you must hold your council while you are here.'

Abbess Eleanor stood over Prioress Ursula's grave. The grave had been filled in. She expected that the body under the soil and gravel would be covered by a slab of stone. The resulting mound would need to settle before the final top stone would be laid as part of the new floor of the chapel. She prayed for forgiveness for the deceit she and little Therese were now involved in, and for Ursula. Wicked Ursula. Funny Ursula. She also prayed for the dead nun, Sister Anna, who'd taken Ursula's place in the grave and for the misguided girl buried outside of hallowed ground for taking her own life.

She'd avoided watching Therese enter the convent and had asked no questions regarding the arrangements for her. She had not wanted to appear too interested.

She would leave directly for Canterbury. The problems here were created from afar, she could almost smell the politics involved in this affair. She could not believe Bishop Odon could have put her and Therese in such a position. Surely Ursula was wrong, Odon himself could not be involved, the commission for the embroidery was his own, and Archbishop Lanfranc, such a great man. He could not have anything to do with the destruction of the hard work of women dedicated to God – could he? But Canterbury, she resolved, was the place to investigate such matters. Perhaps she could solve the problem before Therese became embroiled here.

Therese woke. Her first day, yesterday, was a blur but what stood out in her mind was the fact that she had been shown round but had not been shown the sewing room or any of the needlework done by these accomplished stitchers. She had, however, been shown two large areas that were not in use. One was the room beneath the dorter on the eastern side of the cloister. This was ready for when the priory was finished when more nuns would be able to live here. The other was the area on the ground floor on the south side of the cloister. This was a storage area which was already full of old looms, spinning bobbins, pieces of silk and other fabrics, samples of embroidery and some very old priests' vestments that she was told by Sister Winifred were there for repair.

In the moments before she knew she must rise for Prime, she tried to focus on her tasks for the day. Her main aim must be to encourage the other nuns to trust her so that an early entry to the sewing room could be engineered.

The bell rang and she dressed with the others in her dorter. Each woman was involved in arranging their tunics and tying their girdles about their waists and they paid no attention to her, or any other person. This was no different from home. She was used to sharing and these women were the very people she'd come here to observe, but not now. She counted ten nuns as they made for the stairway directly into the chapel.

The chapel stood on the north side of the cloister and the dorter ranged along the upper storey of the east side. But the cloister was not yet complete and this, for the present, was the only access from the convent to worship even when prayer was not close to sleep time. Therese tried to remember her tour of the priory as the prayers were chanted.

Standing at the south-eastern corner of the cloister, the only part that was accessible because of the building works, Therese had just managed to make out the strange little tower on the south-western corner where Ursula and the Impostor had fallen. So, she assumed, above the south side store room was the sewing room.

Rays from the rising sun flooded through the windows at the altar end of the chapel. So mouthing the words of the prayers and still with her eyes cast down, she knelt in the choir stands and scanned the interior of the chapel. It was plain compared with home. There were some striped stone pillars, but the walls were not yet painted as the builders had not finished making dust. Even shabbier was the temporary back wall put up to keep the weather out for the benefit of the nuns. Half way across it a large sheet was pinned. This had been decorated with a scene of St Thomas meeting Christ after the resurrection and doubting that it was He.

As for the nuns she could only see the backs of those in front, the stooped heads of those opposite her, and the hands clutched in prayer of those beside her. They all were quite still until the Prioress led the way from the church to the refectory which was at the West End of the cloister. To reach it, however, the Prioress led them back through the dorter, across the stairway and along the corridor outside the sewing room. This they were obliged to do in silence. At the far end of the corridor they went down the tower steps and out into the kitchen courtyard. Therese realised this was the only way out of the tower at ground level.

Delicious smells of baking bread and steaming porridge filled the air. The nuns passed through the kitchen lobby and out into the outer courtyard where they could enter the refectory from the visitors entrance. A trough of water stood by the doors for their ablutions. Small rough towels were handed out for drying. The remembered story of a monk that had decided not to wash as a penance made Therese feel a little squeamish.

After a small breakfast the nuns filed nearly all the way back the way that they'd come, except that when they reached the far end of the corridor outside the sewing room they took the stairs down to the ground level. Therese viewed the label on the door there:

Chapter House. Prioress Ethelburga unlocked the door and the nuns filed in. Therese found herself placed, as she expected, in the lowliest position by the door. Next to her was a short, broad elderly nun with coarsened hands, and next to her was a tall slim nun, a little younger than Abbess Eleanor.

The Prioress opened The Rule of Saint Benedict for the daily reading. She glanced around the room. Her scrutiny was fearsome this close up and Therese found it more comfortable not to look at her as she read.

Once Prioress Ethelburga finished reading she closed the book and looked carefully at each of the faces before her. 'Today, I wish to introduce you all to Sister Therese,' she said. 'She has come from Normandy to study our great work. However, this, as you all know, is a great honour and one that has to be earned. Therefore until I say so, no one is to speak of such matters to her. Nor has she access to the work or workroom.'

The group looked at Therese with unbridled suspicion.

'Sister Hilda, you will take Sisters Sybil and Beatrice with you this morning,' continued Prioress Ethelburga. She passed a key to the nun she addressed. Therese noted that these three were all of an age. Mid-twenties? She wasn't very good at guessing ages but they were certainly older than herself and they were smooth faced. But, out of them, the fairest-skinned girl, Sister Hilda, held herself the straightest and carried her well-formed head and features with less modesty than befitted her role.

Prioress Ethelburga barked at the remaining nuns, 'Sisters Winifred, Leofgyth and Aelfgyth you will go to the garden today. Sisters Maude and Mabel are to assume your usual duties with the animals. Much needs to be done if we are to be fed this year.'

So that puts Hilda, Sybil and Beatrice in the sewing room, thought Therese. She looked at them with more care. Sybil was also fair, but her skin did not have the translucent quality of Hilda's and her features were larger. Beatrice was quite different and reminded Therese of the Bretons at home in Normandy, who traded their linens in the market place. She had darker skin, a broad mouth and wide dark eyes.

The gardeners were of mixed ages. Winifred was the eldest. She was similar in age to the Prioress and she matched her height, but she was a more kindly looking woman. However, she carried herself like she was bearing a great weight across her shoulders. Aelfgyth was clearly a bit younger than Winifred, with a lightly lined face and a friendly expression. Therese noted that she looked towards Winifred with respect.

The gardeners shuffled uneasily. 'Prioress, with the greatest respect, why are you sending us to the garden? Is not the work much more important? Will we not be supplied by our benefactor Bishop Odo? Will not the land work damage our hands?' asked the youngest – a girl not much older than Therese. Another pale skinned, blue eyed Anglo-Saxon, thought Therese. But she was scared for her, addressing the Prioress in this way. She held her breath.

'Sister Leofgyth, I have asked you not to talk of such matters in front of Sister Therese and what is more, I am in charge here and you shall do as I say.'

Prioress Ethelburga unbolted a door which opened directly into the garden from the chapter house. The gardening sisters took their leave. As they went out of the door Therese thought she heard Leofgyth say, 'She always sends us to the garden when our needlework is superior to the others.'

The Prioress addressed the tall slim nun, 'Sister Agnes.' She stood up. 'We have visitors, Brother Richard of Caen and his escort are with us again. Fowl will have to be found to feed them. You may use whatever you need to make them a decent meal. You may send out for the supplies to be replenished immediately. If need be you may miss noon prayers.' Sister Agnes bowed and left.

This left just Therese and the short, wide nun.

'Sister Gertrude,' said Prioress Ethelburga. 'You will instruct Sister Therese in the skill of sweeping. All the stairs and corridors are to be done. 'These builders,' she complained, 'make so much dust.'

Sister Gertrude hic-coughed as she rose and left with barely a nod to the Prioress. Therese bowed humbly and followed her. This lowly task – she smiled to herself at the thought – would give her the opportunity to have a better look round than her formal, and limited, showing of yesterday.

'Sister Gertrude,' called Prioress Ethelburga. Sister Gertrude returned from the corridor. 'Come here.' She addressed Therese equally sharply with, 'you can wait outside a moment.'

Therese did not need to know what was being said but she could guess that Gertrude would have to be on her guard with her and keep her away from any of the sensitive areas.

The willow brooms swished along the aisles of the foreshortened church. Gertrude sprinkled water to settle the dust before they swept. She opened the doors to the cloister, which were not yet meant to be in use, to deposit their sweepings. As Therese looked up from her dusty pile her eyes met a plump monk surveying the completed masonry.

'We have finished here, good sisters,' said the monk. 'The carpenters still have cupboards to install, but once this area is cleaned up you might as well make use of it.'

'Brother Richard,' said Sister Gertrude bowing her head in respect.

'I have just informed the Prioress,' said Brother Richard. From his tense reaction to these words Therese was not sure whether he too was a little afraid of Prioress Ethelburga. 'It is strange,' he continued almost to himself. 'I thought if anyone would need to succeed Prioress Ursula it would have been Sister Winifred.'

The two nuns stared at him open mouthed. He harrumphed at his indiscretion.

Therese looked away and over towards the south side of the cloister, which was already in use. Indeed Sister Hilda and her needlewomen were taking a break from their work in that area. But Therese could not see them, just hear their whisperings because of screening placed between the building works and the precious embroidery areas. Such protection was unusual but presumably the idea was to prevent even the stitchers clothes becoming dusty and soiling their work.

'There is too much work for two women here,' said Gertrude. Her jowly face was turning purple with temper.

'The builders have cleared the worst of the rubble,' objected

Brother Richard.

'I do not think Brother Richard means that we are to clean it, Sister Gertrude,' said Therese.

'I am going to see the Prioress about this,' added Gertrude handing her broom to Therese. She padded off over the filth to the screening, lifted a corner and disappeared behind it, heading in the general direction of the chapter house.

Therese smiled at the surveyor and commented on the splendid archways.

'I'm the architect's right hand man,' said the surveyor immodestly. 'Bishop Gundulf himself, sent for me, Brother Richard of Caen, to check on his design. The local masons do not always follow the guidance of the Norman craftsmen we brought over especially for this work.'

'How do you mean?' prompted Therese. She could tell he wanted to have a grumble to a fellow Norman.

'That tower,' continued Brother Richard, puffing out his round belly. 'Is not in the plans at all. Such a bit of nonsense. They tell me an extra stairwell was asked for after that south wing had already been completed.' He waved his pink hand crossly in that general direction. 'Two sets of stairs to a small first floor, quite ridiculous! But it is done now. It will have to be left.'

'How did it come to be?' asked Therese conversationally. His tongue had become quite loose, as Sister Miriam back in Normandy, might have said.

'That, Sister, is the strangest thing. I am told the orders came from the highest level, yet they did not come through me.' Brother Richard paused and looked hard at her. 'This is none of your business, young woman. Get about your work.' His voice was cross with the embarrassment of having said too much.

Therese watched him scuttle out in the same direction as Gertrude, but decided that he would be making for the refectory, ready for the results of Sister Agnes's morning labours. She considered using these moments on her own to slip off and have a look around, but before she could act on the thought Sister Gertrude returned from the direction of the dorter steps. Her clothing had gathered some builders' dust since her departure.

'We can leave the cloister. The Prioress will arrange a special cleaning project for tomorrow involving everyone. She says we are to clean the tower steps.' Gertrude frowned deepening the furrows between her eyes. 'Those stairs are so narrow, so steep and winding. My old bones won't get up there.'

'I'll do it,' said Therese a little too quickly.

'Are you stupid?' asked Gertrude shutting up the chapel. She turned and went under the flap of screening.

'Just keen to do God's work,' said Therese trotting after her.

Gertrude grumbled something about 'the devil's own' and 'Normans', but Therese didn't quite catch it. At the bottom of the tower the old nun said, 'I will wait here.'

So Therese left her sitting on the wood-pile and resting her back on the cool stone wall outside in the yard, while she climbed the tower with her broom.

'Sister Therese!' Gertrude called. Therese peered back down the stairwell, but she couldn't see round the tightly turning stairs. 'You will have to start at the top and work down,' came Gertrude's advice.

'Yes, Sister Gertrude,' she called back. She turned and climbed slowly as if there was something to be gained from inspecting every corner of each step. Steadying herself with her left hand against the curved wall, she reached the opening to the first floor landing. This is where the Impostor had entered the tower with Ursula in pursuit. There were small inky marks on the wall making a pattern trailing upwards. She followed them remembering the Impostor's soul would never be at rest – forever in Purgatory. She tried to rid herself of the thought and increased her speed upwards.

A few steps on, she paused and looked for the door at the top; she couldn't see it yet. But she caught sight of a shadow high up on the sewing room side of the wall. It looked like a hole, as if one of the large stones was missing. She listened but could not hear anything. This did not mean much though as she suspected the nuns worked in silence. She stretched, but was not tall enough to reach it. The tip of her broom-handle could get in though, confirming it as a substantial hole. To one side of the broom-handle she noted a holder in the wall designed to take a lighted taper. She waited to see if there was any reaction to her broom-handle from the other side of the wall.

A scream wrenched at the air above her – not a human scream, nor a shout of surprise given by a nun seeing the end of a broom poking through a wall, it did not come from that direction. This was like the scream of a soul in Purgatory. Her flesh jumped and she brought her broom close to her chest like a staff. She knew it would be useless against a damaged spirit, but it might defend her against worldly obstacles. She rushed up the last twenty or so steps. She flung open the door at the top and threw her broom at whatever was there. A crow's wing span blackened the opening but moved before the wooden handle made contact with it.

Beyond Therese could see the parapet, so close to the door, and her broom was flying towards it. She was following, but she stopped herself from going over the top by catching the high part of the stone castellation.

Hanging over she saw the broom land at Gertrude's feet. It snapped on the wood pile. The old nun visibly jumped, looked at the broken pieces, and then up at Therese. 'There'll be trouble now,' she shouted, struggling to stand. She stooped to collect the smashed broom. 'Heed my warning,' she added, shaking the splintered wood at her.

Chapter Six

On her return to Canterbury Abbess Eleanor had formally introduced herself to Abbott Scotland at St Augustine's monastery. This would be a convenient location within easy walking distance of Christ Church Abbey with the growing structure of Canterbury Cathedral standing by it. Archbishop Lanfranc was so close, yet so out of reach, but Alfred's connections with other people within Saint Augustine's would not be without their uses, and the closeness of Ursula was a comfort.

This was already her second day back in Canterbury and it was time to make substantial inroads into the matters that brought her here. She rose and left the Church of Saint Peter and Paul, within the grounds of St Augustine's, and walked out into the sunshine through the gatehouse to the walls of Canterbury. She entered the town by the South Gates and proceeded north to Christ Church Abbey. Once there she made enquiries about Sir Gilbert's health, but was told he was still poorly and should be allowed to rest.

Once again she decided she must try to speak with Archbishop Lanfranc. She no longer needed his help in getting a spy into the Priory of Saint Thomas the Apostle, but, after her conversation with Ursula she did need to sound out his stance on the embroidery. That was really why she was here, after all. She drew up her reserves of stubbornness and settled in for a siege. She would stay for as long as it would take.

At the visitors hall she was greeted as before and then interviewed again by the stooped clerk, Brother David.

'I will intercede on your behalf,' said Brother David, bowing a little too low. He left, only to return a while later and say, 'Follow me.'

'At last,' muttered Eleanor under her breath. She rehearsed what she would say to the great man, but she soon realised they were heading out of the Archbishop's chambers, not in the direction of the chapter house, to another building behind the main priory.

She followed him up the timber steps. These were external, and she felt the sun warm her back.

'This is a temporary building,' explained Brother David.

Eleanor's nostrils caught the sour smell of ink. 'The scriptorium?' she enquired. This was clearly a diversionary tactic, but it still might be worth looking around, she decided. She walked steadily around peering over the shoulder of each monk.

Some were writing what appeared to be copies of letters for the abbey's records. Others seemed to be making new editions of old books, with the original laid out beside them; pricking the vellum sheets in front of them to mark the position of letters, decorations and lines of text. Some were involved in illustrating works with elaborate pictures of animals and scrolls of red and yellow using paint brushes with only one or two hogs' hair bristles. These were carefully dipped in dishes with tiny amounts of the precious colours. None of the monks looked at her as they concentrated on their work.

While Brother David was answering a query posed by one of the monks Eleanor returned to one of the letters she had noticed earlier, she read the Latin quickly. She had been drawn to it as it was addressed to Bishop Odon de Bayeux, nothing would illustrate the relationship between him and Archbishop Lanfranc better than their correspondence.

While she read, a monk entered with a message for Brother David.

'I have to leave you for a few moments,' he said to Eleanor.

She nodded and he left. She hoped her casual pose had disguised her true activity. The effort, however, was not proving worthwhile, as the letter seemed to be a piece of straightforward business over a piece of land where there was some dispute. The Archbishop addressed his fellow Bishop in the way he addressed all his correspondents, it seemed, as a brother wishing to give advice, even though she doubted whether he always knew the people he was writing to.

The monk stirred at her dallying and she moved on. The smell of ink was too strong for her, so she left the scriptorium and headed uninvited towards the cloister. Often documents were stored there in cupboards so air could keep the vellum fresh, but the cloister was busy with monks leaving the church. It was not time for prayer so she assumed some special service had been said.

Her feet stuttered on the tiles in a panic to escape the flood of monks; but it was impossible. With cowled and bowed heads the monks only saw the ground they were about to tread. One knocked into her and sent her sprawling into one of the pillars supporting the arches edging the cloister. From her position, rolling onto her hands and knees, she saw two large knobbly sandalled male feet in front of her.

'I'm so sorry,' exclaimed the monk, the owner of the feet. He offered her a hand. 'Are you unhurt?'

'I am, thank you,' said Eleanor, rising and brushing herself down. 'However, I will enter the church and take some respite there.'

'I will assist you,' said the monk. 'I am Brother Matthew.'

'Brother Matthew,' she said severely, to cover her embarrassment, 'I can manage perfectly well on my own.'

Brother Matthew bowed and followed the others. She turned towards the southern doors of the church. On entering the eastern end of the nave she found herself alone, but at the western end five people were leaving through the main doors. She tried to adjust her eyes to the contrasting shafts of light from her doorway and theirs, along with the darkness of the church.

These men were important. Their tunics and cloaks caught the light. They wore rich reds, golds and purples: Norman knights and a cleric. One was clearly more important than the others, as they deferred to him at the door. Not the King, the King was older, sturdier – a warrior of many campaigns. These were younger men. One of the Princes perhaps. Eleanor's mind raced. This was why she'd been kept hidden away in the scriptorium. These were visitors she was not meant to see, let alone meet.

As the sun caught the face of their leader she recognised the red hair and sharp face of William Rufus – the King's middle son, and now considered heir to the English throne. 'God preserve us,' she whispered. His brutality was of an ancient kind. His reputation had reached every corner of Normandy and most of England had seen it first-hand. She hoped inflicting such horror would soon be unnecessary in a modern world.

The last person to leave the church was the Archbishop in his robes of office. She started towards them, but stopped herself. This was neither the time nor the place to attract attention. Such an open confrontation could only work against her so she waited until they were quite clear before making her way out. She assumed that by now Rufus and his entourage would be enjoying the Archbishop's hospitality in the visitors hall. As she passed out through the gatehouse she heard voices in the yard and observed Brother David talking to one of Prince William's guards. She turned away and walked through the butter market and onto the main thoroughfare towards Canterbury's south gates.

Out in the town the sun still had warmth in it and the clouds were thin and scattered. Even the breeze, though fresh, was not cold. Abbess Eleanor strode out. She was soon aware of a beggar darting about her in the crowd. At first she tried to ignore him, until she realised it was Agid. She drew into an alleyway and waited for him.

'Did you see that?' he asked breathlessly when he arrived.

'What?' asked Eleanor, not bothering to hide her irritation at having to talk to this filthy man.

'Rufus and his knights.' He plucked at a stained bandage about his wrist. The one about his head had gone. A healed gash marked where it had been.

'Prince William to you,' she said stiffly. 'What did you do to your hand?' she asked.

'Just a cut,' said Agid.

'And your head?' asked Eleanor. She walked on out of the alley-way. He clearly had nothing important to impart.

'I had an argument with a tree,' he replied hopping sideways around a man shovelling up horse droppings. 'You didn't get to see Lanfranc again, did you?' he asked.

'I have no intention of discussing my actions with you.' She turned away.

'I knew you didn't.' He looked pleased with himself.

She turned back and glared at him. 'Who has paid you to follow me today?' He crumpled into a humble slump and peeped up at her with a wily twinkle in his eye. She wanted to poke it.

'Alfred told me to keep an eye on you,' he said. 'I would rather see your Norman bones rot in a pit, but Alfred thinks you're all right.'

'Look what we give you,' said Eleanor making a grand arch with her arm, embracing all the new building works for the cathedral.

'We had perfectly good churches before you lot came along. This is The Conqueror's penance. With all the bloodshed he's caused, the church has conned him into all this building for the sake of his soul. He wouldn't have cared less if they hadn't tried to excommunicate him all those years ago for marrying his cousin.'

'She wasn't his cousin.'

'Old Lanfranc got him off that one, didn't he? That's why he's here. That old Italian. Got the top job for putting matters right with the Pope.'

'You are wrong. Archbishop Lanfranc is a very humble, religious monk. He didn't want to come here.'

'Well then, perhaps the Pope thought he'd better send him here to keep an eye on the old sod.'

Eleanor went to clout the man's ear for calling King William an 'old sod'. She could have him flogged, of course, but part of her couldn't help but agree with Agid's sentiment. She too hoped Lanfranc could control the King's warring. He had, after all, managed to get him to sign up to the church's peace movement last year. Anyway, Agid had disappeared again, so she carried on walking. She was soon aware of the beggar at her heels again.

'Do you know,' he whispered, 'that old Italian monk you hold up so high struck off some of our Anglo-Saxon saints from the calendar.'

'Perhaps,' said Eleanor, her temper rising again, 'he thought you had enough holidays.'

Agid laughed. 'You're not so bad, Abbess.'

Already they stood at the gates of St Augustine's.

They were standing toe to toe. Eleanor stooped slightly and said, 'Now if you'll excuse me, you can tell Alfred that I'm in the best of health.'

'There's one more thing you ought to know about Lanfranc, but that isn't for me to tell you.'

'What is that?'

'Ask your own archbishop – Odo of Bayeux.' With that Agid melted into the throng.

Eleanor called, 'Wait.' But she received no reply.

Therese and the other nuns left the chapel, after vespers, by the priest's door on the north side of the church, which the Prioress unlocked. Prioress Ethelburga had explained earlier that she had decided the builders should clean up the cloisters before a final spring clean by themselves. Perhaps, thought Therese, Richard of Caen had been mellowed into agreement by Agnes's vitals. Anyway, the work was continuing into the evening. Nor did Prioress Ethelburga think it seemly for the nuns to go through the dorter while builders were in the compound.

The setting sun gave the chapel a heavy shadow and this chilled the air about them so they wrapped their semi-circular cloaks tight and pulled their hoods over their veils. Therese felt a strange freedom from just standing outside the priory compound. With her head bowed she followed the others towards the gatehouse. The building site end of the chapel was quiet, with all the builders in the cloister.

She felt the thrumming of hooves through the hillside before glancing sideways and seeing riders coming towards them. Prioress Ethelburga looked alarmed and waved at the nuns, telling them to wait where they were while she spoke to these men at the gatehouse.

Therese looked for somewhere to hide for she had recognised the pony. The brown pony with black mane and tail was broad chested but had neat legs. The last time she'd seen it was when it trotted past her outside Canterbury. The pony rider was now, as it was then, a thick set man. He raised his hand in salute. When she heard the powerful tones behind his shouted greeting she knew it was Michael, the Welsh merchant, riding at the front. His whole entourage seemed to be with him, and an additional wagon – no, two additional wagons.

To her left, Therese caught sight of an open space among the piles of stone ready to construct the rest of St Thomas's church. Once among them she was momentarily distracted by the pieces of dressed stone, many with ornate carvings already made to their surfaces.

She drifted into the centre of the chapel extension works. She tried to get her bearings. She was standing in the area that would one day be the central aisle. A shadowy mound interrupted the ground. It was quite close. She knew it was Anna's grave. She prayed that Anna's soul would remain quiet while she was near. She backed away. Before she realised where she was she had reached the middle of the temporary back wall of the church she had just left, and where her back touched there was a door.

She tried the handle. The door opened and caught on a bar braced against it.

'What was that?' asked Prioress Ethelburga loudly.

'I heard nothing,' said Michael the merchant, equally loudly.

Therese froze. The builders, no doubt, liked having the convenience of ready access to the priory. But, her mind raced, this gave anyone access as long as there was someone on the inside to remove the brace. She withdrew, closing the door as gently as she could. Her heart was thumping, what was Michael doing here? She returned to the place where she'd entered the building site and edged along a half-built stone wall to where Prioress Ethelburga was talking to Michael. She could see also that the Prioress had changed her mind and sent her fellow nuns through the gatehouse and into the priory compound.

Prioress Ethelburga was holding the reins of Michael's pony while she spoke to him. 'You are late,' Therese heard her say.

'I have wagons now. Trade is brisk.'

'You cannot stop the night here. There is no room,' said Ethelburga.

'The builders are camped yonder.' He waved over to the east, at the twinkling lights of fires and torches. 'We can make camp with them. There is plenty of level ground there between the banks of the stream and the hill beyond.'

Therese looked in the direction of his gesture and saw the shadowed tents she'd seen on her arrival. She could just make out, in the flickering light, people moving about up there, no doubt preparing a meal.

'I will not do business at this hour,' stated Ethelburga. 'You will have to return in the morning.'

Michael conceded the matter with a bow and waved the ponies and wagons back down the hill, complete with the priest and the boy who'd attended to Sir Gilbert on the way to Canterbury. She watched them slow to pass over the stream at the bottom of the hill.

Therese jumped, realising that Prioress Ethelburga had already gone through the gatehouse. She felt alone and was sure she would be locked out. She made a dive for the gate when she heard Michael call,

'Sister, you have big ears.'

'You cannot see my ears,' said Therese crossly. He must have looked back and seen her.

'Is that the little sister from the forest, who jumps on robber's shoulders?' he said riding up.

'No,' said Therese annoyed at being drawn so easily to give her voice away.

'All the nuns here are Anglo-Saxons. You are Norman. You have the accent.'

She wanted to tell him that this was the land of her birth, but this teasing man could be using his wiles to trick her, so she pulled her plain woollen cloak about her.

'Sir, I was not listening to you. My sandal became loose and I tripped. When I stopped to repair it I became separated from the others. That is all.'

'That is possibly the weakest lie I have ever heard. I heard you, you know, in among the works there. I covered for you. But I will let it go, and you, this once. But you owe me for my silence. I will not tell Prioress Ethelburga about this little mishap, Sister Therese.'

'Thank you,' said Therese feeling as if a trap had been sprung about her. She slipped through to the gatehouse as quickly as she could. The guard was talking to the builders who were grumbling as they carted out the last of the rubble and dust collected from the cloister area. He complained in colourful language that it was a nuisance that the new Prioress had stopped them using the back

door in the chapel.
She passed through unnoticed.

Chapter Seven

Therese arrived at the refectory table trying to hide her shortness of breath. Grace was said and they sat down to their fish and bread. Any lateness would go against her and unreliability would not get her into the embroidery room. Yet she wanted desperately to tell Alfred of St Edmundsbury about Michael's arrival, perhaps he ought to speak to Abbess Eleanor. She was grateful that the meal would be taken in silence, as always, but she would still have to stay alert to the signals given by the other nuns. Sister Leofgyth was already making a gesture to indicate she wanted the jug passed to her. She would think Therese was ignoring her if she failed to hand it to her promptly. Sister Winifred was charged with reading the bible text while they ate. Most of the nuns seemed to phase out the gentle rolling sound of her voice and tuck into their food.

At least sleep came early in a priory and soon she was lying down with the others in the dorter. Already she knew how she would leave the priory. So, as soon as the nuns succumbed to their tiredness, she rose and put her tunic over her chemise and her cloak about her shoulders. She flicked her cape hood up over her cap. She left her veil on the stool next to her bed. She stole her way into the chapel from the dorter stairway. Despite the dark she felt her way along the pews to the temporary end wall. Her fingers made contact with the soft wall hanging of Saint Thomas the Apostle. Moving it to one side with as much respect as she could muster, she felt for the wooden brace and lifted it from its hangers. The builders had clearly not used it for some time and as she opened the door dust spewed up and descended upon her. A sneeze took hold in her nose and she nearly choked trying to stifle it.

Closing the door she was grateful that the wooden formers for the arches were being assembled and the walls on the priory side of the church were well advanced. This gave her a solid screen against any curious eyes. She noted that the piles of stone blocks and structures on the other side had not been touched since she'd hidden from Michael there, earlier that evening. But she sought out the view of the builders' campfires and, in particular, the new fire that would have been set by Michael's party. Alfred was encamped on the other, southern, side of the priory hill – that was what he'd told her. She sensed the warmth coming from the lively camp on the eastern side of the stream. There was a hint of laughter on the breeze. It was like being drawn on a line into the sea by a very strong fish.

Running down from the priory towards the camp she reasoned with herself that she would hide on the hillside below Michael's camp and listen to his talk. Afterwards she would be able to work her way round the bottom of the hills that surrounded the priory to its southern side. By then she might have more to tell Alfred than just that Michael had arrived.

At the bottom of the priory hill she splashed through the river using the flagstones laid on its bed by the builders, to ease their journeys with the heavy loads of limestone brought from the port at Reculver. The Isle of Thanet was not far from there, so she'd learnt through Gertrude's chattering – Gertrude had been born there and then taken north by her family, to return close to the area of her birth many years later. Therese went more cautiously up the slope at the base of the hill facing her until she was just below the level ground, which held the camps. There she crouched down, out of the line of sight of the campers.

Listening to the rhythm and lilt of the languages spoken above her she worked her way along from the builders' camp and soon heard the Welsh of Michael's group. With ale and food, perhaps his guard would be down and she might hear something useful. What deal was he involved in at the priory with Prioress Ethelburga? Why was a man, who had little respect for the King, here at such a sensitive time? She settled herself on the hillside below the level of his fire.

Soon she realised that this was pointless as this was one language she did not know. It was similar to a language used by Normandy's neighbours, Breton, but even so it was beyond her. She was about to move on when she heard footfalls coming up from behind. Flattening herself into the grass she avoided creating a shadow against the fire that would give away her position. She could feel the spring dew seeping through her layers of clothing while she waited for the walker to pass by her. She shut her eyes as if that act would make her invisible.

'Greetings, Michael the Merchant.' Therese recognised the voice. Her eyes snapped open, it was an English voice.

'Greetings to you, Alfred,' said Michael speaking English.

Trying to control her surprise Therese gripped the grass.

'What brings you this way?' asked Alfred. His accent was so different to Michael's. His vowel sounds were flat like monks chanting whereas Michael's voice almost sang with each part of his words pitched at a different musical note.

'Trade, same as you,' said Michael. 'You are here on foot?'

'I've made my own camp a little downstream.'

Therese assumed Alfred to be lying to prevent unwelcome callers – surely he was upstream from here? He had clearly come to check on this new arrival to the vale for himself. Her strength seeped away with her purpose. She let go of the damp grass. She noticed her clothes were wet and heavy about her. She shivered and considered leaving until she caught a change in the tone of their conversation. Their voices had become tentative as if they were testing each other, or sharing a secret hidden in the words.

'You were turned away by Prioress Ethelburga, then?' asked Alfred.

'You saw?' asked Michael.

'We are here for the same thing, are we not?' asked Alfred.

'Aren't we always?' said Michael. 'But we are not working against each other.'

'That is good,' said Alfred, 'for I would not like to be opposed to a man with your strength and youth.'

'Your age gives you skills I have yet to learn,' replied Michael.

They were laughing now. Therese was confused by their apparent friendship. What could this mean? Were they joined in some political endeavour, or was Alfred trying to find out more about Michael by assuming his friendship? Therese crawled away down the hill. Supposing this meant that she could no longer trust Alfred? She would be lost and alone. She ran back all the way to the priory, and returned to her bed the way she'd come. Slipping off the damp woollen over-clothing she hoped the straw mattress and wool blanket would help dry out her linen chemise.

In the middle of the night all the nuns rose for vigils. Therese had hardly slept and her clothes were still wet. They made their way down the stairs she'd used earlier and Therese, seated in the choir stands with the others, stole glances at the hanging over the disused builder's door while bending over deeply in apparent meditation. The dust had settled but she imagined, for she could not see in this light, that her footprints would be clear to all in the dust by morning.

They returned to bed and Therese lay shivering with fear and cold when a hand touched her arm. She kept it still as she did not wish to show any emotion, until she found herself looking into the steady eyes of Sister Agnes. In an instant she recalled Ursula's warmth and the help Sister Agnes had given the ex-prioress of St Thomas's. Even now Agnes had the comforting smell of the kitchen about her.

The older nun beckoned to her to follow. Her mind raced. If Alfred was connected to Michael then Ursula might be, too – and Agnes? Sister Agnes took her along the corridor past the sewing room, down the tower steps, outside and across the yard to the kitchen.

Inside Agnes stoked the fire in the central hearth with two logs, each about the length of Agnes's forearm and stood Therese in front of it.

'They'll soon burn through. It will help keep the fire going for the morning. No-one will know we've been here.'

She passed Therese a dry habit and placed the wet one, once removed, in front of the blaze on a wooden stand, without speaking but with kindly gestures. Therese followed her instructions as gently as she could. She was not encouraged to speak and their silence protected them both.

Agnes drew up a short bench for them to sit on and they stayed there for over an hour. But still the garments hung onto the wetness from the grass, so Agnes sent her back to bed with the ones she'd given her. Before parting, the only words she spoke were, 'The nun who wore this has no need of it now.' It was said in tones meant to comfort Therese, but instead they unsettled her.

When Bishop Odon disembarked at Dover, his ship was just one of many pulled up along the river's sand and gravel shoreline. Casks of wine and other necessities from the continent were being unloaded, while other boats were being loaded with the first of the season's wool. He'd brought just two men with him as a bodyguard, but he was confident as he had many more stationed at Dover Castle. This England was like a missing piece of Normandy. He was pleased to be back and sighed, knowing the English would always consider him a foreigner here. He turned the sigh into a deep breath. This was his Earldom and he would take rest and change into dry clothes at the castle. He thanked God for a good crossing.

He kept a simple but comfortable home here, and at the other castles he had to use. Just two good chairs made from beech wood in his father's day, softened by pads of goose down and covered in trimmed and stitched deerskin stood by the hearth in the castle's keep. He sat down and fingered the chess pieces on the board in front of him.

He looked at the chessboard: a game of power; Kings, Queens, Knights, Bishops, and so many pawns – but no Princes. He had only considered two as potential kings since the death of King William's eldest son: William Rufus and Robert. Henry was too young to be considered, just thirteen, but growing fast by all accounts and speaking English like a native, so they say. Perhaps it would take another generation for the Normans and the English people to adapt to each other.

His reverie was broken by the entrance of one of his personal bodyguards.

'My Lord Bishop, Prince William has sent word that he will be arriving shortly.'

'Make ready for him,' instructed Odon. He allowed himself another sigh once he was alone again. He was reluctant to see William Rufus, but he could not possibly turn down the King's son.

The clatter of horses in the courtyard caused him to look through the slit of a window, down at the King's second son. He dismounted with expertise and unnecessary swagger, he rode with three others. He left the horses with the grooms Odon had sent to attend them. Rufus directed his men to follow him. Odon recognised the distinctive height of Roger and the fair head of Simon. The last of the three looked up. It was Ralph with his aquiline nose, lips like a long-bow at rest, dark eyes and hair. They made for the entrance to the keep.

They entered Odon's room still with their chain mail and swords. Their red cloaks were thrust back to show linings made from wild cats of Africa. Their hands rested on the hilts of their swords. Roger, Simon and Ralph stood by the double entrance door to Odon's apartment and William Rufus was playing with a short jewel encrusted dagger. This was rudeness barely tolerable to Odon, but he contained his anger. 'Prince William.' Odon bowed to his nephew.

'Uncle,' said Rufus, his face as cool as his blade.

'Please, as my honoured guests, feel free to remove your encumbrances from your journey and relax with me. Take some sustenance?'

'You are too kind,' snapped Rufus looking about him as if he expected to be run through by a sword at any moment.

'Dover castle has to be the safest in England,' said Odon. 'My guards are totally trustworthy. Your equipment will be well cared for.'

'I have no time to stay. The King is intent on securing Wales this year.'

'Surely Earl Montgomery has already broken the back of that task? With his border castle and the strong arm he has shown the area.'

'He has done well, as have the other Earls along the Welsh border, but it is not enough. My father wants these Welsh to declare their fealty to him as the English have done.'

'With respect to your great father and my beloved brother, the King, I think he may be asking a great deal of those wild people. They share a past with our Bretons and we have had many a fierce battle against them.'

'Normandy is all-powerful,' said Rufus. 'We follow the Roman Empire in our magnificence.' There was a general nod of agreement from his men.

Odon turned away. The fury of war was in their blood; it was honourable to fight. It was more honourable to fight for convictions than to win. This was as strong in his blood as in any of his family, yet he was a Bishop.

'I know,' said Rufus, 'that you would rather see Robert on the throne of England. But it will never be.'

'I desire only what is right.' Odon hoped the neutrality of the statement would be lost on Rufus, and that he might even consider them words of support.

He looked as a sailor might who had suddenly found himself sailing into the wind, so he said, 'The King holds sway on all things, Your Grace. And you have put down uprisings all over this England, Bishop Odon, by the sword. Your hands are as bloodied as any of ours.'

'And I pay my penance daily,' snapped Odon. 'Surely all that business is now settled?'

'I have heard, Uncle…' said Rufus as if dangling a baited line. He seemed calmer now Odon's temper had been roused.

'Heard what?' Odon rose again to the enticement.

'I hear that there are Welsh spies infiltrating into England causing unrest.'

'I have heard no such rumours myself.'

'I am surprised. For I believe Alfred of St Edmundsbury, a brother of a former Kentish Prioress of your acquaintance, Prioress Ursula, is a man who moves between these worlds.' Prioress Ursula, herself, I believe, stayed for a while some years ago in the Scottish court with Queen Margaret and King Malcolm.'

Odon felt as if he'd been struck a blow in the back. How easy it was to make a little information look treasonous by adding a slight twist to a few select details. 'Prioress Ursula is dead and I believe,' he said evenly, 'that Alfred of St Edmundsbury is a wool trader. Our monasteries need to sell their wool to survive.

'Your monasteries gather riches to themselves like squirrels gather acorns. What need has God of gold and ivory?'

Odon hid his anger by poking at the fire's embers. The clean smell of wood smoke filled his lungs. He let the words hang, hoping Rufus would become embarrassed at his own coarseness.

But when he looked at his pale eyes the young man's gaze was steady.

'Earl Montgomery tells me he does not trust a trader from his own area, a man called Michael,' added Rufus. 'I believe you know him also.'

Odon felt the blood drain from his face, despite his proximity to the fire. This was a man who held a great trust, not in words but in the goods he traded. He must have truly worked out the political value of his trade with the embroidery workshop at the Priory of St Thomas the Apostle and even know the importance of the work going on there. For this man to even have the slightest smell of deceit lingering in his behaviour or motives was unacceptable. And Alfred would have to be drawn into his cleansing net in case he was involved too. He could not risk anything happening at this stage to the embroidery. Perhaps all he'd heard about the poor dead Prioress Ursula had been true. Perhaps she had been the traitor. Odon turned to his visitor and said,

'Thank you, nephew, for your information. I will have these men arrested directly. This will be carried out under my personal supervision.'

Chapter Eight

Therese bowed her head. She stood in the lowliest position in the chapter house and waited her turn to make her confession. She'd been dreading this ordeal. It was, of course, inevitable as she could not take the sacrament of communion without purging her soul. But her soul would not be purged, for she held in her heart so many secrets that had given rise to falsehoods. She had, therefore, composed a version of events that she thought would cover matters for now. She would rely on a total confession to Abbess Eleanor at a later date when she would be free to tell all. She would have to feign illness to avoid Mass the following day. Her list of sins seemed to be growing at an alarming rate. No doubt, Sister Miriam, back in Normandy, would have had no trouble over her conscience with such matters. Her fellow confessors seemed particularly eager to hear the sins of their fellows and were clearly leaning forward in a restrained manner. So Therese just told the community of nuns about the breaking of the broom.

'Three rosaries to be said this morning in church after Terce, Sister. And after our midday prayers you will go down to the woods to collect willow for new brooms. Sister Gertrude will go with you and supervise. Her knowledge on such matters is without equal.'

Therese had been so worried about what she was going to say she'd hardly heard the others make their confessions. One, Sister Sybil, spoke so quietly she couldn't hear what she said at all and another, Sister Maude, gabbled. But she became alert when Sister Agnes spoke. Sister Agnes's confession was also incomplete, she noticed. There was no mention of her giving clothing to a wet novice in the night. That was not really a sin though, surely? But then Sister Agnes must already have difficulties over the replacement of Ursula's body with that of a dead colleague. She shivered, thinking of the dead Sister Anna's clothing about her body. Finally, Prioress Ethelburga announced the benefit of a united effort to clean the cloister now the builders had cleared it.

'Equipment has been laid out ready for your use,' she directed.

As they left the chapter house Prioress Ethelburga placed her hand on Sister Agnes's arm. Sister Agnes stopped and they both looked at the arresting hand. Some battle of wills seemed to be taking place until Prioress Ethelburga saw Sister Gertrude and Therese waiting to leave. She released Sister Agnes. Sister Gertrude walked off but Therese paused behind the timber banister of the sewing room stairs to listen.

'I have been wondering about how Sister Anna is faring,' Prioress Ethelburga asked Sister Agnes.

'She's gone to her family, Prioress. They came for her the morning of Prioress Ursula's funeral. I have heard since that she passed away peacefully among her own folk.'

Listening made her nervous and listening to lies made Therese nauseous. She scurried off. She did not hear the end of the conversation but she did not want to be caught listening. Her clothing seemed to wrap itself about her legs as if it were trying to trip her up. She thought of it being worn by Sister Anna, who now wore Ursula's shroud. She felt chilled until she reached the cloister where the nuns were already hard at work. She shook off the burden of Sister Anna's wronged soul and took on the merriment of the others.

First the women brushed down the walls and arches with goose wings and then they sprinkled the new patterned floor tiles with water and swept. The work was soon finished and Therese was left to tidy the brooms and dusters before prayers.

While stooped over her work she heard the deep, Welsh tones that had become carved into her like the zigzag patterns made by the masons on the beautiful stones around her. His laugh came from the western end of the cloister by the refectory. By rights Michael should only have passage through to the outer courtyard. In case she was noticed she tried to conceal that she knew him. She pretended to ignore his conversation with Prioress Ethelburga.

She wondered if they sounded like conspirators. She could not hear their words, just the drift of tone and measured volume, in keeping with their location close to the chapel.

Sister Hilda appeared on the far side with her fellow stitchers; the dust rinsed away from their skin and wiped off their clothing.

As they turned away from Prioress Ethelburga and Michael to walk round to the church entrance, the Prioress called out,

'Sister Hilda, I would like your opinion with regard to the threads the merchant, Michael, has brought us. Perhaps you will join us in the chapter house?'

'Immediately,' said Sister Hilda, swishing her skirts as she turned towards them. Her translucent skin was flushed with self-importance.

The others entered the church while Sister Hilda joined Michael and the Prioress. They walked towards the chapter house entrance, which was off a corridor in the southeast corner of the cloister. Therese collected the dusters and brooms. She took them over to the store close to the kitchen, her heart lightened by what she'd heard. She felt her mind had been making complications where none existed and she blamed the devil for making such mischief in her head. Alfred was a wool merchant and Michael was a thread merchant. They both would surely deal with the same people – spinners and dyers. It was not surprising they knew each other. She could let go of the fears created by last night's trip across to the builder's campsites.

Gertrude grumbled as Therese darted past her down the southern slope of the hill where the tower of the Priory of St Thomas the Apostle looked out across the Kent countryside. At the bottom, near the wood, she turned back to see Sister Gertrude descending at a much steadier pace. Behind the old woman the building appeared complete. This was the sewing room side. The sunlight was shimmering on the freshly hewn stones. She focused her attention on the wall. There were four windows. These were high and large to let in light to the work. Three were close together and a fourth was some distance from the other three, closer to the tower. This brought to her mind the hole in the wall she'd found in the stairwell. She'd thought it went directly into the sewing room. Yet there'd been no sign that the nuns had seen her broom-handle when she'd poked it through. It was no good, she would have to see inside the sewing room before she could work out what this could mean. The hole could be in a cupboard. She just did not know. She turned away from the building. This collecting of willow for broom-making was, at last, a little bit of freedom and she intended to enjoy it.

Gertrude was catching up so she turned to her task. The wood of willow and alder had been well coppiced. The alders looked almost ghostly with their small purple cones and leaves. She could see why these trees had thrived here. Their roots and part of their trunks were submerged in the water drained from the surrounding slopes, and somewhere in the midst of the woods the stream flowed. In winter it had spilled out, and the ground here would take a summer to dry. She guessed the water would cover her ankles, and would possibly reach her knees. The older nun was already wrapping the tail end of her skirts around the cord girdle around her waist. Therese did the same. They slipped off their sandals and entered the muddy water.

Having cut a wand of willow, Gertrude passed her knife to Therese. 'Like that,' she said, 'you cut it like that.' She wedged her rear into a stump, which was shaped like a chair with wands of willow sprouting out around its edge on three sides. Her action had the fluency of habit as she shuffled back. Her feet cleared the water and she leaned on the fine branches of willow. 'I'll watch you, so make sure you do it right,' said Gertrude.

This was a chore she'd often done back in Normandy, so Therese set about her task, reducing the number of willow stems on each stump, but not taking them all, before moving on to the next. She waded back out of the woodland to stack the bundle on the dry ground. Gertrude watched her, steadily at first and then less so, her head dropping onto her chest from time to time. So Therese continued, the sunshine and the work warmed her until she heard someone approach from the far side of the wood.

She glanced at Gertrude and wondered whether she should wake her, as they might need to run for safety. She was close to the old nun, her hand reaching out to touch her when she heard Michael's rich voice very quietly say, 'Sister, I need help.'

Turning to the sound further into the woods, she saw him. He was out of sight of the priory, but too close to Gertrude to avoid disturbing her if he said any more. She was in enough trouble as it was, but her investigations at present were not going well and he might know something useful if only she could quiz him without Sister Gertrude hearing. She flicked her hands at him, shooing him away and pointing out the slumbering nun. He did as he was bid and walked back through the water, across the stream – bridged by a fallen tree in the middle – and out to the far side. Therese followed. He sat down and invited her to sit with him on the grassy hillside. She looked about her. Michael's bay pony was standing grazing quietly. There was no-one else to be seen and behind them nearly at the top of the hill was a mound of earth in the distinctive shape of a grave. She guessed it must belong to the Impostor.

'My town is well under the thumb of the Normans,' he said.

'Then your town is a safe town,' retorted Therese. 'If this is going to be your line of conversation, I would rather not hear it.'

'My town may be safe, as you call it, for now, but the Welsh will not stand to be controlled by foreigners.'

'What business is this of yours?' Her confidence in Michael being a simple merchant was failing. She wondered for a moment whether he might invite her to join with him in some conspiracy. He ignored her question.

'There is a boy in my party,' he said. 'You have seen him, he is the son of a priest. Your Archbishop Lanfranc is against such things. He wants clerics to be celibate. My outspokenness may well bring my little companion into danger.'

'Then hold your tongue,' said Therese.

'Most of my group are grown men and we can fend for ourselves. It is the boy I fear for.'

'What do you want?'

'I want you to hide him in the priory.'

'A boy?'

'There must be a place you can hide him.'

Therese wondered about the hole in the wall, but she could not be sure where it led. She frowned. 'You could take him to the infirmary,' countered Therese. She wanted her mind to work faster, find a solution before she agreed to something she might regret.

'I don't want him around all those sick people,' said Michael. He signalled with his hand over to the eastern end of the woods and a boy scampered out, tripping on a loosened cross garter. It was the boy who'd held Michael's ponies in the woods. He seemed too young to be away from his mother, she thought as he bobbed down and tied his lace. His little face with big green eyes and freckled nose turned up to greet her gaze and she knew she had already lost the argument.

'You can take him now,' said Michael. 'Bundle him in your cloak like the willow you're collecting.'

'I cannot make a broom from him, and he is the weight of a dozen brooms. I cannot explain away the disappearance of that much wood.'

Michael laughed. 'You are right. He is a wooden boy.' He waggled the boy's sandy-haired head and the boy allowed his head to be waggled.

'Sister Therese!' It was Sister Gertrude's voice.

'Bring him to the church wall on the northern side of the compound tonight. I will find somewhere for him,' whispered Therese hastily as she ran back into the woodland. Each step felt as if she'd caught herself up in a rope that was tightening about her. The going was difficult, but it was not because of any impediment about her legs, the rope was in her mind. It was the added complication of having a child to care for.

She was still unsure of Michael's motives. He had landed a new responsibility on her and she had not gained one straight answer out of him. He must have been watching Gertrude and herself to make such a calculated approach. And where was Alfred? She thought he was going to set up camp at the very place where she and Michael had just sat. Was he in some way party to the arrangement that Michael had brokered with her about the boy?

As dusk approached Therese finished whipping the bristles to a new broom-handle.

'No need for formalities, Sister,' said Prioress Ethelburga swooping into the kitchen yard from the base of the tower. Therese twitched to stand but was arrested by the firm grasp of the Prioress on her shoulder, Prioress Ethelburga continued, 'I have just the job for a new broom.' She sounded almost friendly until she added sharply, 'Come with me.'

They ascended the tower steps to the first floor and walked towards the sewing room door. The community had been filing along this corridor several times a day with the cloister out of use. Her feet knew the way and almost without counting she knew the distance from the tower to the door: fifty-five steps. She nearly said it. She couldn't believe that she had gained access to the sewing room so soon.

Prioress Ethelburga unwrapped the priory keys from the folds in her skirts. From those she chose a key that was the length of her hand. The thin chain connecting it to her girdle jingled as she turned it. Inside the evening light poured through linen screens at the windows onto a fabric laid loosely over a frame in the middle of the room. Therese hoped it was the embroidery but it was a dust-cover protecting it from prying eyes. The Prioress didn't offer to show Therese the covered work, she simply instructed her to sweep as she'd been shown using water to lay the dust. Slightly disappointed at not being shown the embroidery, she set about her work studiously, for while she swept she summed up the length of the room. This was quite hard to do without looking as if she were counting. But, she managed to sweep with short vigorous strokes the dampened timbers and keep a check on her feet at the same time with the Prioress watching her. It was barely thirty steps long, and she knew that as she'd stood and watched Gertrude come down the hill she'd seen a fourth window along this wing, but there were only three in here.

Therese scooped a handful of water from the bucket and scattered it low over the floor.

'Good, good,' said Prioress Ethelburga, 'you mustn't splash the work.'

As Therese gingerly swished her broom around the floor by the embroidery frame she observed the ornate wooden screen at the end where the embroiderers had left their threads and needles. She wondered how many of the other nuns had worked out that there was a secret room. But for now that did not matter, for she had somewhere to hide the boy.

Threads and lint from the fabric made fluffy balls and tangles among the sticks of her broom.

'Shovel up the threads, Sister. But don't put them into the bucket until we're out of the room, just in case the dust flies up.'

Therese backed out keeping an eye on her load. For a moment her pan wobbled and the Prioress commanded her, 'Be alert, girl!' This made all her sinews snap to attention and the pan steadied long enough for Prioress Ethelburga to shut the door and for Therese to safely deposit the load in the bucket.

When they turned away from the door Sister Hilda was standing behind them. Her translucent skin was pulled tight over her small features. She was clearly on an unwelcome errand. She was not showing the swagger she displayed when she was charged with the sewing room key.

'Yes?' asked Prioress Ethelburga. Her mouth pinched up tightly behind the question.

Hilda bowed respectfully. 'Prioress, I've been sent by Sister Winifred to say it is time for our devotions.'

Prioress Ethelburga shot Hilda a severe glance. Then nodded to Therese. 'Young people,' snapped Ethelburga, 'never do jobs properly unless they are carefully watched, Sister Hilda.'

'Yes, Prioress,' said Hilda meekly, and Therese could see her trembling.

'Lead on,' said Prioress Ethelburga to Hilda and Therese followed Prioress Ethelburga's stiff back. It was clear that Hilda felt equally admonished.

The nights were still chilled and Therese rubbed her arms as she stood outside the temporary door in the church. The night was very dark with cloud covering the moon and stars. Even after some time she could make out little among the stones. She felt her way along to the edge of the building works.

Michael was already there, his brown pony at his side, the child almost invisible between the pony and the man's stocky legs. Michael pulled him out to the front. The sandy-haired boy seemed so much smaller than when she'd seen him burst from his hiding place in the woods.

'How old is he?' she asked, wondering about her ability to look after a child.

'He's seen six summers,' answered Michael. 'He's strong and can look after himself mostly. Hurry now, you must take him.'

Therese could hear the thunder of hooves and the rattle of metal somewhere beyond the hill where the builders and Michael were encamped. 'What's going on?' she asked.

'I do not know, Sister. But whatever it is, remember the boy's father is a Norman and has no part in what I do.'

'How can a small boy not be influenced?' she asked Michael, but he was already taking his leave. 'What shall I call him?' she asked as he swung his pony round.

'Call him Eric,' suggested Michael as he drove his pony away with his legs.

Taking the boy into the church she realised her gullibility. She'd been taken in by the boy's smiling green eyes and her own sense of adventure, and, not least, by Michael's confidence in her. That now seemed like flattery. She shouldn't be doing this. It was, at the very least, against the priory rules, but she was already halfway round the cloister.

Michael was, in attitude, if not in fact, an enemy of the Normans. Without saying anything she turned around and took the boy back to the chapel. When she reached the builders' door the child hung back.

'You must go back to Michael,' she said. Silently he shook his head. She picked him up and, with one hand, lifted the brace, opened the door and carried him out. 'You can't stay here.' She put him down outside the building works and held onto his sleeve. He resisted enough to show his reluctance as she took him down the valley and steered him across the stream towards the campsite. The valley was quiet. The sound of horses had gone. It was not unusual, she guessed, for such groups of her countrymen to travel through the night.

She made her way to the place where she'd seen Alfred and Michael talking around the fire, but the fire had been kicked out and the tents were lying slashed to pieces. Eric tugged at her sleeve and it started to rain. She trembled, but she could see no bodies, and she had no time to listen in on the builders' conversations as they picked over Michael's camp. Even though she might learn something from them, she would have to be in church for dawn prayers. Eric had started to sob when he saw the empty camp, she could only guess at Michael's fate; but whatever had happened, he was no longer here.

There was no choice. In the same way Bishop Odon de Bayeux had plucked her from her flaming village, she was obliged to care for Eric. Bending down she wrapped her arms about him and picked him up. She ran back to the priory against the rain and with the child weighting her steps. She thought her will might break until she reached the sanctuary of the church. The structure held a physical strength she needed. The boy was quiet now. She let him slip down as she clutched a nearby pillar and held it till she caught her breath. She wanted to enter the church quietly.

Eric tugged at her habit. Therese looked down.

'Is it my fault?' asked the boy in English. The four words were spoken like a ballad, almost sung. Just the way Michael would say them.

She wiped her face with her sleeve, and said, 'No.'

'What has happened to Michael?' he asked. Eric faltered over what, to him, was clearly a foreign language.

'I don't know,' she replied. Composing herself, she took him into the church and to the tower. She counted the steps and stopped below the hole. 'Climb on my shoulders,' she instructed, bracing her hands to form a stirrup for him. The tower was almost completely black with the rain clouds still covering the moon. He felt for her hands. His fingers were small but strong and his leather-clad foot made a firm purchase and soon the boy was on her shoulders.

'There's a hole in the wall up on the left. Can you see it?' she asked.

'I can feel something,' he said. 'A metal thing, a light holder.'

'It's higher and on your left.'

'Found it.'

'Climb in,' said Therese, 'but be careful. I do not know what is in there.' The weight on her shoulders pushed her down on one side and then it was gone. He made no sound, so she called to him, 'Are you all right?'

'Yes,' said Eric poking his head out. 'I only just fit in the hole. It's like a hay-loft up here.' He sounded excited, but still there was little in his voice to indicate a Norman father. He seemed more like Michael.

'Do you need any food?' she asked.

'I've eaten, thank you.'

'Good, but wait.' Therese went downstairs into the kitchen yard and collected a pot. She returned and gave it to him with the words: 'There are no hedges up there so use this.' He reached down to collect it and disappeared into his hideaway.

'You will look after me, won't you, Sister?' he asked, peeping out again.

'Yes, of course,' said Therese. Her heart sank with the burden of his little life.

Chapter Nine

Abbess Eleanor left the refectory at St Augustine's Abbey. She had eaten more than she had intended and she felt slightly uncomfortable. She decided to take a walk in the grounds and see if she could gain a casual audience with Abbot Scotland. She thought he might be able to shed some light on the local political situation.

She saw him walking – a big man with red hair, a larger version of Archbishop Odon. He had his head bowed, the sun shining on his tonsure. It made him look as if he might have a tight-fitting halo, but she banished this thought from her mind. This was a practical man, not a saint. She approached cautiously, not wanting to disturb any private prayers he may be making, but as she got closer it was clear he was inspecting the plants.

After a few moments discussing the progress of the herbs growing in the border Eleanor tried to sound conversational as she broached the subject of the neighbouring abbey inside the city walls of Canterbury. 'How do two such important abbeys cope running along beside each other as they do?' she asked.

'You know, Abbess, that we come under the rule of the Pope here?' replied Scotland. 'Because Saint Augustine himself was sent here by the Pope.'

Eleanor was taken aback by his Scottish accent though she realised she should have expected he might be from Scotland as he was named after the country. 'I do now,' she said. The thought of a possible Scottish conspiracy to add to the possibilities surrounding the attempt on the embroidery blocked out any other thought for a moment. She floundered. 'You are from Scotland?' she asked stupidly.

'I am, and what of it?'

'Is it very different here?'

'Not really. People are people and God is God.' He thought for a moment clearly humouring her. 'The hills are bigger in Scotland.'

'Do you miss home?' She felt she might be stretching his good manners, but he was in a powerful position. Could he be involved in a plot?

'Nay, Abbess. I have been here over twenty-five years.' He looked at her in a way that indicated he would not be answering any more questions about it.

She returned to her original reason for the interview. The thought of Agid challenging her in the Canterbury street provoked her. She had to know what the conflict was between Bishop Odon and Archbishop Lanfranc. And if Abbot Scotland was as neutral in this area as he seemed, she may get her answer from him. 'So you have very little to do with Christ Church Abbey?'

'Very little directly,' said Scotland. 'I'm so busy with the rebuilding of this place. But I shall soon have it in good order.' He sighed with satisfaction. 'It was virtually falling down when I came. We have the very best builders here. Bishop Gundulf is organising much of it.'

'I hear his name mentioned a lot,' said Eleanor. She thought for a moment. The conversation had drifted from her original intention, but this seemed a suitable area to explore. Bishop Gundulf was involved with all this building – the whole country seemed to be a building site, perhaps there might be some falling out among them? 'I wonder,' she asked, 'if there might be some jealousy between the builders, some competitiveness that might cause problems to develop? Not all the masons are from Normandy.'

Abbot Scotland rounded on her, his face red. 'The masons are sworn to secrecy and allegiance. They have to behave with honour. I am offended on their behalf.'

'I apologise for any offence, but none was intended,' said Eleanor stiffly.

'This amounts to gossip, Abbess, and I will not gossip.' The Abbot's skin reddened further around his neck.

'I do not intend to gossip. I see us as equals, exchanging views for the benefit of our respective communities.'

'Then you will know, perhaps, that Bishop Odo has been making that priory, which is under your control, St Thomas the Apostle, a little safer.'

'I have not heard, Abbot Scotland.' Her blood ran cold and she bowed her head to hide her fear for Therese and her friends.

'Bishop Odo has had people arrested. I hear that it was at the command of Prince Rufus.'

'I thought you didn't gossip?' said Eleanor. She regretted annoying him over the masons especially as she couldn't see that they were in any way relevant, but his reaction had brought a fire to her temper.

'This is just a frank exchange,' said Scotland sharply.

'Who has been arrested?' She tried to keep the tremble from her voice.

'A Welsh merchant from Montgomery. I believe his name is Michael.'

Eleanor kept her sigh of relief hidden. Michael the merchant may have saved herself and Therese, but he was not important to her in the same way as Alfred and at least Scotland had not mentioned him. Hopefully he was still there for Therese. Eleanor went to take her leave – she wanted to check what had happened – but the Abbot wished to change the subject.

'So for now the balance of power between the King's sons seems to be with Prince Rufus. So what do you think the elder brother, Robert, would think of that?'

Eleanor managed a Gallic shrug. She did not wish this conversation to continue any longer, yet he'd thrown up another possibility. Could the Princes be trying to destroy the embroidery in some kind of power game? She could not believe that they would destroy something that was intended to honour their father. Yet would that be any stranger than Ursula's idea of warring bishops. Or, indeed, a Welsh or Scottish plot. She felt overwhelmed.

Abbot Scotland's face softened. 'You are concerned for your priory. I understand.' He laid a hand over hers touching Odon's ring. He looked into her eyes and said, 'Take care, Abbess. I speak to you as equal to equal. Such things go on in Canterbury even I cannot keep a check on. I warn you, do not pry. It can be dangerous.'

Eleanor bowed and started to walk away.

'Oh, Abbess,' he called after her. 'There was someone else arrested with the merchant's group, an East Anglian man called Alfred. We had some dealings with him ourselves over wool, so my prior tells me.'

She bowed again and hurried away. Therese was without protection. She could not bear the thought of that child at risk. What had she been doing allowing Therese and Ursula to talk her into such nonsense?

She looked up. Her footsteps had brought her through to the kitchens. She would have to tell Ursula about her brother's arrest. She opened the door. The kitchen was quiet. Clearing up after the meal was complete and the servants had taken themselves off for a break. Only one remained poking the hearth.

'Ursula,' said Eleanor. The ex-prioress looked up. Her broad face was pink and tearful. 'You know about Alfred?' she asked.

Ursula nodded. 'And he was worried about what we were getting ourselves into!'

'It means that Therese is at St Thomas's on her own.'

'Sister Agnes will help her.'

'She can do little against someone prepared to murder.'

'They will not try to murder her.'

'Why not? They tried to murder you.'

'I knew too much.' Ursula was going to ask her a question, but Eleanor did not have time for it.

'But Sister Therese might already know too much,' said Eleanor. 'We should get her out of St Thomas's.' Ursula turned away. There was such sadness in her movement Eleanor put her arm out and touched her hand, red raw with scrubbing and peeling. 'What is it, Ursula?'

'We need to act quickly. We must leave Sister Therese there. She is the one person who can find something out. Your knight, Sir Gilbert, must be able to replace my brother as her protector.'

'I will check on his health.'

'But I need to find a way of freeing Alfred. And the only way to do that is to resolve this issue at the Priory.'

'What do you mean?

'I hear Rufus has been to visit Lanfranc as well as your employer.' Ursula's tone had hardened. Eleanor winced at her leaving out the titles of these important people, but she forgave her – after all her bishop had just arrested her brother.

'Look,' said Eleanor, 'I was at Christ Church when Prince Rufus was there with his guard. I was sent to the scriptorium out of the way. I am concerned about Archbishop Lanfranc. I find it hard, however, to believe that he would have the embroidery destroyed just to get at Bishop Odon, but right now I can't be sure.'

'Then I will go and get employment in the kitchen,' said Ursula.

'No, Ursula you've done enough. I have not been in any danger so far. I cannot leave it all to you and Sister Therese. I will go. But the kitchen is too far away, I will only hear gossip there. I need to be inside the monastery.'

Ursula dried her eyes on her sleeve. 'I can get you a monk's habit and as no new monks are let in without a letter of commendation I can get one of those too.'

'You know a forger?' Eleanor looked at her old friend aghast.

'I know someone with the right skills. All letters are written by scribes. There is just the matter of the signature and seal.'

'What of my voice?' asked Eleanor.

'There are many monks with high voices.' Ursula smiled reassuringly and Eleanor smiled back with dawning confidence.

St Augustine's was well supplied with visitor accommodation, so the corridor to Eleanor's apartment was quite long. While she walked down the length of it to her room, she could see a page waiting by her door. She stopped in front of the young boy, and he presented her with a note. She looked at the seal. It was from Bishop Odon.

'I am to return with a reply, Abbess,' said the lad, bowing.

'Wait here and you shall have one,' she replied. She entered her room and broke the seal. Her hands seemed chilled. She did not want any interference; she had too much to do. The words she read felt as if they were building a high wall around her. Bishop Odon was summoning her to meet him at Dover Castle. She could not refuse and yet she did not wish to find herself in the position of having to explain her actions since arriving in England.

She wrote her reply, sealed it with wax and her personal seal which she kept in a small wooden box in her pocket. She returned it to the page in the corridor and followed him back to the end. He handed the scroll to a messenger in the outer court, seated on a fast-looking chestnut horse. It would not be long before Odon had his reply. She would follow the note to Dover within the day, but she would travel at her own speed.

Before going to Christ Church infirmary to see Sir Gilbert, she decided to call on Ursula to explain where and why she was going.

'Instructions have already been received to put together a retinue for your journey,' said Ursula as they stood in the kitchen yard. She rubbed her hands on her skirts. 'Old friend, I must ask you…' Her voice faltered.

'What?' asked Eleanor.

'There is another way to get my brother released and that is for you to intercede on his behalf.'

Eleanor looked into Ursula's eyes. The dark anguish that lurked there disturbed her. 'I will try, but I cannot promise anything.'

'But do not tell him about your investigations. Not yet. And don't tell him about me. It could all look so wrong.'

'What do you mean, Ursula?'

'If he suspects Alfred then he could suspect me, and it could look as if we were tricking you into believing that we are innocent.'

'But you are innocent, aren't you?'

'Yes, of course we are.'

'You do not sound very sure,' said Eleanor.

'I am sure of my heart, Abbess Eleanor. I beseech you to intercede on his behalf.'

'Then I shall try. Now I must see Sir Gilbert before I leave. Hopefully I will be able to return directly.'

'Everything will be ready for you,' said Ursula with a knowing smile.

Brother Matthew met Eleanor at the infirmary door. She introduced herself more formally this time and Brother Matthew bowed. As she lowered her head to go through a second doorway, he allowed her to pass first.

Eleanor glanced at Brother Matthew as he went across to grind some herbs in his pestle and mortar. He had a rugged face and he clearly had difficulty maintaining a clean-shaven appearance. His steel-grey eyebrows were bushy with little tufts growing in random directions out of them.

'Where is he?'

Brother Matthew showed her through to Sir Gilbert's bed which was in its own annex, but without a door. 'Thank you,' she said, dismissing him politely. He nodded and left her with the knight who was sitting up. Sir Gilbert acknowledged her with a small bow.

His skin was blotchy and white. The bruising had receded into discoloured lumps. Eleanor started their conversation in Norman-French. This would not keep their conversation completely private but it might prevent idle listeners understanding her plans and then a thought struck her. Perhaps he could answer the riddle set by Agid when he accosted her in the lanes outside Christ Church Abbey – the story of division between Bishop Odon and Archbishop Lanfranc. So she asked him outright about any incident since Archbishop Lanfranc came to England that would have set the two in opposition.

'There was a matter some time ago and it was related to the Crown of England,' said Sir Gilbert. 'It goes back to 1066. On the death of Harold Godwinson at the battle of Hastings the Bishop of York swore in Edgar the Aethling as the King of England. He had the power to do so as well as the Archbishop of Canterbury. I suspect this goes back to the time before England was one kingdom.'

'But all that was sorted out,' complained Eleanor. 'Edgar the Aethling has come to terms with King William.' She found it strange that she should be saying to Bishop Odon's knight the same thing she'd said to the Welsh merchant so recently.

'That may be so, but the Bishopric of York was given to Thomas. Before he went there he was Bishop Odon's treasurer at Bayeux. You may remember him. Archbishop Lanfranc insisted that he swore fealty to him.'

'Yes, I remember him, but that was more years ago than I care to remember. So why should Archbishop Lanfranc insist on this public display of loyalty?' Eleanor frowned.

'Because Bishop Thomas might be tempted, as other York Bishops had been, to enthrone a king and this time it might be on

Bishop Odon's say so.'

'That sounds incredible,' said Eleanor.

'Why? Bishop Odon supports Robert, King William's eldest son, while Archbishop Lanfranc supports the King's choice, William Rufus, for the crown of England. Supposing Bishop Odon arranged for Robert to be sworn in at York while Rufus is sworn in by the Archbishop of Canterbury. There would be chaos.'

'This surely is more a matter for a sensible solution to be worked out amicably between colleagues, than some great intrigue.'

'They went to the Pope for a resolution but the matter was eventually resolved in England and Bishop Thomas swore his fealty to Archbishop Lanfranc. But this will not necessarily stabilise matters when the King dies.'

Eleanor crossed herself. She felt almost tainted by hearing the political manoeuvrings that the church involved itself in. Was this the seed of competition that had grown up between these two powerful men? Was this why there was trouble at her priory? And it was more trouble at the priory that she had to guard against.

'I need you to guard Sister Therese at the Priory of St Thomas the Apostle as soon as possible,' she said briskly.

'I did not know she was there,' said Sir Gilbert with concern. 'Has she been there all this time on her own?'

Eleanor felt a stab of guilt. 'This is my business. All you need know is that she has been kept safe until now. Your position is to be on the rising ground beyond the small coppiced wood to the south of the priory. You must tell no-one of this.' This was where Alfred had agreed to make his camp; if Therese wanted help that is where she had been told to go. Eleanor did not mention her involvement with Ursula. He was still Bishop Odon's knight. But, she did inform him of the arrest of their saviour in the woods, and she did tell him that Michael's whole group and Alfred had also been arrested.

'I will set out before the end of the day,' said Bishop Odon's knight. 'My horse is rested and I'm sure I am up to the ride. I feel better by the hour.'

Eleanor thanked him and rose. Brother Matthew was not about so she slipped through the door quietly. On leaving the infirmary she saw the stooped figure of Archbishop Lanfranc's clerk, Brother

David, coming towards her. She felt tightness about her heart.

'Abbess Eleanor,' he hailed her, his right hand up and his palm facing her.

'Brother David, has Archbishop Lanfranc found time to see me yet?' she asked as he reached her. A morsel of hope lightened her heart.

'No, I'm afraid not. That is not why I've come,' replied Brother David. His red-rimmed grey eyes reproached her.

'So, Brother, what is the reason for your approach. I assume it is not to pass the time of day?'

'You are quite right, Abbess. We have rested and restored your knight here to health at our expense, of course. However, what we spend on him and his horse we cannot spend on the poor. I'm sure you understand our predicament.'

She thought she saw David's hands tremble slightly before he tucked them up opposite sleeves. 'Indeed, I do understand.' Eleanor sighed. The morsel of hope left her but this was a matter that could be readily fixed. 'He will not be in need of your good offices any longer and I will ensure your funds are more than restored.'

Brother David took his leave and Eleanor started to walk back to St Augustine's. With every step she doubted more her ability to spy within Christ Church Abbey. Even dressed as a monk, surely Brother David, if no one else, would recognise her?

Chapter Ten

After cleaning the cloister, Prioress Ethelburga had ordered the laundry of the nuns' habits. So Therese sat opposite Sister Agnes, at last, in her own dry clothes. Sister Agnes's long features looked serious. Neither of them spoke for a moment as they examined the wooden table.

There were two ways she could get help from her for the boy. One was just to ask for it and hope she did not question her and the second was to tell her all and hope Sister Agnes was discreet and loyal and not part of the conspiracy to destroy the embroidery. Despite the fact that Eric was hidden in the tower, she had to continue to look into the details of what went on here at St Thomas's the day the Impostor fell to her death and took Ursula with her. She did not want to be thrown out of St Thomas's yet. A thought struck her. There might be another way to make the approach.

Agnes nodded and smiled. The kitchen servants had gone home and Agnes passed her a bowl of porridge. 'Please, what is the matter, Sister?' asked the older nun. 'Come let's sit by the fire.'

Therese took a deep breath. 'I know about Prioress Ursula,' she said testily.

'What about the Prioress?' asked Agnes, guardedly.

'She's not dead.'

'Hush,' said Agnes, going to the door and checking no-one was behind it.

'But there is a rumour that she was as guilty as the other one, the Impostor who fell from the tower.'

'That's not true!' said Agnes. She covered her mouth briefly as if she wanted to catch the words but she was already too late. 'I ask you again, what do you know?'

'I know where Prioress Ursula is now,' ventured Therese.

'You must say nothing of this,' warned Agnes.

'I am not the one I do not trust here, Sister Agnes.' Therese was unused to talking in this tight-lipped way.

'In what way do you think me untrustworthy? I have been a

nun for twenty years.' Sister Agnes pulled her dignity about her.

Therese took a deep breath. 'You are Anglo-Saxon.'

'I am, so what?' Agnes's eyes narrowed.

'You could be wishing to destroy the embroidery,' suggested Therese, already starting to lose the suspicious tones in her voice.

'Why should I want to do that?' asked Agnes.

Therese realised that this line of questioning was, after all, appropriate; she tried to sound angry. 'To discredit the King,' she said.

'I have been here since this place opened. I have had plenty of time to destroy each panel as it was made. Now they are on the last panel and the others have been taken away under guard, so all that can be destroyed here is the last panel. If I wanted to do such a thing I would have done it long ago.'

Therese looked at her long and hard in the firelight. Her eyes were shadowed by the flickering flame. Therese couldn't read them. 'So if Prioress Ursula and yourself are both innocent, where has the rumour come from that Prioress Ursula is as guilty as the Impostor,' she asked with simple curiosity, all pretence at anger gone.

Sister Agnes stirred the fire with a poker. 'I don't really know. I assumed it was Sister Ethelburga.'

'Why would she do that?' asked Therese.

'I thought it was to discredit Prioress Ursula's choice of successor.'

'I thought Sister Ethelburga was the obvious choice to succeed.'

'She was equal with Sister Winifred, but Sister Winifred had Prioress Ursula's favour. As soon as we'd buried Sister Anna as Prioress Ursula...' Agnes looked down. 'I'm sorry. I am still carrying the guilt for such a sacrilege – but we did not know what else to do.' Her eyes were pleading with Therese. 'Anyway,' she continued, pulling herself straight. 'Sister Ethelburga took Bishop Odo aside and told him her version of events. As soon as she was given the keys she locked up the sewing room and had it thoroughly cleaned.'

'So she removed the evidence of the fight between Prioress Ursula and the Impostor? So,' deduced Therese, 'she could have created the story about Prioress Ursula to hide the person who had passed the key on to the Impostor?'

'I may not like Prioress Ethelburga, but I do not think she is like that. The sewing could not have been restarted in a room in that condition.' Sister Agnes stood up. 'Now if that is all, Sister Therese, I would like some sleep before our next session in church.'

'I'm sorry, Sister Agnes. I have had to offend you. Otherwise I could not have known exactly how you feel. I did not really come here to examine you in this way. I just did not know whether I could trust you or not.'

'And do you?'

'I wish I could. I want to trust you. But you, Prioress Ursula and Alfred are all connected and to trust one I have to trust all of you and possibly Michael the merchant from Montgomery too. And he is gone. And he has left me a boy to care for.'

Agnes was already by the door lifting the latch. She dropped it, and it fell back into its holder. 'A boy?'

'A six-year-old boy. He is harmless and I have hidden him, but he needs food and I need you for that.'

'Someone you don't wholly trust?'

'I know, I know. I have to trust you.'

'Even though you don't want to have to?'

'Yes.'

'I will leave him some food under a pot in the kitchen yard each day.'

'Thank you, thank you,' said Therese catching her arm.

'Mind you, I don't want to know where he is or anything else for that matter.'

'You won't.' Therese followed Agnes to the door.

'And in the meantime I will see if I can find him somewhere else to live.'

'Thank you, Sister Agnes.'

'Abbess Eleanor brought you here. You are clearly under her direction. I will do what I can for you. But you must be careful not to let others make the connection by asking too many questions.' Agnes paused. 'You found me disturbed by recent events, Sister Therese. Michael the merchant and his group were arrested by

Bishop Odo. One of the servants told me. I personally have had nothing to do with the Welshman, and have no intention of doing so. I have only ever seen him speak to Prioress Ethelburga and Sister Hilda since the incident with the embroidery.'

'What about before that?' asked Therese.

'When Prioress Ursula was here she spoke to him, of course. But so did Sister Winifred and Sister Sybil as well as the two I've just mentioned.'

'Prioress Ethelburga and Sister Hilda?'

'Yes.'

Therese squeezed Agnes's hand and kissed her cheek with gratitude.

'That'll do,' said Agnes. 'Your young blood is up. Now calm down or someone'll guess you've got something to hide.' As Therese settled herself Agnes continued. 'I must also tell you that Alfred of St Edmundsbury was arrested with Michael the Merchant. If you know about Prioress Ursula you will be acquainted with her brother, perhaps.'

'He was there to help me and to get messages to the Abbess.' The excess of energy dispersed and Therese felt her mouth drop open, then she shut it firmly before saying, 'Abbess Eleanor will find someone else to take my messages to her. She will know of this, and she is the one person I can trust.'

'You are determined to carry on here?' asked Agnes. 'You don't have to, you know?'

'I am determined to stay, Sister Agnes.'

'You are young. The young do not know of danger.'

Therese kept her head down in the chapter house the next morning. She was exhausted from seeing to Eric overnight. The food, some porridge, had been there as Sister Agnes promised but it was nearly impossible to keep him quiet and allow him to exercise. Her neck seemed to be without strength and she had to avoid anyone seeing her eyes. She did have so much to conceal.

Prioress Ethelburga called her name. Therese jumped. The day's duties must already have been allocated to the others; she was last on the list and closest to the door. The others were all looking at her.

'Sister Therese,' repeated the Prioress, her pasty skin blotching slightly with temper. 'I wish you to go into the garden today and help Sisters Winifred, Aelfgyth and Leofgyth. You are looking pale. I think the fresh air will do you good.'

Therese was surprised by these unusually kind words from Prioress Ethelburga.

The gardeners slid from their places and as she filed out with her fellow nuns she found herself next to Leofgyth, who whispered, 'What have you done to get kicked out of the sewing room?'

Therese frowned. Could Prioress Ethelburga have seen her working out the size of the sewing room? Did she suspect her of spying? She turned and watched the Prioress march away, her skirts rustling. There was no way to tell.

'There is much planting to do,' said Sister Winifred as the party of gardeners reached the fresh air. Therese could see small white marks on her already tanned face. These vanished when she smiled as she did now. She must always be smiling for the sun to miss those places, thought Therese, and she returned the smile. 'But the young plants must be cared for as we care for all young things. So I will leave you with Sister Leofgyth to hoe along these rows here in the middle of the garden, while Sister Aelfgyth and I will be over there, down the bottom end, setting bean seeds. Call me if you need me.'

Therese dropped her smile at the reference to looking after the young and wondered if Sister Winifred knew about Eric. But she nodded as innocently as she could and a moment later Leofgyth was talking.

'She doesn't mind us chatting as long as we get on with our work,' she said. She rubbed her pointy chin. 'I think she and Sister Aelfgyth like to talk too. Anyway we're far enough away from anybody not to be heard.'

The garden was located behind the dorter, chapter house and infirmary. At the southern end there was a large barn with doors that stood open to air the building after the long winter. She could just see that the doors were also open on the other side of the barn. Where the garden was not enclosed by buildings there was a high stone wall. Fat doves sat sunning themselves in the small arches of the dovecot in front of the barn.

The two older nuns were clearly talking as they went down the garden towards the barn with Sister Winifred's height stooped over to listen to the much shorter Sister Aelfgyth. She carried a wicker trug containing trowels and seeds. Sister Aelfgyth carried a draw-hoe.

'I've given up minding about not being allowed to work in the sewing room,' said Leofgyth. 'I'm proud of the work I've already done on the other panels.'

'We nuns aren't allowed to be proud,' said Therese. 'It is a sin.' She drew her hoe back and pushed it forward over the dry soil.

'They are all proud,' said Leofgyth waving her hand as if showing Therese the whole world.

'Who?' asked Therese.

'The Bishops and Priests, the Abbots, the Priors, the Prioresses et al. A humble churchman? I've not found one. And why should they be? In a country where every other year there is famine they always have enough to eat. They have power over the laity, which they use and say it is in the name of God. It has nothing to do with God.'

'But the monasteries look after the sick and the poor,' Therese pointed out.

'And this place makes expensive embroideries for a conqueror.'

'You cannot be proud of your work, but angry that it is done.' Therese stopped work and leaned on her hoe.

'Perhaps you are right,' said Leofgyth, 'but it's the way I feel.'

'Do the others feel as you do?'

'I don't know. Sister Hilda is always tight-lipped, but since Prioress Ursula died she has been given a lot of responsibilities that used to be Sister Winifred's.'

'Is Sister Winifred suspected of being involved with what happened? Is that why she's been put on gardening duties?' Therese looked at her companion. She had hardly noticed the change in the conversation from the general to the specific information she was seeking. She started hoeing again; she did not want to attract attention to herself.

'I don't think so,' replied Leofgyth. 'Sister Aelfgyth said it was for Sister Winifred's health. She'd worked so hard on the sewing her eyes were sore.'

'So why has Sister Hilda been promoted, then?'

'That's what we'd all like to know. I suspect she comes from a good family with influence. They've probably endowed the priory with funds. That's usually the reason.' Leofgyth stopped and leaned on her hoe, staring at Therese. Therese kept hoeing and Leofgyth returned to it when they saw Sister Aelfgyth straighten up and look at them. Aelfgyth turned away.

'What do you know of the others?' asked Therese. It was normal enough to want to know about your new community. Surely, Leofgyth would not think the enquiry strange?

The young nun launched into the subject with vigour: 'Mabel and Maude are sisters by birth, twins in fact, but not identical. They're loyal to each other and inseparable. They barely communicate with the rest of us.' Leofgyth was flushed with the pleasure of telling the new girl all. 'You know they work with the animals mostly.'

They finished hoeing their rows and started on the next two.

'And Sister Sybil?' asked Therese.

'She's all right, I suppose. She's another one from old Anglo-Saxon aristocracy. The families sent their daughters to the church so they wouldn't have to marry Normans.' Leofgyth looked up from her hoeing. 'No disrespect intended.'

Therese nodded, but said nothing of her own Anglo-Saxon origins.

'Anyway,' continued Leofgyth, 'her family lost their lands to the Normans so they've lost their influence.'

'And Sister Beatrice?'

Leofgyth smiled. 'She's beautiful inside and out. She's our guardian angel on Earth. She has patience and kindness beyond that which is human. We all love her. She is so easy to love.'

'So,' said Therese, as casually as she could, 'who was in the sewing room the day Prioress Ursula died?'

'You know of that?'

'Everyone knows of it.'

Leofgyth accepted this with a nod. 'I was there. It was my turn to help by threading needles and the like. Prioress Ursula was keen to get the work finished so Sisters Winifred and Aelfgyth were working on one end with Sisters Sybil and Hilda on the other. Sister Ethelburga and Prioress Ursula worked the middle section. Sister Beatrice was in the infirmary with a cold and the twins were overseeing the servants feeding and cleaning the animals over-wintering in the barn. Sister Beatrice wasn't too poorly because she was able to go to the funeral in all that snow.'

Leofgyth paused for breath and her face changed. She clearly remembered Prioress Ethelburga's warning against talking to Therese about the sewing room. 'Anyway,' she added, 'that all happened before you came here, so why do you need to know all that?'

'Just curiosity,' said Therese. Her hoe barely paused.

'I can get into trouble for telling you.'

'I won't tell on you, if you don't tell on me,' said Therese. She fixed Leofgyth with an earnest gaze. Leofgyth may look completely different to Sister Miriam at home but she was just like her. She would prefer to keep an indiscretion a secret than have to proceed with a burdensome penance.

'Hmm,' said Leofgyth in reluctant agreement. 'It's time to take a short break. We normally sit by the barn.'

The sheep and cattle had left the barn for the pastures around the priory and only the odd wisp of winter hay and straw remained. Sister Aelfgyth had left Sister Winifred planting beans and was gathering eggs from the dovecot. Therese and Leofgyth sat on the ground and leaned against the barn wall. It was shady and sheltered. The girls relaxed and Sister Winifred joined them.

'Which of our good sisters is the Infirmarer,' asked Therese as she made herself comfortable.

'Sister Aelfgyth takes some of the duties with Sister Agnes,' Sister Winifred informed her. 'I also like to take my turn nursing the sick.' Sister Winifred looked at Therese with concern.

Resting was easy, but she thought she might not be able to rise at the end of the break. In a sleepy haze she thought that this is where Sisters Mabel and Maude had been the day of the incident in the sewing room. Could they have seen something? Therese looked up towards the priory. They would have seen nothing of the events that day. Their view of the tower was blocked by the chapter house and infirmary. Her eyes closed. 'Just a few moments,' she muttered as she felt herself slip away into slumber.

'Wake up, Sister Therese. You must wake up!' Leofgyth's voice was a penetrating shriek. Therese stirred and stared at her waker.

Chapter Eleven

Eleanor stopped her pony at the gate of Dover castle. He was of a small grey breed with short, jolting strides and Eleanor was already a little saddle sore from the day before. Her small retinue of a guard and a servant from St Augustine's had stayed with her overnight just outside Dover in modest lodgings. She hadn't wanted the scrutiny that would accompany an evening at Dover Castle.

The castle guards were looking at her now. She announced with quiet authority who she was and that she was here to see the Earl of Kent, Bishop Odon de Bayeux. She was clearly expected as they readily let her in. As her pony carefully brought his rider to the yard in front of the castle keep she realised how difficult it would be to plead for Alfred. He was an old friend as was Ursula. Whatever she said she could not help but betray Ursula to her Bishop. Nevertheless, she decided that if the opportunity arose she would try. A house guard accompanied her up the steps of the keep and opened the Bishop's door for her.

He was by the window looking down into the courtyard. 'How is my little Therese?' he asked.

'Well, Your Grace.' Eleanor bobbed down respectfully and kissed his ring of office which he held out for her.

'She isn't with you? I thought she would come too.' He sounded disappointed.

Eleanor felt sweat break out on her brow. 'With the greatest respect, you did not ask me to bring her. I have left her in a priory near Canterbury, Your Grace.'

'Not St Thomas the Apostle, I hope?' Bishop Odon asked with a frown.

'Would I do such a thing?' Eleanor smiled. Was that a lie? She hoped not. She looked at Odon, his thoughts had already moved on.

'What does she think of her homeland?'

'She is very excited about it.'

'Good, good. Do you think she will take her final vows and fully enter the service of the church?'

'I don't know yet. If she does not, her future would be very uncertain. But she has such a wild side to her nature. Her zest for life may be too great for the confines of a monastic life.'

'There is no hurry. I will not rush her,' said Bishop Odon. 'Now let us take a seat. We must discuss your investigations. Who are your suspects?'

'I have come across various possibilities. The obvious one is an Anglo-Saxon group.'

'The same group Prioress Ursula was involved in?'

'She may not have been involved,' Protested Eleanor.

'She was the one with the key to the room. The feeling among the nuns there was that she was involved.'

'You mean the new Prioress Ethelburga thinks she was involved.'

'I find her loyal to the Normans.'

'And I am Norman, or have you forgotten?' Eleanor felt slightly disgusted at him accepting Ethelburga's word so readily, almost in preference to her own views, especially as she was the woman's superior.

'I understand it must be difficult for you, the fact that I appointed Prioress Ethelburga when that would normally have been your job to do so. But, the situation was an emergency. I thought when we discussed it in Normandy you accepted that, along with the fact that I had to stop the work on the embroidery until you came over here.'

Back in Normandy, it had been difficult to argue against the decision of Sister Ethelburga as Prioress but now, in her mind Ursula was still Prioress. 'I understand why you appointed her. You had to maintain order at the Priory.'

He accepted her concession with a nod. 'I am sure now that the plot against the embroidery was of Anglo-Saxon origin,' said Odon. 'I have been informed that there has been complicity with the Welsh.'

'So you have arrested people around the Priory, I have heard. It is difficult to condemn those who have been friends. And, did you know the Welshman saved us from the thieves who took Sir

Gilbert's chain-mail and sword.'

'This is the first that I have heard of the incident. Was Sir Gilbert's equipment recovered?'

'No, Your Grace.'

'I will arrange to send what he will need. I do not want to hear any more about the Welshman. As he has done a kindness to you he will keep his life, but no more.'

'Thank you, Your Grace,' said Eleanor bowing. This was a concession she had not expected. She continued her theme: 'Whoever is involved at the Priory of St Thomas the Apostle will only be foot-soldiers. I have also heard that there are political pressures on our highest people, and these are muddying the waters.'

'Speak plainly, Abbess.' He stood. He spread his feet and placed his fists on his hips.

'There is conflict between yourself and Archbishop Lanfranc.'

'If you mean I am not a monk, then that is clear for all to see. I make no apology for that. But there is no conflict; we are both men of the church. You can't be accusing me, so you must be accusing the Archbishop of Canterbury!'

'I know that sounds beyond reason but...'

'No buts, Abbess.' She could see that he considered this the end of that particular area of enquiry.

She started on the next doubt that nagged at her. 'You give support to your nephew, Robert de Curthose, while the Archbishop supports Prince Rufus for King of England when the Conqueror dies.'

'This has nothing to do with the embroidery,' said Odon. 'It is of no concern of yours.'

'You have made this my concern. This is another of my possibilities. I have come back here to England after many years and I find people fear you – a man of the church.'

'I have had to govern this country as king, while the King is away. I have had to quell rebellions on the Conqueror's behalf. This is not going to make me popular, nor does it give me credit with the church, but as you see I am an Earl and the King's half-brother. I have no choice in the matter. I have not called you here to listen to my confession.'

Surely he could express some useful opinions! She persisted, 'But Robert de Curthose is in the same position in Normandy. He is the eldest son. He is angry at his father's lack of trust in him. He might not want his father to be honoured by this embroidery.'

'He would not do such a thing.' He was clearly adamant.

'Because of his friendship with you? If he is a true Norman warrior he will do whatever it takes to succeed.'

'Enough!' roared Odon. His pale face flushed crimson. He checked himself, and the colour faded. He spoke through tightened lips; 'Rest assured if Robert has been involved, there will be no more trouble from him.'

Eleanor felt herself dismissed and yet she had not told him of Prince Rufus and how little she trusted him, nor the possibility of interference from a Scottish influence. Nor had she had the opportunity to plead for Alfred's freedom though, at least, no imminent execution had been mentioned. This was clearly not the time to broach the subject. She would have to be satisfied with Odon's promise regarding Robert de Curthose. Clearly only proof of the true culprits would be enough to satisfy him, and for him to release Alfred. She bowed and left. She could not wait for the Bishop to see her view, she would have to return to Canterbury.

During noon prayers Therese scrutinised each of the community that had been in the sewing room when the Impostor had struck. Her nap, she discovered, had been sanctioned by Sister Winifred. Sister Leofgyth's urgency in waking her had been nothing more than an attempt to prevent lateness for prayers. The sleep had left her much brighter and made her see all of the nuns as good women. Their heads were bowed and their faces smooth with contemplation. She had to tell herself quite firmly that, if Ursula was to be believed, one of these people was not as innocent as they looked. One of them had hidden the key for the Impostor.

Even though Therese could only see the back of Sybil in front of her she could tell it was her by the slight tilt of her head. Sybil certainly had a motive to be involved in the wanton destruction of an honour to the Conqueror, with her disinherited family. Leofgyth herself had been unhappy about the unworthiness of the enterprise, but could this open, chatty, friendly, young woman be able to hide such a thing. Therese doubted it.

And what of Sister Winifred, Prioress Ursula's chosen successor, and her friend Aelfgyth, was their closeness and constant whispering a sign of duplicity? She realised the immaculate face of Sister Hilda was watching her, so she dropped her forehead down onto the steeple of her middle fingers and joined in with the prayers. She included little Eric in her thoughts and wished she could arrange to see him more.

As they filed out of the chapel Sister Aelfgyth approached Therese and drew her close so her voice would not be heard. Therese lowered her head to match her ear to the mouth of the whispering nun. 'I wonder if you could collect the eggs from the garden, Sister?' she asked. 'I left them there this morning and forgot to bring them up for the kitchen.'

'Of course, Sister,' said Therese. She half-hoped that Aelfgyth was going to make a clandestine meeting with her at the dovecot. She hoped Leofgyth had told Aelfgyth of her interest and that she might have something important to tell her, but all she found was the basket of eggs. She picked it up and took it back up the garden through the refectory door from the western cloister to the kitchen. When Therese reached the daylight of the kitchen yard on the far side of the tower she found the yard full of children playing and doing small tasks such as tying bundles of kindling and fetching small logs for the kitchen fires.

Sister Agnes was playing skittles with a sandy-haired boy and when he turned round and winked at her, she saw he was Eric.

'They belong to the servants,' said Agnes, embracing the yard with a sweeping wave of her arms. 'Except this one.'

'That's...'

'I know. He told me. He just appeared. Children need fresh air. One of the women says she'll take him home and look after him. She's one of the builder's wives living up on the encampment. He'll go today so you'd better have a word with him. He knows he's going.'

Therese sat down on the woodpile and called him over. He sat next to her. She let him speak first.

'You know that hole I've been living in?' he asked wrinkling his freckled nose.

She nodded. It had clearly been too much to ask a six-year-old boy to stay there. She was relieved Sister Agnes had arranged new lodgings for him. 'How did you get out without help?'

'I can get out all right. I just jumped, but I can't get back in on my own.' He wriggled excitedly. 'But that's not the point, Sister.' He managed an expression of seriousness worthy of the oldest nun in the Priory as he continued, 'That hole goes into a bit like a hayloft. A kind of floor at the top of a room. And there's stuff stored in there. There's even steps down into the room and there's more stuff stored in that bit too. The room has a window. It's covered over, but I took a peek through.'

'You could have been seen!'

'It was only a peek; no-one would have had a chance to see me. Anyway, aren't you interested?'

'Yes, of course I am!' Therese patted his arm. 'What sort of stuff is stored there?'

'Cloth, all embroidered. It is beautiful. There are piles of it covered with plain sheets. They're really dusty. I sneezed when I pulled them back to take a look. The dust just whooshed up.'

'You must have drawn back the window covering to see all this.' Therese was trying to put what she already knew together with Eric's information.

'Well, yes, of course. But it doesn't matter.'

Her wild thoughts fell together as neatly as psalms in a Psalter. 'Oh my,' said Therese. She was not concerned that Eric's hiding place might be found for he would no longer be there. But surely, the other panels of the embroidery must be hidden there? Even though everyone was under the impression that they'd been removed under heavy-armed guard, and yet, could that have been an elaborate hoax? Surely, leaving the panels here unguarded was crazy? But a secret room? Who else would know of it and had Eric's actions led to others discovering it? 'Eric, is there a door to this room?'

'Yes, it goes through the wall on the far end. I tried it but it wouldn't open.'

This must lead through to the sewing room, behind the wood screen the stitchers used to place their threads and needles, she decided. How easily doorways could be hidden, as Sister Miriam had shown her at home in Bayeux. 'Has any of this material been damaged?' she asked Eric.

'I haven't done anything to them.' He drew himself up, his green eyes full of indignation.

'I was not accusing you of damaging them,' said Therese, 'but someone else could have.'

'Only if they know about them,' said Eric. 'No,' he added. 'They have not been damaged and no-one has been in that room except for me since I arrived.'

She hugged Eric's shoulders. 'Be good and happy at your new place. At least you can see it is not right for you here.'

'If I don't like it,' said Eric, 'I'll be back. Michael left me in your care, remember.'

Therese smiled uncertainly. 'Tell no-one about your hiding place, Eric.'

'I won't,' he replied.

Agnes called her from the kitchen door and she left him with a wave. Agnes drew her in to the hot shade of the cooking room.

'The eggs,' she said loudly, 'are a particular favourite with Bishop Gundulf, the architect.'

'I've heard of him. The monk, Richard of Caen, mentioned his name.' Therese grasped the charade, but wasn't sure why they were behaving like this in front of the servants.

Agnes picked up the egg basket. 'You must take this back. It's stored with the garden equipment.' She tilted it so Therese could see the scrap of bark in the bottom with a name written on it. She read it and Agnes said, 'You won't need this,' and flicked it into the fire.

Therese blinked as the heat of the burning material reached her eyes. There had been one word there, 'Hilda', preceded by the letter 'S' for Sister.

In a wood just south of Canterbury Eleanor wrapped a towel

around her shoulders and sat on the stump in front of Ursula. Her grey pony was tied nearby dozing in the sunshine.

Ursula wiped away the last tear and sniffed.

'We'll get Alfred out one way or another,' she said with a defiant toss of her head. 'Your journey to Dover was not really wasted. At least we know where we stand.'

'But it has delayed me, and I have lied about Sister Therese to Bishop Odon. I do worry about her so.'

'She's a clever girl. Trust her,' advised Ursula trimming the hair on the nape of Eleanor's neck.

'Watch what you are doing with those scissors,' advised Eleanor. 'I agreed to come out here to be turned into a monk, not to have my throat cut.'

'I shall have to use a blade for the tonsure.'

'Have you used one before?' Eleanor was nervous enough without this. She felt her dignity had been removed with her veil.

'Fortitude, Abbess. You have to look like a monk, if you are going to live with them. And, yes I have. I used to shave my father.'

'Anglo-Saxons wore beards and long hair, everyone knows that.'

'Not all Anglo-Saxons,' said Ursula defiantly. 'Sit still.'

Eleanor watched tufts of her greying hair fall among the fronds of new growth reaching through the leaf litter of the woodland floor. The cold blade swept over the crown of her head. She stood up and shook the cloth around her shoulders and her clothing.

'Here,' said Ursula handing her a monk's garb.

Eleanor changed behind some bushes. Being very slim made it easy to hide any feminine curves, and she felt quite pleased with the over-all effect. She returned to Ursula and handed over her nun's habit.

'Now, I have your letter. The monk who did this is a craftsman, no-one will know it's not from a Norman Abbot.'

'Do you think the Archbishop's clerk, Brother David, will recognise me?'

'I do not recognise you! No, certainly not in a monk's habit. Although you need to lower your voice a little, you need to sound just a little bit more masculine.'

'How's this?' asked Eleanor lowering her voice. The tensions broke through and Ursula giggled. 'This is serious,' Eleanor complained, but she started to giggle too. After a few moments and once a small tear of mirth had been wiped away, she said, 'Ursula, pull yourself together.'

'Yes, Abbess,' said Ursula straightening her rough kitchen servant's clothing.

'My letter is even sealed,' said Eleanor, wondering at how much forgery this monk did. 'You keep some strange friends, Ursula.'

The former Prioress stiffened. 'I have to,' she said.

Eleanor looked away from her old friend. They had always been equals, despite Eleanor's higher rank, but now she felt Ursula to be of higher rank than her in the art of watching without being seen.

'You will keep your ears open for news of me?' she asked.

'A new monk at Christ Church Abbey? I will know when you go to the lower dorter before you even take a pee.'

'Such Anglo-Saxon crudity,' replied Eleanor and Ursula laughed.

'Turn round and let me inspect you,' said Ursula.

By the time Eleanor turned back Ursula was frowning. 'What's the matter?' she asked.

In reply Ursula reached into a bag that she'd brought with her and pulled out a pair of socks.

'Monks don't wear those things,' observed Eleanor.

'They were good enough for the Roman legions over here in Britain; they will have to do for you. Your feet will give you away. No man has such dainty toes.'

Eleanor took them and, in return, handed Ursula Odon's ring. 'You will need to be me, at least as far as St Augustine's. Once you are in my room feign illness. You can then become yourself again and state that I wish you and only you to serve me as I have developed a slight fever following my trip to Dover.'

'You are getting the idea of this escapade, aren't you?' said Ursula clapping her hands in delight. 'Brother James of Caen.'

'Ursula, if we are caught this will not seem such a lark.' Eleanor leaned forward and gripped the tops of her friend's arms and gave her a little shake. 'Use the ring to get help if anything goes wrong. Promise me.'

'I promise,' said Ursula her eyes steadying as Eleanor gazed into them. A rumble of wheels on the track nearby caught Ursula's attention. 'Your wagon is here Brother James,' she called loudly.

Eleanor took her leave and mounted the driving bench without being offered help by the driver. She looked back towards the woods but could not see Ursula. Shortly afterwards the wagon was overtaken by Ursula on Eleanor's grey pony. The nun put her hand up in acknowledgement. Odon's ring flashed in the sunlight, but the rider did not stop. Eleanor thought Ursula's salute a shade brash compared to her own dignified style.

Chapter Twelve

Therese swept the sewing room with Sister Hilda supervising her. Over the last few days this had become the pattern of her work as Sister Gertrude was resting some bruising in the infirmary. Therese remembered the incident, and blamed herself. It had been a combination of Gertrude's keenness to get to the refectory and her own slowness to remove her broom from her path. When she'd visited Gertrude in the infirmary she seemed well pleased with her lot and so she felt less guilty for arranging the change in cleaning partner. The first time Hilda had been quiet and strict with her. Therese had felt very young in her company but the self-important swagger Therese had noticed in her early days at the Priory had gone. Therese was aware of Hilda's cool skin, small features and blue eyes pulled tight by concentration, but the second time Hilda had smiled and her features had softened as she talked about her brothers and sisters, all older than herself, with families and farming land not far from the Priory. At first Therese had been wary of Hilda because of the note left in the egg basket. Now, on their third turn together, Hilda was chatting freely about the different threads and stitches employed in the panel. This Hilda classed as generally educational so she was allowed to talk about it.

Therese had put the message written in bark to the back of her mind half-hoping that Hilda's name had been given to her as the contact for an Anglo-Saxon plot. At the forefront of her mind was the thought that she still hadn't seen any of the embroidery.

Hilda ran her dainty fingers along the edge of the workbench. 'The story of William Duke of Normandy's succession to the English throne,' she said proudly, and she bit her lower lip. It was clear she knew she'd said too much.

Therese caught her glance and steadied her with her own searching gaze. 'May I see the panel?' she asked.

Hilda considered for a moment. 'I will show you a small piece. We will not need any more embroiderers now. We have nearly finished.' She sounded excited. She lifted a corner of the protective cloth and exposed a Norman knight on his horse. Therese wanted to touch the bright threads, but did not. Her eyes feasted on the small, neat stitches.

The horse and rider were outlined in a darker colour and the body was filled with another giving a distinct outline that appeared to lift the character from the fabric. The detail of the chain mail vest, neck-guard and helmet thrilled her. Along the bottom were patterns and animals, and she could just see the corner of a piece of fabric with all its drapes carefully depicted.

Therese exclaimed with sheer pleasure.

'You know,' said Hilda. 'That many years ago there was a great English battle against the Vikings at Maldon?' Hilda didn't wait for a reply but continued, 'A great English Warrior died there and his wife had an embroidery made telling her husband's story. It was hung at the Isle of Ely. Odon saw it there and wanted one depicting his brother's triumph.'

Therese tried to work out the emotions behind Hilda's words, but there were footfalls in the corridor so Hilda pulled the cloth back over the work. They returned to their task as Prioress Ethelburga entered.

'Sisters!' It was almost a growl. 'Your tardiness is sinful, you will make us all late for vespers. I want to get locked up here.'

'Yes, Prioress,' the two young women chimed, but as soon as she was gone they struggled to smother their giggles.

'She sounded like my brother's dog,' said Hilda, and they both lapsed into laughter.

In prayers Therese realised how easily she'd become friends with Leofgyth and now with Hilda, and yet there was the warning in the egg basket about Hilda. She did not want any of them to be guilty of betrayal. The nuns' voices were lifting and falling with the cadences of the psalm they were singing and she found she loved her sisters. If she were to single one of these women out, it would be she who would feel the traitor.

Hilda's jovial demeanour had changed after a few moments of singing. She looked uncomfortable and during their meal afterwards in the refectory she only picked at her fish. Therese liked perch and tucked in. She was hungry but her upbringing helped her to retain some of her table manners. She paused to take a sip of water and observe Hilda. Hilda noticed her looking and she returned to her beaker.

After compline, the nuns settled down in the dorter and readied themselves for sleep. Therese had been enjoying her sleep since Eric went to live in the builders' camp so she took off her outer garments ready to settle onto her straw mattress in her chemise. She noticed, however, that Hilda did not remove her outer clothing, just her veil as she pulled her bed covers over her. This was just as Therese had done on the nights she'd been up in the night. She put her hand out and dragged her habit under the blankets with her. In the dying light the others were only interested in their own slumbers and she was sure their actions had gone unnoticed.

Therese slipped her tunic back on and waited for any sound of Hilda rising. She did not have to wait long. She was soon aware of Hilda's light steps, heading for the stairway into the church, so she followed. Therese had become almost expert at gliding noiselessly over the floorboards. On entering the chapel she paused behind the choir and looked for Hilda. She could not see her but she could hear her at the back of the chapel, near the temporary wall. She remembered her own feet making dusty footprints there and realised why no one had seen them: someone else had been there and swept them away – and that someone was Hilda. Therese moved closer, hiding behind an altar screen.

Now the virgin moonlight in the eastern sky came through the window behind the altar, highlighting Hilda. She was lifting the door hanging. Therese heard a brick slide out of place and then slide back. She leapt from her hiding place, bounded down the aisle and caught Hilda's wrist.

Hilda turned away from the door to look at the person who'd arrested her, but Therese was looking at the hand she gripped firmly. A small pottery bottle with a narrow neck and stained with ink was clasped between her fingers.

'Why do you have this ink bottle, Sister?' asked Therese in a hushed but angry voice.

'Don't be a martyr, Sister Therese. This has nothing to do with you.'

'It seems you have something you wish to hide?' Therese gave the young woman's wrist a little shake and the bottle slipped from her fingers into Therese's other hand, which she held underneath ready.

'This isn't as it seems. Believe me.'

'Tell me what it is, and I might believe you.' Therese was surprised by her boldness with the older girl.

'This is the inkbottle that was used to try and destroy the panel in the sewing room. You must have heard about the incident from the others?'

'Some rumours have it that there was no ink; that the deaf nun wasn't deaf and that she and Prioress Ursula were fighting with each other; that they were together in the plot and somehow came to blows. They fought and fell from the tower.'

'There is,' said Hilda, 'another version of the story. The true one. If I tell you, this must go no further or I will be finished here.'

'Who am I to tell anyone?' asked Therese.

'I don't know who you are, but I know you are Norman.'

Therese nodded. 'Hurry, tell me, before we are found down here.'

Still a little reluctant, Hilda continued, 'On the day of the incident I had gone on break a little behind the others. Prioress Ursula ushered me out. I was dawdling on the stairs when I heard shouts. So I went back to the sewing room, but Prioress Ursula and the deaf girl had already left. I was the first one back. I could hear them in the tower. There was ink everywhere and there was this inkbottle in the middle of the floor. Sister Ethelburga, as she was then, came in behind me. She told me to pick it up and hide it. We didn't know the Prioress was about to fall to her death. Sister Ethelburga said that if I did as she said when she was Prioress she would make me head of the needle workers. She wanted to discredit Prioress Ursula. And, God forgive me, I took it and hid it. Sister Ethelburga locked the room and when Prioress Ursula was found dead she had the room cleaned. Some of the floorboards were planed and some had to be replaced. The carpenter was dismissed shortly afterwards.'

'Did you not feel this was wrong, Sister Hilda?'

'I knew I'd made a terrible mistake. I went to Sister Ethelburga and said to her that she didn't need to discredit Prioress Ursula now that she was dead, and she pointed out that Sister Winifred would be likely to get the post and anyway my hands were stained with ink. She said she would expose me as one of the traitors. What could I do?'

'So what are you going to do with the bottle now?' asked Therese.

'I'm going to destroy it. The ink has faded on my hands. No-one can connect me with this any more.'

'What do you mean?'

'She will look to remove me, because I know.' Hilda trembled.

'Others who have power over the Prioress will soon know too.'

'What do you mean?' asked Hilda. 'Who are you?'

'Does Prioress Ethelburga know the bottle is here?' asked Therese as calmly as she could.

'No. No she doesn't.'

'Then put it back, Sister Hilda. All will be well. I will tell no-one if you keep your secret a little longer and you must tell no-one about this or about me.'

'Are you sure you can make this right?'

'Soon, Sister Hilda.'

The bottle slid back inside its hiding place and the loose brick was put in over the top. The two nuns returned to their beds to catch a little sleep before the next set of prayers. As Therese snuggled down she smiled to herself. At last there was real proof of Ursula's story. There had been the ink on the tower wall. But that might have easily been explained away, and then there was Agnes's story, confirming Ursula's. But she could be dismissed by some, as she was a close friend of hers. No. This was hard evidence, not offered, but found from a reluctant witness.

Sister Aelfgyth had noted Hilda's suspicious behaviour and passed that note to her in the egg basket. No doubt Aelfgyth was defending her friend Sister Winifred, who'd had the position of Prioress snatched from her. This complication seemed to have arisen due to conflicting ambitions for power among the members of this small community. Ethelburga used the opportunity that arose in the sewing room to her advantage. So if it wasn't Prioress Ethelburga or Sister Hilda who were in league with the Impostor, thought Therese, who was it?

Chapter Thirteen

Eleanor looked up from her script. She felt quite naked without her head covered as she watched the other monks stooped over their work in the temporary scriptorium of Christ Church Abbey. Being Brother James of Caen had not been as difficult as she'd thought it would be. The Rule of St Benedict, which they lived by, was the same, although here it was kept to more rigorously than most of the English priories she'd visited.

Ursula had arranged for the letter of introduction to say that Brother James was excellent at colouring so she would gain access to the scriptorium. However, letters of any significance were not elaborately coloured so she found herself painting glorious patterns, animals and plants around the edges of pages for a Psalter. Brother David seemed pleased with her work and paid little attention to the person who was creating it. She'd become used to the smell of the ink and the various tinctures – though she tried to sit near the door, which was left open on warm days, to get as much fresh air as she could.

A week had already gone by and she had completed plenty of pictures but she had nothing of significance to show for her presence here. The bell rang for noon prayers and the monks rose. She opened the door and descended the steps into the cloister. They entered the church through the cloister, where she entered the church through the cloister door.

Some of the laity had clearly braved the building works to join them and Eleanor couldn't resist a sideways glance to see who was there. Her heart seemed to spin in her chest. Prince Rufus, with his crop of blazing red hair, stood in the centre aisle, his guard of three knights slightly behind him.

The chanting rose and fell melodically, but Eleanor could not find a suitably low singing voice, so she mimed. She could no longer see the Prince and his guard due to an altar screen, but on leaving she saw him cross the cloister to speak to Archbishop Lanfranc, resplendent in his purple robe. She stopped to adjust her sock and sandal. The two men were talking so quietly that Eleanor could hardly hear them. She leaned forward to listen, staying like this until her elbow was gripped and her arm was jerked sharply. Perhaps one of the Prince's guards had come up behind her. If she were to die now she could help no-one. She tried to control her rising panic. She toppled slightly, stumbled and regained her balance, while being propelled along the walkway. She managed to turn and see the person who'd arrested her. He was a large monk, cloaked and cowled. Her fear subsided slightly. She heard the Prince call his guards to him by their names: Simon, Roger and Ralph. On looking back she could not work out which was which although one was taller than the other two and without their helmets she could see one of the shorter ones was quite fair in colouring. The large monk at her elbow propelled her out to the infirmary before he stopped. At least she knew how to deal with this sort of enemy.

'I will say, Brother James, that you were taken ill,' said Brother Matthew, lowering his hood.

Eleanor looked at his feet. She should have looked before. They were unmistakable. She smiled.

'Anyone would think you were spying on the Prince and the Bishop, loitering like that. The Prince's guard were giving you some very suspicious looks, especially the blonde one, Simon.' Brother Matthew frowned at her.

She wondered if he recognised her, but she spoke in her "Brother James" voice anyway.

'Which of the Prince's guards is Roger?'

'The tall one,' answered Brother Matthew.

That made Ralph the shorter, brown-haired one, thought Eleanor.

'You ask a lot of questions about people who should not concern you,' complained Brother Matthew.

'I am just fascinated by royalty,' she said like an awe-struck novice.

'It is best to keep away from royalty. Power creates turmoil. Any rift between people can be prized open by their so-called advisors for their own advantage.'

'Does Prince Rufus seek advice from the Archbishop?' she

asked.

'Among others, Brother James.' Brother Matthew's bushy brows folded into a frown. 'But he is not one of those types of advisors I have mentioned. He is a clever man, but a good one too.'

'I understand the Archbishop favours Prince Rufus, over his elder brother, for King of England?' She inflected her voice making a question out of the statement.

'I think that is only because the Conqueror himself is in favour of this arrangement. What the King wishes, will be the rule of law.' Brother Matthew went to enter the infirmary, he paused. 'Brother James, I would not wear those socks if I were you. It is not usual here and you will be asked to remove them.'

'I have bad feet. They need to be covered.' Eleanor could not keep the irritation at his nosiness out of her voice.

'I have not seen you lame,' stated the Infirmarer.

'But I will be if I do not keep my feet warm,' she said, now feeling defensive.

Brother Matthew frowned again. 'Let me see your feet.'

Eleanor looked at him. He was examining her hairless face. She wondered if she could trust him. 'Ah well,' she sighed in her own voice while she sat on the step. She took off her socks and showed him her feet.

'Abbess Eleanor?'

'Yes, I've been a bit of a fool. I thought I could come here as a monk and find out what was going on. I guessed there might be some trickery between Archbishop Lanfranc and Prince Rufus, but, of course, there cannot be. If the Archbishop is an honourable man, as you say, and Rufus is recognised as heir by his father there is no reason for discord.'

'I will not ask for the details of your being here, Abbess. But I think your instincts are right. I am sure there has been an excessive amount of comings and goings here lately by the Prince. And, no doubt these matters need looking into but, even so, I have to say I think your behaviour is extraordinary. You take such risks in dressing in this manner and taking on the role of a monk.'

'Others have taken more risks than I,' said Eleanor.

He looked at her steadily as if there was no void between them of hierarchy or gender, examining her intent and her constancy. 'I think you ought to stay and see what is going on. It may be relevant to you as well as to us.'

'Why should such things bother you, Brother Matthew?'

'Everyone has been worrying themselves about it. They are concerned for the church's treasure. Christ Church Abbey draws a considerable income. Kings often like to take for themselves what was given to the church. And Princes are not always patient about waiting for crowns.'

'You talk of treason.'

'I am not making any accusations, Abbess. I just appreciate your interest. It gives me an incentive to look further myself and I will tell you all I find out. Between us we should be able to make some sense of it. Hopefully I will be able to put my brothers' minds at rest.'

'If I am to stay, what am I to do about my feet and my socks?' she asked.

'I will give you a note from the Infirmarer saying that you have to wear them for your health. Hopefully that will resolve the issue.'

Prioress Ethelburga was reading the morning's chapter from the Rule of St Benedict while Therese sat on her hands so she would not be seen wringing them as hard as sodden washing, for that is what she wanted to do. The chapter house seemed too small for what was inside her head. Frustrations were building inside her until the tension made her want to scream, but she could not. That would cause chaos, and disrupt her investigations. That was her main frustration, she may have been back sweeping the sewing room, but she was doing it when all the nuns had left – and Sister Gertrude was back as her guide. But Sister Hilda had not left her conscience. A week had passed since Therese had promised her a resolution and Hilda was still waiting to be made safe from Sister Ethelburga's machinations. Therese had made no progress.

She had to gain access to Sister Sybil. Sybil was, after all, from an Anglo-Saxon family dispossessed by the Normans. She was about the same age and she looked much like Hilda, but Therese knew so little about her views. She had not come across any occasion when she could talk to her and Sybil kept herself to herself except for an occasional conversation with Winifred and Aelfgyth. She took a peek at her. She was sitting with her head tilted in a listening stance. Her features, although larger than Hilda's, gave her a sophisticated air. Therese could read nothing from her steady expression.

She hadn't spoken to Beatrice, but she had not been well the day of the incident. The broad-faced young woman was missing again today as she was back in the infirmary. Therese was running out of individuals who could be the link between the key and the Impostor, for now Sybil seemed the most likely.

Prioress Ethelburga finished reading and started giving out the morning's work. She pointed out that the growing season was getting the better of the gardening team of Sisters Leofgyth, Winifred and Aelfgyth and that they would need additional help.

'Sisters Maude, Mildred and Therese will join them in their labours this morning,' she directed. 'The animals are out on their summer grazing now and the servants can deal with what jobs are left.'

Therese had hoped she might be asked to thread needles in the sewing room. She felt she had been at the Priory long enough, but, yet again, she would have to wait to talk to Sister Sybil. Nothing would be gained from making a fuss, so she followed the others out into the garden where, once again, she was given the task of hoeing. Maude and Mildred joined her. Their brown hair poked out of their veils as they grumbled to each other about being taken away from their usual tasks of animal husbandry, which they far preferred.

Their conversation drifted over different subjects as they progressed down the rows until they started arguing about the day it snowed late in February. Mildred insisted it occurred on the Sunday and Maude said it did not. Until then Therese had been only half listening to them, now she was attentive. They both remembered that some of the plants and animals had already been responding to a few days of spring-like weather when a cold, gusty wind blew up, but which actual day it happened was in dispute.

'That was the day Prioress Ursula and the Impostor fell to their deaths,' said Maude.

'I'm sure it was the day before,' complained Mildred, sounding more interested in their argument than the plight of the fallen nuns. 'We'd opened the top doors in the great barn to let in the air.'

'Yes that's right, but we opened the bottom doors too,' said Maude, 'to let out the muck wagon on the far side of the barn. The servants had filled it and it needed to go out to the muck-heap.'

'That wasn't the day the snow came though,' said Mildred.

'Did you see what happened?' Therese asked them, enthralled.

'That's why I know that was the day of the snow,' said Maude clearly forgetting her shyness in her eagerness to prove her sibling wrong. 'The wagon had just left for the muckheap. I was hooking back the door. It was difficult in the gusting wind, and then I heard a scream. It came from the direction of the tower, I ran down the hill a little bit to get a better look and I saw them fall.'

'What happened then?' asked Therese.

'I called out to Mildred, but we couldn't leave the animals. There were plenty of people to help over there and we smelt a bit high by then so I don't expect they'd have wanted us around anyhow.'

'I see,' said Therese leaning on her hoe. 'But did you see anything else. Anything else at all?'

'I did,' said Mildred, happy to out-do her sister. 'And so did you, Maude.'

'I don't remember anything,' said Maude pouting.

'Well I do,' snapped Mildred. 'There was someone in the woods. I saw him and so did you, Maude.'

'A man?' asked Therese.

'I'm sure of it,' replied Mildred.

'Didn't you tell anyone at the time about him?' asked Therese.

'No, what of it?' asked Mildred. 'He could have been collecting kindling for the camp on the other side of the stream. It really does not matter. Does it matter to you?'

Therese regretted forgetting that the twins had already opened up to her more than she could have hoped and she had pushed too far, but this was important information – and unexpected too. She smiled. 'No, it doesn't matter to me. I was just curious, you know.'

Maude was frowning. 'I don't remember. I think I was seeing to one of the sheep. It had caught its head in the side of its pen.'

They re-engaged in their sibling squabbles and Therese turned back to her work. She used her hoe as rigorously as her mind was working.

Who could have been the man in the woods? Could the Impostor have had another accomplice – or could it have even been the designer of the conspiracy to damage the embroidery? Perhaps she'd gone to the tower not to just try to escape but to signal to him, and when she saw all hope was gone she killed herself. She might even have hoped he'd seen her fall, and if that was the case, who could that man be?

She stopped hoeing. Michael the merchant? And if it was? Her mind raced. The child Eric could even be the Impostor's son! That was unthinkable. Eric gave no hint of having the Norman father Michael stated. Perhaps little though he was, he was a spy. Such dangerous possibilities. Thankfully the child was no longer in the Priory, but from what he'd told her, he already had vital information others could make use of. All he had to do was wait to be contacted by one of the conspirators.

She told herself this was nonsense. Michael was too open. He had no spirit for subterfuge. You don't express your opinions openly to a Norman if you are plotting treason and, anyway, Michael had been arrested. If he ever was a danger that danger was now removed. But if she could make such rash conclusions there were, no doubt, others who could make the same connection. Michael would be slain. No proof would be needed. She would not be mentioning this to anyone.

Chapter Fourteen

As Brother Matthew came towards Eleanor, nothing in his manner gave away his knowledge of her identity. The scriptorium at Christ Church Abbey was on a short break and the monks were taking exercise on the walkway behind the infirmary. Eleanor had slipped her hands up opposite sleeves and bowed her head to give the impression that she, or rather Brother James, was in deep contemplation and not to be disturbed lightly.

Brother Matthew showed suitable respect as he bowed and engaged Eleanor in conversation. 'Brother James, I have some news,' he told her, his voice barely above a whisper.

'What is it?' asked Eleanor in the same manner. Their behaviour, she realised, would not seem unusual as other monks were talking quietly to each other. But a noticeably female voice even in these circumstances would carry like a bell across the drone of male ones so she used a hushed version of her Brother James voice.

'I have found out why Prince Rufus goes to see Archbishop Lanfranc.'

'Why?' asked Eleanor through gritted teeth. She was already irritated at Matthew's slow, deliberate manner.

'Prince Rufus goes to see him because the Archbishop has told the Conqueror he does not approve of the Prince's behaviour. He is trying to stop his brawling, womanising and he wishes to modify his expensive tastes.'

'So,' said Eleanor, 'he may be disgruntled with his father after all?'

'That looks a definite possibility.'

'What happens during these interviews?' asked Eleanor. Even speaking quietly she sounded crisp, more so than she intended.

'They are in private,' said Matthew. His wiggling toes were the only outward sign of excitement. 'What I have told you has slipped through overheard conversations between one of the Prince's guards and Brother David. Indeed the Prince's pride is somewhat hurt by it.'

'Thank you, Brother Matthew. I haven't been here long enough to be trusted with the gossip.' Eleanor noticed a change among the monks. They were separating to make a path through the middle of their number. Brother David was giving sly little glances to each monk, expecting them to defer to him and receiving their excessive respects as if he himself were a Bishop. There was no mistake, however, that he was making his stooped progress towards Matthew and herself.

'That information was not just ordinary gossip, Abb..., Brother James,' Matthew faltered. Brother David was almost upon them.

On his arrival they both bowed deeply as the others had done and he nodded his head in recognition.

'Brother James of Caen,' Brother David addressed Eleanor.

She bowed again.

'I have news of one of your brethren.' Brother David's persistently rude tone was what she'd come to expect. The whites of his eyes were heavily veined and the flesh about them grey. This was more than age, thought Eleanor. Perhaps he was aiding his sleep with the contents of the cellar. He seemed sober enough now.

'Oh?' asked Eleanor trying to contain her embarrassment – as far as she knew she had no 'brethren'.

'Brother Richard of Caen. He is one of Bishop Gundulf's men involved in the building program.'

'I see. I'm not sure if I've met the man. Our skills are of a different order. I work in the scriptorium, he works on buildings.'

'You must know him. He is about your age. You must have been novices together.'

She was about to say that she undertook her training in Bayeux but realised that this would be a mistake as there would be immediate suspicions raised about her loyalty with the shadow of Bishop Odon cast across her. 'I do not remember him in particular,' she said instead.

'You will have much to talk about. He will be here in a couple of days. I will arrange for you to sit close to each other at meal times so that afterwards you and Brother Richard will be able to talk. He will be most impressed to have the company of someone he has so much in common with.'

'Yes, Brother David,' said Eleanor, this time bowing so low he could not see her reddening neck and cheeks.

When Brother David had reached the doorway, Brother Matthew turned to her and said, 'Two days.'

'I know, I know,' she snapped. She was beginning to realise that the scribe used by Ursula for her letter of commendation must have had access to Richard of Caen's correspondence to copy the seal of letters sent to that august monk. Meeting this man was always going to threaten her disguise.

Odon embraced his nephew. It was good to hold young Robert de Curthose close to him. They broke apart and made their way up the embankment of the river at Dover docks.

'Did you have a good journey?' asked Odon.

'Yes thank you, Uncle. All is well with me. The little sea was calm and we made good time.'

'We will ride up to the castle. I've brought horses down for you and your men.'

'You treat me well,' Robert replied.

Odon clapped him on the shoulder. 'Your mother favours you, even if your father does not,' he said. 'And I respect your mother. It is good to see you, but what brings you to England in such haste?'

'I came as soon as I got your letter. Such rumours of my interference with the embroidery will do me no good.' Robert showed due respect and concern.

'You did not need to come yourself,' said Odon smiling upon his nephew. 'Your written assurance would have been enough for me.'

'I wanted to have confidence of your trust in me, Uncle.'

'Of course I trust you, Robert. So much so I plan for you to take the embroidery back to Bayeux with me when it is finished. They are on the last panel and soon all will be ready.'

'That will be a great honour, Uncle. Hopefully the King will be pleased with us for once.' Robert smiled back with a measure of relief.

Odon laughed. 'You might be right, but we shall have to wait and see.'

Time passed slowly for Therese in St Thomas's Priory, it made her feel she must act and that she must act quickly. There was no doubt that the last panel of the embroidery would soon be complete and if anyone was going to attack it here then it must happen soon. She had yet to converse with Sybil. In fact she was so quietly spoken, she wasn't sure if she'd ever really heard her speak. Therese doubted that she would be able to make useful contact with her before the embroidery was removed without a little deviousness of her own. This morning she had an opportunity to lay some bait to tempt any Anglo-Saxon activists out into her view because she was following Aelfgyth down towards the dovecot, and Aelfgyth would be the carrier of that bait, hopefully to Sybil.

They passed the dovecot and went into the garden store. Aelfgyth's small body wriggled into the crowded shed and brought out two egg baskets one of which, just days before, had been the bearer of that tiny note giving Hilda's name. Therese had to be sure Aelfgyth had been the one who put it there, but she did not wish to give away that she'd acted upon it, so she said innocently, 'I was interested in your note about Sister Hilda.'

'I shouldn't have sent it to you. Sister Leofgyth said you had talked of nothing but our little tragedy.' Aelfgyth opened the dovecot door and went in.

Therese followed. The doves cooed in harmony around them as gentle as the sweet sound of Beatrice's singing voice. 'Just curiosity,' said Therese offering up one of the baskets for filling.

'That won't work with me. You are the only Norman here. A fact that has not exactly gone unnoticed. We thought you were checking on us so I threw you that name to see what you would do with it. But it is clear you are not as intent on pursuing the matter as we thought.'

'What do you mean?' asked Therese. She was getting nearly as good as Sister Miriam at looking incredulous, when inside her throat was tightening with fear. Her outward expression betrayed nothing of her inner turmoil. She stood motionless with her basket outstretched.

'I thought you would pursue Sister Hilda. But you clearly haven't, or you would not be here now.' Aelfgyth put a handful of eggs in the basket.

'I'm sorry?' asked Therese. The air was heavy with the scent of the birds.

'Sister Hilda is an ambitious woman. If Sister Winifred had become Prioress and not Sister Ethelburga who do you think would have gained the position of leader in the sewing room?' She did not wait for a reply. 'Yes. Me,' said Aelfgyth hitching up her skirts and climbing the pointed ladder, its end tucked into the higher roosts.

This confirmed that Aelfgyth's note had been passed to her not because of any real knowledge, but just because of the spite Ethelburga had provoked by getting the position of Prioress.

'Excuse me, Sister Aelfgyth, why wouldn't I be here now, if I'd gone after Sister Hilda?'

'That's obvious. Prioress Ethelburga would have been rid of you as quickly as an egg falls to the ground from its nest.' Aelfgyth demonstrated this effect by dropping one of the dove eggs. It broke open, yoke splattering the edge of Therese's tunic.

Therese jumped back. 'Why would Prioress Ethelburga know?' Therese asked.

'Prioress Ethelburga gave her the sewing room position. It is clear they are loyal to each other.'

She realised how little the nuns really knew of each other. They spoke in their own little groups but beyond that the extensive silences meant that they could easily keep their secrets hidden. Aelfgyth and the others had not received any sense of Hilda's and Prioress Ethelburga's relationship becoming strained. Therese let the conversation lapse for a few moments and then piped up with, 'I find myself thinking about my identity, who I am.'

'That is natural. You have doubts about taking your vows?'

'That as well, but it is my nationality that gives me my biggest problem. You said that the fact that I was a Norman was obvious.'

'You are a Norman in England,' confirmed Aelfgyth. 'You are instantly higher in status than Anglo-Saxons. You will not have any problems in the church. Before you know it you will be a Prioress yourself.'

'But that's not the point I'm trying to make,' said Therese. 'I'm not Norman. I was born Anglo-Saxon and brought up by Normans in Normandy.' For a moment she wasn't sure if she felt a traitor or whether she felt liberated. She let it pass. In the darkness of the dovecot Aelfgyth would have difficulty reading her features, but she still had to remain calm. She hoped she was the only one who could hear her heart thumping.

'Well I never,' said Aelfgyth as she came down the ladder. A cluster of feathers floated down with her. The delight in her voice was clear. Aelfgyth took the egg baskets from Therese, put them outside, took her by the hands and stood her out in the sunshine. She raised herself up on her tiptoes and took a good look at her face. 'Are you sure?' she asked. 'You have Norman ways?'

'I cannot help those,' said Therese. 'But in my chest beats an Anglo-Saxon heart.'

Aelfgyth smiled. 'And your loyalties?'

'My loyalties are not what they were. I find myself increasingly unable to decide. In fact I feel cheated out of my own nationality to the point where I want to actively support my fellow Anglo-Saxons.' Therese was surprised by just how much she believed in her own words.

'You are a dear child,' said Aelfgyth dropping down from her toes. 'You will find your way, I'm sure. Bring the eggs up to the kitchen for Sister Agnes.'

Therese watched her small figure almost bounce as she walked away and she thought that she'd laid the bait well. But if there really was an Anglo-Saxon plot here among the nuns, could she pluck it out – not only were these people her friends, but they were her countrywomen.

Chapter Fifteen

A hearty breeze blew off the sea, cooling Bishop Odon and his large cream-dun stallion as he watched his knights and their mounts exercising on the downs. The sun glinted on their harness as they raced their animals at full tilt below him. A horse broke from the main group and galloped towards him. He recognised the familial red hair, which was sandier and less fiery on Robert than his brother Rufus.

Robert de Curthose reined in his horse and bowed his head. Odon acknowledged this show of respect.

'I have news,' said Robert. 'Edgar the Aethling has landed.' His face was full of enthusiasm. It was no secret that Robert and the Aethling were, if not friends, then at least aligned in their basic views.

'This is a complication I could do without,' complained Odon. 'What is he doing here?'

'He didn't say.' Robert sounded defensive.

'Tell him to turn round and go back. England is not the place for him now.'

'As England and Normandy are not the right places for me, Uncle?' Robert said this with a flash of anger, which he clearly regretted almost instantly.

'Edgar had to sign up to the inevitable power machine that is William the Conqueror. He was allocated lands on the continent to keep him out of England.'

'He is not ambitious for himself,' insisted Robert.

'There is not a knight who is not ambitious for himself,' warned Odon. 'How do we know he has not been behind the attack on the embroidery?'

'His allegiance is strong and he builds bridges between people. That is his nature. With his sister married to the King of Scotland, we must recognise him as a friend in order to keep the North quiet. How else will the Conqueror bring Wales into his fold? We cannot afford to be stretched on all fronts. You and I have both been to the North to put down uprisings. I would not wish to do so again.'

'It looks,' said Odon, almost persuaded by his nephew to accept the inevitable, 'that he is already here.' For ascending the hill towards them was Edgar. He was ahead of two horsemen. But Odon was not happy. The Conqueror and his middle son, Rufus, would be suspicious of so many powerful men and allies gathering in Kent.

Edgar approached. He was not dressed in armour as Odon's exercising knights but he wore the robes of an earl. His cloak was lined with beaver skin and clearly of the finest cloth produced in Europe, as were his breeches and the leather of his boots. However, the colours were muted shades of green and brown, not the purples of aristocracy, his dress was too Anglo-Saxon for Odon's comfort.

Leading his retinue, the Aethling dismounted and bowed before them. His dark shock of hair fell forward, far longer than the Norman fashion. He lifted his head. The brown-eyed youth had matured into an able looking warrior. He was about the same age as Robert Curthose. His even features, aquiline nose and fine bone structure were the picture of a well bred nobleman. In his manner Odon could also see the gentility of the Hungarian Court of his early childhood and the solid bearing of the English Court of King Edward from his youth.

'My Lord, Earl of Kent,' said Edgar bowing low again. 'I am honoured to be in your earldom. As are Sir Guy and Sir Alun.' He gestured towards his men, who remained mounted, but bowed their respect. Odon noted the lack of any vestiges of a Hungarian accent.

'Have you been in England for a while, Aethling?' asked Odon, an edge of suspicion to his voice.

'Just a couple of weeks, Your Grace. I have been visiting my sister Christine at Wilton.'

Odon thought that was an excessive time to give a sister in a convent, but he looked at Robert and let it go.

'Take food with us, Edgar Aethling, and refresh yourself after your journey. If you remount your horse we will go directly to Dover Castle. Your men are also welcome.'

Edgar did as was suggested and Odon led the way with Edgar beside him.

'I understand my presence may bring you embarrassment,' said Edgar.

'So why are you here?' asked Odon unable to hide his irritation.

'I am just stopping off on my way to see my sister in Scotland.'

'You will not be staying long?'

'Only a few days, Bishop Odon de Bayeux.'

'Good.' Odon's frown darkened his countenance.

'I am not staying here, however. I have not given you notice of my arrival, so I could not presume on your hospitality. I will be moving on to Canterbury. It has been arranged with Abbot Scotland that I will stay at St Augustine's. There are presents to pick up and then the rest of my journey will be by sea.'

'Your youth protected you after King William conquered England, Edgar. And your battles with the Conqueror are long over. And, for the present, all is settled with your brother-in-law, the Scottish King. We accept your allegiance, but you must never again give King William reason to doubt your fealty.'

'Why do you greet me with such suspicion, Your Grace?'

Odon shook his head. Perhaps all would be well. Edgar's responses were either well disguised or had the ring of genuine innocence. Odon remembered that Edgar may know more than he had said so tested him with, 'You have heard the news of Prioress Ursula? She was a nun whom, I believe, your sister, the Queen of Scotland was acquainted with.'

'Yes, I knew her.' There was simple curiosity on Edgar's face. 'She worked as a needlewoman in the service of my sister Margaret, Queen of Scotland, for the beautification of the church buildings.'

'Prioress Ursula has been killed,' said Odon.

'I'm sorry to hear that,' said Edgar. Odon noted a brief sadness change his expression.

'I have had Abbess Eleanor look into the matter,' explained Odon.

'Was there any reason for that?' asked Edgar.

'I thought so at the time. But I am not so sure now,' said Odon. 'I am thinking of bringing the investigations to a close and calling back the Abbess and her young protégé, Sister Therese. The Abbess is staying at St Augustine's. Perhaps, you would be good enough to pass on the message to her when you see her. But first I would be insulted if you did not spend the night here.' He looked over his shoulder at Robert, who smiled back. 'My nephew would greatly enjoy your company.'

'I would be honoured,' replied Edgar, turning and nodding at Robert in a friendly manner.

As they neared the castle Odon bade Edgar the Aethling enter the fortress, which he did so, followed by Sir Guy and Sir Alun.

Outside Abbess Eleanor's room, Ursula adjusted her clothes. The scheme had worked well. All she had to do when she was tired was claim she had to attend to the Abbess and she could take a nap in her room. She was still fiddling with the latch when a barked command of, 'Kitchen servant!' made her turn. She kept her head low, and not only out of respect, for she knew the voice well and did not want to be recognised by its owner, Abbot Scotland.

'How is the Abbess today?' he asked.

'She is over the worst, Abbot.'

'It is a great favour she does to you to allow you to care for her,' said Scotland.

'I know, Abbot.'

'May I see her?'

'She is not yet well enough for visitors, Abbott.'

'I see,' said Scotland. He looked thoughtful. 'Do I know you from somewhere, servant?'

'Only the kitchen, Abbott.'

'Then return there with all haste!' he replied taking his own leave along the passage. His strides made his robes rustle about his legs.

She decided to walk the opposite way to the kitchens but as she turned she saw a shadow of someone at the far end, someone much smaller than Abbot Scotland. She hesitated, but the person didn't. The gait of this individual was rolling and the path he took deviated from the straight way most people would walk down a corridor. This person was keeping to the shadows, but Ursula had recognised him even before her nostrils were attacked by his acrid smell.

'How have you gained access to this part of St Augustine's?' she demanded of him.

'I have my ways, kitchen servant,' said Agid with a wicked grin.

'You hear too much,' said Ursula. 'That was none of your business.'

'You only dislike it because you don't carry the respect you used to, do you?' Agid smirked.

Ursula ignored his taunt. 'And what, may I ask, are you doing here?'

'I have come to see Abbess Eleanor.'

'And why would she want to see you, Agid?'

'I am only a messenger.'

'Who for?' Ursula was intrigued. Agid had strange loyalties, mostly dependent on who paid him best, but he would never take a Norman's silver.

'I cannot say, kitchen servant. Now which is her room?'

'You do not know as much as you claim, Agid, for I told the Abbot that Abbess Eleanor has a slight fever. She is not receiving visitors.' Ursula blocked the little man's way.

'Then you must take the message to her. A man will see her. He has important information to give her. He will wait in a clearing in the woods an hour's ride to the south of Canterbury. There are some tree-stumps that were once great oaks, felled by the Normans for all their grand buildings. Do you know it?' His contempt was clear as he spat out the words.

This was the very place in which Ursula had transformed Abbess Eleanor into Brother James. 'I know it,' she said. 'Now both of us must leave here. I do not want anyone seeing us together. Go!'

Abbess Eleanor's robes caught on the stirrup and then wrapped themselves around the saddle. Ursula had gathered up the skirts as best she could with the belt, but Eleanor's extra height made wearing her clothes more of a trial than she'd expected. On the first occasion she'd worn them coming away from the woods she was now heading towards, her excitement had made them less of a burden. This time she feared what she would find and the clothes snagged on branches tugging at her as Abbess Eleanor's pony carried her steadily towards her meeting with Agid's informant. She admired Odon's ring on her finger, it comforted her. This would give her the power and authority to deal with whatever she would find.

She turned off the main road and carried on along the track made by oxen pulling felled tree trunks out of the woods. The clearing was upon her before she had really thought through her actions. There was a breeze in the tops of the trees and she looked up. She heard a whoosh from behind and an arm about her neck. She was being dragged off the pony and down onto the ground by her assailant. She choked against the pressure, pulling at his arm with both her hands. She remembered her fight with the Impostor but this was different, then she'd been the stronger one.

To come here had been foolish. She'd told no-one. She'd thought that she must act quickly and come in Abbess Eleanor's place, but now Agid had shown his true colours and there was no hope for her. Unconsciousness was almost welcome in removing the thought of her own stupidity.

Chapter Sixteen

Therese hadn't been in St Thomas's infirmary before, Sister Aelfgyth was on duty this morning. She sniffed the air. It was full of the smell of herbs. Therese stood just inside the door clutching a cut finger. She hadn't intended to cut it. As she told Sister Aelfgyth, she'd caught it on a sharp stone while shifting some weeds.

Aelfgyth sat her on a chair and examined the cut. 'It's quite deep,' she said. 'I'll fetch some speedwell wash.'

Therese could just see into the dormitory area and she knew Beatrice was still in the infirmary somewhere. She tried to catch a glimpse of her or at least the sound of someone. She thought Beatrice was the only patient in the infirmary at the moment.

'Sit still,' said Sister Aelfgyth.

Therese sat still and held the little bowl underneath her finger to catch the liquid as it was poured over the wound.

'Stay like that, with the bowl there to catch the drips. I will fetch some lavender and rose oils.'

'Thank you, Sister Aelfgyth.' While she went over to the shelves to collect the promised salves, Therese again twisted on her stool to view the inhabitants of the infirmary beds. She was rewarded by a capped head with a coil of black hair running down a woman's back. Beatrice was reaching for a steaming cup of mint tea. The smell wafted towards Therese just as Aelfgyth arrived with the ointments.

As she put the rose and lavender oils on Aelfgyth said, 'I will need to fetch some Shepherds Purse. It should be used fresh.' She wrapped a bandage around the wound and said, 'stay here.'

As soon as Aelfgyth left the infirmary Therese went through the doorway into where Beatrice was resting.

Sister Beatrice tilted her angelic face up at Therese. 'Hello,' she said.

Therese looked away. She composed herself and smiled back at Beatrice. 'Hello,' she replied as gently as she could.

In turn, Beatrice closed her soft brown eyes and turned away. 'I've been wanting to talk to you,' she said. Beatrice seemed to be trying to recall a speech that she had rehearsed. 'I know Sister Anna is dead. I was in the infirmary at the time. Sister Agnes closed the door. Sister Anna was in that room at the end. But I saw and I know what they did with her body. It would be easy to tell.'

'So why didn't you, why don't you tell someone – Prioress Ethelburga, for instance?' Therese tried to catch her gaze.

'I don't know if I would be doing good or bad. I don't know what is going on.' Beatrice looked long and hard at Therese, clearly searching for an answer.

'Well don't look at me. It may have come to your attention that I am curious about the events surrounding the death of your Impostor…'

'You didn't say, "And Prioress Ursula"', said Beatrice.

'You didn't give me time to say, "And Prioress Ursula"', Therese replied a little crossly.

'She is alive, isn't she? I know Sister Anna didn't go back to visit her family, that was Prioress Ursula leaving under cover of darkness. Perhaps you're right. Perhaps I ought to tell Prioress Ethelburga.'

'No don't,' said Therese, realising almost as she spoke that she had exposed the fact that she did have prior knowledge of Ursula being alive and that she had a reason to keep the matter quiet.

Beatrice smiled at her small triumph. 'I will not tell as long as you do not harm anyone here.'

'I assure you I have no intention of harming anyone.'

'You will. If you carry on like you have been, someone will be hurt.' The angelic glow of Beatrice's face was gone, replaced by iciness.

'What do you know about me? Who has been talking with you about me?' asked Therese.

The infirmary door opened and Aelfgyth came in. Both Therese and Beatrice provided the entering nun with smooth untroubled faces as she came through to where they were talking.

'I told Sister Beatrice when she insisted on going to the funeral that she had left her bed too early and that is why she developed this cough. It is nearly better. The shepherds' purse will be of benefit to both my patients.' Aelfgyth waved the greenery at them as they both dutifully awaited their medicine.

Therese tried to look anywhere in the church other than the wall hanging that hid the temporary doorway and the hiding place of the inkbottle. Noon prayers had been completed yet she hadn't left. Extra time here was not wasted. She could think clearly among the pillars and vaulted roof uncomplicated by the decorations that would come when the church was completed. She slid along the pew, stood, genuflected and crossed herself before turning and making her way to the chapel doors.

Before she got there another nun entered, made her respects and stood in front of Therese. It was Sybil.

Was this the person that Beatrice was thinking of when she was concerned Therese might harm one of the fold? Was this the person who had clearly discussed her activities with the poorly Beatrice?

'You claim to be Anglo-Saxon,' she remarked in a singsong accent. She was so softly spoken that only Therese, sitting close to her would be able to hear.

'You're Welsh!' gasped Therese. This was the first time she'd heard her properly.

'Not really. I come from the marches – the land between Wales and England, where Offa built his dyke. I am Anglo-Saxon, but that is not why I am here.'

'Isn't it?' asked Therese.

'No, I am here to talk about you. You claim to be of Anglo-Saxon birth?'

'I am.'

'Well, if you think you can join in our fight against the Normans you are quite mistaken.'

'Why?' asked Therese.

'Because there is no fight against the Normans. We are, of course, delighted that you are English but then so are we all. The church prays for the Crown of England whoever that might be. So I advise loyalty to those who brought you up, the Normans – the nuns.'

'Weren't your family dispossessed by the Normans?'

'So what? I have no possessions myself. I gave up all worldly goods when I came here as a Sister. I suggest you forget the outside world if you are to become a nun, Sister Therese.' There was a hard edge to Sybil's voice. Therese was not sure whether it was anger against Therese for her lack of gratitude towards the Normans or a kind of irony. Perhaps she was testing Therese.

'I mean what I say,' persisted Therese. 'I am Anglo-Saxon.'

'We shall see where your loyalties lie when they are tested.'

'What do you mean?' asked Therese.

Sybil did not reply. Instead, she turned and left.

Therese felt exposed. These cloistered women although quiet were sharp and thoughtful. They could make dangerous enemies and even now she still did not really know whether Sybil was involved in the plot to destroy the embroidery or not. But she came from an area which had the Welsh on one side plotting against the Normans and Anglo-Saxons on the other, doing exactly the same. Also, it seemed, that none of them cared for their new masters. Therese was not convinced of Sybil's innocence.

Dappled patterns on her eyelids were the first things Ursula saw. She opened her eyes only to squint at the sunlight coming through the leafy canopy. She focussed on the sounds of men talking. One in particular had a rough voice as if he'd swallowed stones. There was a tightness around her wrists and ankles and her discomfort told her she was lying on rough ground. She was firmly bound with strips of leather. Lifting her hands to block out the sun she observed that Odon's ring was missing from her finger.

'She's awake,' said Agid, placing his filthy face close to hers.

'Don't give me away,' hissed Ursula to Agid, 'or the Devil will take your bones as well as your soul. Common thief.' Ursula almost spat the words at him.

'I didn't know it was you,' wheedled Agid. 'I thought you were the Abbess Eleanor.'

'What do you think you were doing?' asked Ursula.

'Ah, Tancred, she's awake,' repeated Agid to the heavy man with the gruff voice.

Tancred stabbed Sir Gilbert's sword in the ground and hung the wolf-skin lined cape he'd also stolen on the hilt. Most of the garment lay in the dust. He ambled over.

He lifted her by her arms – Ursula resisted the urge to scream in pain – and he shoved her against a tree. He secured her to the tree with rope and reached inside his tunic. He pulled out a small drawstring bag and shook out Odon's ring into his hand.

'You will hang for this,' said Ursula.

'They've got to catch me first, Abbess,' he replied.

'Don't you worry, they will,' said Ursula.

Tancred turned away following the odour of cooked hare drifting across the clearing to its source. She looked about. They were not in the place where she'd cut Abbess Eleanor's hair. This was some other place, an established hideout with tents and hearths.

She thought of the Abbess. The thieves knew now that she was not Abbess Eleanor. St Augustine's would soon discover that Abbess Eleanor was missing, and soon they would look for the curious kitchen servant who didn't know her place. They would never work out what had happened to them. She would never be rescued. She had to get out of here. Agid was still close by, she called to him.

'Agid, you'll have to set me free,' she said when he came close.

'I can't.'

'Why not?'

'They'll kill me.'

'Of course they won't. You can run away with me? Where is the Abbess's pony?'

'We will not get that. It is to be given to Tancred's son. And, have you seen their dogs?' complained Agid. 'I've pleaded for your life already. They were going to kill you.'

'So why have they kept me alive?'

'I told them you knew of a great treasure and you would tell them where it was.'

'What do you know of a great treasure, Agid?' Ursula strained at her bindings.

'I know whisperings, and I know you sent Sister Therese to the Priory of St Thomas the Apostle.'

Ursula flopped back against the tree and shook her head in total despair. All the fight had gone out of her. 'The treasure at St Thomas's has no value in itself. It is a great work of art, a historical document. It is not gold and precious stones.'

'You tell them it is, Prioress, and we'll be all right.'

'No, we won't be all right, Agid. Not only would we be committing a huge crime, and a sin, but we would be killed by these thugs as soon as they gain our knowledge! You will have to go and get help.'

'Who should I go to?'

Ursula could not trust him to go to Eleanor – after all, he would have been happy to let Tancred kill her. She still harboured concerns about Archbishop Lanfranc's motives, so she could not send him there either. There would be little in the way of fighting men at St Thomas's. Sir Gilbert was needed to guard Therese. 'Go to the Earl of Kent. Go to Bishop Odo.'

'He holds your brother!' gasped Agid. Clearly his fear was for himself.

'You will be safe. Tell him that Abbess Eleanor has been abducted by thieves. That will get him here. With any luck we will be able to escape in the ensuing battle.'

'I'm getting my food first,' said Agid.

'You will go?' asked Ursula as he turned away.

'I'll go. I never meant for any harm to come to you.' Agid trailed away with his head down, though he perked up as he got close to the cooking pot and came among the hungry banter of the thieves watching their food being dished out.

Ursula felt no hunger. She watched the camp wind down for sleep and wondered why they hadn't bothered to extract any information out of her about the treasure at St Thomas's.

As night fell Agid brought her some food and told her, 'I've fixed it. I've told them you've given me some information and that I am going to check it out.'

'They won't let you go alone?'

'No, they are sending someone with me. He has been bragging about his role in ambushing Abbess Eleanor and Sister Therese on the night of their arrival in England. He drove their wagon, apparently. Thorkell.'

'You do not admire this man?' accused Ursula.

'It matters not, Prioress.' Agid got up and left.

Ursula called after him, 'What do you mean?' But he was lost to the shadows.

Chapter Seventeen

Agid left the wagoner, Thorkell, where he fell. Carrion would strip the carcass. He didn't even look back at the body. The man had been in the way, that was all. He bore him no malice. His strangulation was not because he was a thief – no sense of justice had driven Agid. He made his way back to the track.

The vibration of hooves on the ground reached him almost as soon as he started back towards Dover; only knights rode that fast. He glanced back in the direction of the body. When he saw the three horsemen before him he realised they were not carrying shields or wearing helmets. He knew, though, that they would not be without their swords, and one carried a lance. The horses slowed even though he moved to one side to let them pass and bowed his head, partly to hide his features. He knew he should stop them. They must be Odon's men so close to Dover but his fear was too great. He fancied sidling up to the castle gate and presenting his message anonymously.

Their leader drew his horse in to a standstill beside Agid. 'Who do you belong to?' he asked.

Agid froze; he hated the assumption that he was a slave. And there was something else, he knew those soft elegant tones so well. He never expected to hear them again. The man who used to speak like that was dead. He looked up to see what ghost spoke in this way and he saw a man the image of the one he expected to see, but younger with fine features and a shock of dark hair. Then he realised there was little in the way of an accent attached to this voice. This was not Edward the Exile who came to visit King Edward long before the battle of Hastings. This was the son, Edgar Aethling, but grown from a lad whom he could remember running around the castle, to manhood.

'Sir, you are my master,' said Agid nervously bowing.

'I have no lands in England,' said Edgar the Aethling clearly realising that he'd been recognised. But worse than that, his countenance became suspicious as he examined Agid. Agid squirmed.

'I must have been mistaken,' said Agid. He was about to turn away when he thought that perhaps he might be safer asking the Aethling for help rather than Bishop Odon. As he looked up he was caught by the weight of Edgar throwing himself at him. He was pushed to the ground. Agid screamed and kicked as Edgar's hands gripped his throat. He managed to bring one of his short sturdy legs up and place his foot on the Aethling's belly and push him away. Edgar's guards moved forward. One, still on his horse thrust the point of his lance at Agid's chest.

This was just the behaviour Agid expected from the aristocracy – Norman or Saxon. He would have told them so if it wasn't for the lance blade so close to his heart. 'I apologise for any offence I may have caused,' he said with caution.

'It is more than offence you have given,' said Edgar. 'I know you. Your face, every inch of you was carved into my soul – not least your shifty little eyes. Why have you not left this land like the others?'

'What others? I don't know what you mean?' Agid squirmed again under his gaze.

'You claim to be my man. In what way were you ever my man? There was only one family you looked to and that was Harold's. You were his sister's man. You were a servant of that evil Queen Edith. She saw to the removal of anyone with any claim to the throne of England, including my father.'

'I assure you that was not the case, my lord,' said Agid feeling that he might yet avoid death.

'I am not your lord,' said Edgar. 'I ought to have you run through here and now. No-one would miss you, and England would be a cleaner place without you.'

'I protected you,' Agid claimed. 'They wanted you dead, but I was there to make sure no harm came to you or your sisters. I am not the bad man you think me to be. You were a child. You cannot be sure that I meant you harm. Think back, can you really remember what happened?'

'My father was announced dead and I had seen you leaving his room earlier,' Edgar claimed with certainty. His guard pressed the lance into Agid's clothing, piercing the cloth.

'It was he who charged me with your safety before his death. But before you kill me I must give you a message from Prioress Ursula.'

'Prioress Ursula? Edgar paused. 'The same good lady, who was among the needle-women of Queen Margaret's court in Scotland?'

'Yes, the same.'

'This is the second time I have heard of her in as many days. I have been told that she is dead.'

'She is not dead. Let me up and I will tell you all you need to know.' Agid frowned at Edgar Aethling and wondered how much he already knew. He was, after all, on the road to Canterbury and beyond there was the Priory of St Thomas the Apostle. He shook his head. He had long since had enough of the aristocracy's in-fighting. Prioress Ursula was his priority now.

Edgar nodded at the guard whom he addressed as 'Sir Alun' who let Agid rise. 'You run and Sir Alun will kill you before you reach the first tree,' threatened Edgar.

Agid sat down and invited Edgar to do the same. Edgar crouched down opposite Agid and tilted his head towards him, he was clearly listening. So Agid told him about Prioress Ursula's fall, her hiding and her kidnapping. He did not include her exchange of identity with Abbess Eleanor or his part in her attack by the robbers. Nor did he say anything about the secret treasure that wasn't treasure that Prioress Ursula knew of.

Edgar leapt to his feet. 'Quick, man! Show me the way!' He directed his other guard, Sir Guy, to put Agid on the animal they'd brought to carry the baggage which was as yet unladen. Sir Guy slung him on as if he were a sack of wheat.

Agid wriggled astride the horse and settled himself. A feeling of importance pushed up through his feet and ankles, straightened his back and squared his shoulders. As far as he was concerned he was riding with the most important man in England.

Eleanor lifted her head and viewed the monks of Christ Church Abbey. She was beginning to recognise their faces. She scanned along the row, just checking that all was in order. Her eyes stopped. There was an unfamiliar round face next to Brother David. He was deeply coloured from hours spent outside. The prayer ritual required them to bow. While the others dropped their heads Eleanor did a head-count. There was no doubt about it: Richard of Caen had arrived.

When the others rose to leave, Eleanor followed the brothers towards the door into the cloisters. Daring to glance round, she saw Brother David leave with Richard of Caen through the public entrance. Clearly, some of Brother Richard's time would be taken up in looking at the works to the new cathedral. She wondered how long she could avoid him as she made her way to the infirmary. A flame of indignation burnt below her ribs. Her questions about Archbishop Lanfranc and Prince William Rufus were still unanswered.

After some miles of riding on a route that avoided any main roads, Agid was still enjoying the fact that he was not on foot, however, he could feel the bones in his rear end. It was as if they were trying to poke through his leathery flesh. Even though he was giving directions to Edgar, the Aethling and Sir Alun rode in front while Sir Guy rode beside him. 'Edgar Aethling,' he called out.

Edgar turned in his saddle, 'what is it?'

'Can you give me a better ride than this?' asked Agid.

'I advise you not to get above yourself, Agid. My knight, Sir Guy, may be big but he's short on patience and you are at best only tolerated here. I do not think that you are the sort of man my father would have charged with our safety. It is more likely that Queen Edith set you to spy on us as children.'

Agid reined in his animal. 'So how do you think you and your sisters grew up to leave court?'

Edgar stopped and turned his horse to face Agid. 'I suspect the King threatened her.'

Trembling slightly at the young warrior's intensity, Agid explained, 'He dared not threaten the Queen. Her brothers held sway in the land. It was I who told her you were young and kind and that you and your sisters held a great interest in the church. It is what kept you safe.'

'All that you said was blatantly true,' said Edgar.

'But I could have said you looked likely to grow into a fine young warrior with more grace and dignity than any of her brothers – just like the son she would never have. Then what do you think your fate would have been?'

There was rustling just off the road ahead of them. Agid was sure they were still a half hour or so from the thieves' camp site, yet he could hear the distinctive tones of Tancred's voice approaching.

Sir Guy directed them off the track and Agid felt himself pulled off his mount and pushed behind a thorn bush. He complained bitterly as Edgar, already dismounted, told him to hold his tongue or he would cut it out for him.

A train of people and goods straggled past them. Some were on foot, others on donkeys and a couple on ponies. Tancred walked along near the front swinging his sword. Towards the back there were two creaking carts. In the back of one was the distinctive shape of Prioress Ursula. All her good humour seemed to have been punched out of her. Agid instinctively moved forwards. 'We must attack them,' he said. 'They have Prioress Ursula and she does not look right at all.'

'Not yet,' said the Aethling.

'Why not?' Agid was furious with the young upstart.

'There are too many of them.'

Agid looked carefully at Edgar's face, but he could not tell what he was thinking. He could be right. If they followed them they could snatch Prioress Ursula from the thieves at a more suitable moment. Or was his decision of a different nature? Had he not only recognised Prioress Ursula but also the thieves? They could, indeed, be under his own employment with Prioress Ursula's demise an unauthorised action by Tancred because of his greed for the ring. He took another look at the young man's strong profile. No, he could not tell.

'It seems, Agid, that they've tried to beat something out of her. Nor have they waited for your return before setting out again. Perhaps they did not trust you either?'

'If any harm comes to the Prioress…' Agid started, but he could not finish for Edgar was already mounted on his horse and moving away.

Chapter Eighteen

Therese paced the cloister of St Thomas the Apostle. Exposing her past had achieved nothing except suspicion from those who barely trusted her anyway and an expectation of success at putting all things right, which she could not believe she could fulfil, from others. She approached the corridor that led off to the chapter house and to the stairway to the sewing room. As she started to pass it a broom shot out and tripped her up. She stumbled but did not fall.

'That Prioress Ethelburga has me sweep for no reason,' complained Gertrude. She pulled a face at Therese. 'Just getting my own back, you tripped me up. And don't look so shocked, I haven't heard you confess to it yet.'

Therese dropped her head guiltily and scratched the newly-tiled floor with the toe of her sandal. 'Why are you here, if you dislike it so much at St Thomas's? I'm sure there are plenty of other places you could be. You don't sew.'

'I don't have the skill. That is true,' said Gertrude sitting down on the wall next to the unplanted garden in the centre of the cloister. Her dumpy figure and the arch of the cloister were picked out by the bright sunshine behind her. 'The skill was well established in England before your lot came. Many of the experts we have here came from Winchester – and that remains an Anglo-Saxon stronghold even now.'

'You've heard about me, my place of birth?' asked Therese.

'You wanted everyone to know, didn't you?' Gertrude looked down at her weathered hands.

'So how come you're here?' persisted Therese. 'At St Thomas's.'

'As you know, I've spent most of my life in the north of England, the land of Bede. I have well-placed relatives in Winchester. I am an embarrassment to them, I speak my mind in the Anglo-Saxon tradition and now we must be careful.'

'Do you want to damage the embroidery?' asked Therese.

'Do you?' replied Gertrude.

'No, I don't,' said Therese thoughtfully. She hadn't considered it before, but even if she did hold Anglo-Saxon sympathies she knew she could not bring herself to damage the labour of others. And the small piece she'd seen had been so carefully worked.

'Well neither do I,' said Gertrude. 'I don't care for fine things particularly, nor do I care for most of the stuck up women here, but I do care for my safety and that is being endangered.'

'By me?' asked Therese.

Gertrude's face softened. 'No, girl.' Her fleshy jowls rattled as she shook her head. 'You have no control over what is about to happen. None of us have. I suggest you take your leave tonight. I tell you this because despite you tripping me up, I quite like you, and you are in more danger than I.'

'What is going to happen tonight?' She remembered her promise to Bishop Odon de Bayeux. It seemed such a long time ago now, though it was only a few weeks. 'I vowed to protect the embroidery. Who is it? Who's going to damage it?'

'Damage. Hah! You don't know the half of it!'

'Tell me!' Therese moved forwards.

Gertrude held her broom defensively. 'That is all I know.'

'Who is behind all this?' The bell rang for prayers and Therese stamped her foot in frustration while Gertrude ignored her last question and went into the church. Therese followed. But her mind was already made up, and on the conclusion of prayers she remained behind while the others filed out. The wall-hanging and the brace in the builder's door of the temporary back wall gave little resistance. She had to warn Abbess Eleanor. Alfred would not be there but Abbess Eleanor would have ensured the placement of another guard, of that she was sure.

Therese would try the far side of the southern woods first. That was where Alfred was meant to have set up camp, even though there had been no sign of it when she visited the place before, but his replacement might well be directed to go there too. The shortest route from here meant passing the gatehouse and going round the western end of the priory complex. The builders ignored her as she walked through their works; luckily they were sitting with their wives eating lunch and thus distracted. The children were down at the stream chucking stones in the water. She did not take the time to see if Eric was among them. She felt invisible as she passed the gatehouse. The porter was eating too. She did not feel hungry. The nuns did not usually eat until later, so there was no fear of being caught out by an empty seat in the refectory.

Soon the priory was behind her; the sewing room, with its sheets of linen strung across the windows to filter the harsh light, and the heavily covered window of the secret room. She could almost feel them watching her go down the hill. In front, and coming upon her fast, was the swamped woodland. She waded straight in. The water level was lower than before, but the mud was thick and she sank into it. Dragging her legs through was exhausting and after a short distance her breath was rasping in her throat. She stopped by the crossing to the stream and leaned on a tree.

Having caught her breath she pulled her feet from the mud and slithered across the fallen tree-trunk bridge she'd used before when she'd met Michael in the woods. Suddenly there was more sky showing through the trees but another fallen trunk barred her way. Beyond it she saw a Norman knight in full battle dress – a sword resting in his scabbard, a mail shirt protecting his body, a helmet and a wing-shaped shield. The knight seemed deep in thought, or prayer. She did not recognise his armoury, but Sir Gilbert's own pieces had been stolen by the thieves in the forest. It had to be him in some different garb. At last she could unburden herself, let someone else sort the problems out, she was exhausted. She was about to call out to him when another Norman knight ran down the slope facing her, his sword aloft. The first knight turned, saw him and drew his sword.

On reaching the first knight the second swung his sword at his opponent's neck, letting out a horrendous yell, but the blow was parried by the first knight's sword. The two continued to fight, turning and twisting until she lost track of which one was which. She dared not move. How could such a thing be happening? Norman against Norman on English soil? She knew, of course, something about the past unrest in England but she'd assumed any invaded country would resist a new order. This was something quite different, and she wondered if she could trust any Norman knight who chose to fight a compatriot. She had no idea which one was Sir Gilbert, though she was sure one of them must be. She looked about for his and the other's horse but saw none, but they could be over the brow of the hill.

Their weighty long swords crashed into each other making an ear-shattering din. They were so close, just beyond the fallen tree-trunk. She covered her ears but dared not shut her eyes in case they saw her and turned on her, she had to be ready to flee.

Both men were staggering now with exhaustion. Therese could barely watch. She knew one must die and that the end would come soon. One of the knights lifted his sword, swung it with practised expertise and took the other's head off in one swing. Still with its helmet on, the head rolled away while the body it was once attached to slumped to the ground. Therese stuck her fist in her mouth and bit her hand to stop herself from screaming.

The remaining knight grabbed the head and strode up the hill. He stopped almost at its ridge and examined a mound of black earth there – the Impostor's grave. He dropped the head onto it and stood for a moment over the grave. He turned and walked back down the hill towards Therese. She was still unable to work out who he was. He had not even removed his helmet and the nose-guard concealed most of his face.

She shrunk down behind the tree-trunk. He must be something to do with the Impostor, she thought. Had he killed Sir Gilbert and was he offering his dead body up to her? She was sure that he was returning to collect the dead knight's body. The blood no longer flowed from its neck. The warm liquid was mixing with the damp soil. She swallowed hard; she would have to make her own way to get help. The thought must have made her move imperceptibly, but clearly enough to alert the knight lifting the body, for he turned in her direction. She swung away and started to run along the edge of the wood, her wet muddy clothing wrapping around her legs.

She knew she did not have the speed or strength of a knight, even one who had just done battle, and when she felt herself fall she expected to feel briefly the cold of metal of his sword then she would meet her maker. Instead she felt a firm hand grab the clothing across her back and pull her up straight. When she looked around, she saw Sir Gilbert's eyes smiling apologetically at her.

Even so she was unsure whether to trust him.

'It is me. I had to borrow armour from Archbishop Lanfranc's armoury. You know mine was stolen. Abbess Eleanor told me that Archbishop Odon has promised me more, but I have yet to receive it. I'm sorry I frightened you.' He paused. 'Did you see what just happened?'

'I saw you fight with that Norman knight and I saw him die.'

'You did not see what happened before that?'

Therese shook her head.

'The knight I killed was the one we all thought drowned on the sea crossing from Normandy, Sir Brian. I've been stationed here since Alfred was arrested – I assume you know about that?'

Therese nodded. She felt a little reassured. 'I knew the Abbess would not leave me unguarded. I came to find Alfred's replacement, but when I saw two Norman knights fighting I did not know what to think…'

'Listen, you need to know this, Sister Therese. I am not a traitor. While I was waiting today I brought my horse down to eat the rich grass by the woods. I was sitting on that very trunk you were hiding behind when Sir Brian came by. He did not see me, but went to that grave and started praying, then weeping over it. I knew it to be the Impostor's grave as the builders had told me when I first arrived. I think they feared me after the arrests in the neighbouring camp.'

'And you approached him?'

'I did. We spoke. I've known him many years. This woman who lies here was definitely not a nun. She was as Sir Brian put it, "My love." Many of us have taken Anglo-Saxon wives. I understood his difficulty. I said to him to do what he had to, and then surrender himself to me, that I would take him to Bishop Odon de Bayeux and ask for his mercy.'

'You didn't expect Sir Brian to turn on you.'

'I know that you will not understand, Sister, as you do not believe in such things, but I expected him to take his own life to join her in purgatory, and I would have buried them together.'

'They can still be laid together,' observed Therese. 'I do not think we should take him to the priory. That would cause too much of a disruption, so we must bury him with great haste. I need you to take a message to Abbess Eleanor. I need help. They are going to act against the embroidery tonight. I have been warned. But I still don't know who will be carrying out the attack.' She was almost breathless with urgency.

Therese and Gilbert completed a makeshift burial. Therese knelt by it and patted the soil whilst she prayed for a moment.

Gilbert whistled his horse and the animal trotted over the hill to his master, with the fallen knight's horse following it. 'Come back with me, Sister Therese. It is too dangerous here.'

Therese shook her head. Even with Gertrude's warning still ringing in her ears, she knew she could not leave. 'No, there may be something else I can do here. Be quick.' They wiped the soil from their hands on the grass and Therese watched him leave before wading back through the woods towards the priory.

Chapter Nineteen

Therese burst into the kitchen and crashed into Agnes, who was on her way out with vegetable trimmings. Agnes brought the basket up above her head to avoid spilling it and as Therese recovered herself Agnes took it outside to the animal feed tub. Therese followed her, wanting to tell her what she knew.

'Sister Agnes, you must leave here. It's too dangerous to stay. There's something planned for tonight, but I don't know what it is. Sister Gertrude told me.'

'Where would I go?' asked Agnes.

'Any priory would take you in, you know that,' argued Therese.

'Are you going?' asked Agnes.

'No,' replied Therese. 'I can't. I promised.'

'Then neither am I,' said Agnes.

'I have sent the news to Abbess Eleanor, Sister Agnes. She will send help.'

Agnes viewed her and Therese shivered. Seeing the way Sir Brian had been killed had shocked her. Her previous life in Normandy had, she realised been very sheltered. It had not prepared her for this. Her wet clothes chilled her.

'There is a fresh habit waiting for you and you look as if you need it,' observed Agnes going to a cupboard in the corner. 'It's well aired.'

Therese thankfully donned the dry linen chemise and the warm woollen tunic, before leaving the sanctuary of the kitchen. She decided she would have to find Gertrude as it was already getting to the time of day when they were required to sweep the workroom. She made for the sewing room. Hilda was coming from the direction of the chapter house, she waved and strode up to her.

'Where have you been?' she demanded. 'Never mind. I can't find Sister Gertrude anywhere. Prioress Ethelburga will be rightfully annoyed if the room is not clean. Could you manage it on your own this evening? I'll let you in and come and let you out when you've finished. Prioress Ethelburga wants to see me.'

Hilda's blue eyes were particularly cool as her gaze met

Therese's. Therese understood from it that she feared Ethelburga would now destroy her reputation over the ink container. There was also acceptance of her fate, and all because Therese had failed to deliver a solution to her.

Therese fetched the broom, pan and bucket from the new cupboard fitted in the cloister and returned up the timber stairway towards the sewing room. She realised that going into the sewing room by herself was what she'd wanted for so long but now she felt her heart thumping in her throat. Her mind was full of Sybil. Could anyone be dispossessed by the Normans and still be so stoic about such a thing? She doubted it somehow. 'Have you seen Sister Sybil?' asked Therese.

'Not for a while,' said Hilda impatiently.

Therese was sorry that she had caused Hilda this grief. 'I'm sorry,' she managed to say. 'There's going to be…'

'What has that to do with anything?' snapped Hilda. 'Your work will be checked and it will soon be time for prayers. You haven't got long,' she said as she let her in.

As the door locked behind her Therese felt trapped.

Against a darkening Dover sky, Bishop Odon de Bayeux organised his guard with shouts to his horsemen and to those who would fight and travel on foot. As he expected, he heard no complaints, and when Robert de Curthose approached already mounted on his horse he explained to him, 'I am restless. I can wait no longer. We will travel overnight so we might collect the embroidery in the morning. Our enemies will not be expecting us.'

'No-one would dare attack a troop such as this,' agreed Robert. 'You must have over a hundred men here.'

Odon was aware of Robert's frown even though he was not looking at him. 'You do not expect trouble from me, I hope?' Robert asked. 'Or Edgar?'

'Of course not,' snapped Odon. If either of these young men, or anyone else for that matter, gave him any trouble, he was fully capable of dealing with it.

Eleanor snatched at the clean dressings as she rolled them up. The light was going and the bell for vespers at Christ Church Abbey had already rung.

'We must go to prayers,' said Brother Matthew. He was clearly a little circumspect because of her temper.

Eleanor's frustration was at boiling point and soon her disguise would be useless. She forced her anger down. She wished she could cast it out, as she was meant to, but of all the passions that she was meant to control, this one gave her the most difficulty.

'I have just received news from St Augustine's,' added Matthew.

Eleanor looked up at him questioningly.

'They know Abbess Eleanor is missing,' he told her.

'How?' asked Eleanor, hardly able to maintain her "Brother James" voice.

'Abbott Scotland became concerned because the servant who had been attending to her could not be found, so another was sent to take her food and care for her. She entered the Abbess's chamber, and we can guess the rest.'

Eleanor wanted to move out of earshot of those on their sickbeds so she went to the door, which had been left open, for Matthew believed in ample fresh air. Matthew followed her. 'Something must have happened to Ursula,' she said.

'Ursula?' asked Brother Matthew.

'It is too complicated to explain, but I must leave Christ Church Abbey now.'

'No, you mustn't. You are so close to uncovering what is going on here.'

Eleanor brushed herself down. 'You are right. But I have had enough of all this nonsense. It will not be long before Bishop Odon is informed of my absence. I cannot imagine what problems that will cause. I am going directly to Archbishop Lanfranc and will put all this before him. I will not be turned away.'

'After vespers, Brother James,' said Matthew as they spotted Brother David heading belatedly to prayers with a curious stumbling gait.

She nodded her consent. After all it would give her time to compose herself and to consider what she would say. She closed the infirmary door behind them.

North of Canterbury the thieves took a roundabout route towards St Thomas's. No doubt thought Agid, scratching at the healing scabs on his wrist, to avoid so many of them having to take the ferry across the river. He spent the evening ride pulling ageing catkins off the birch trees and pinging them at Edgar's mountainous guard beside him riding on an enormous horse which matched his size. This passed the time well enough whilst they followed and waited for Tancred and his gang to rest. He disagreed with Edgar's insistence that they did not follow the thieves too closely.

There was barely any light left and Agid was sure that they had lost them until his stomach was stirred by the smell of a cooking pot. Moments later, off the track, the sight of a flame flickering from the fire underneath it, confirmed the gang's presence.

Slithering close to the camp Agid glanced round at his companions. Sir Guy had been in favour of an all-out attack, but the much slighter Sir Alun agreed with Edgar Aethling, the advantages of them being mounted and the thieves full of food were still insufficient considering their numbers. Agid located Ursula without difficulty. She was secured to a tree away from the fire.

Crouching, the Aethling crept towards her. The ground was dry but the spring grass and new ferns made no sound.

If the thieves saw a shadow move, they gave it no heed. Already many were snoring with the heavy sleep of the well fed and drunk. Agid envied them and was looking longingly at the cooking pot when Ursula's guard, who was snoring the loudest, snorted as if he were about to wake.

The Aethling stayed still within an arm's length of Ursula until the guard settled back into sleep. Having slit through her ropes with his knife, he carried the weakened woman back to his guard.

Agid was relieved to have Ursula back and allowed his mind to return to the demise of his stomach. He viewed the fire and wondered if he could re-enter the group and feed from the pot without being discovered. But Agid spotted a glint of silver, he screwed up his eyes to try and make it out. It was a sword – a fine Norman sword. And beside it lay the bulk of Tancred wrapped in his stolen cloak. Agid shivered and pulled back behind the

Aethling's men. He knew such a man with such a sword would make short work of a man who trades in information and not muscle, such as himself.

Sir Guy growled at him under his breath and he slipped further away from the small raiding party of Norman knights and Ursula. He was soon aware that they were following him with Ursula now being carried by Sir Guy.

Back near their own horses Sir Guy laid her down. Her face was bruised and she had difficulty opening her eyes. She looked up, and the Aethling stooped over her. Ursula reached out her hand and touched his face.

'Am I in heaven?' she said.

'Not likely,' said Agid without thinking.

'Oh, Agid, you got help!' she said. Her voice was a weak mixture of pleasure and amazement. 'But they beat me and I …'

'Hush, Prioress,' said the Aethling. 'You and Agid must return directly to Canterbury and report this to Abbott Scotland.'

'I cannot go there,' said Ursula.

'Well, Archbishop Lanfranc then.'

'No,' said Ursula. 'There is a monk there, though, that will understand, James of Caen.' She pulled herself upright. 'I must speak to her…him.'

Agid squinted at her. 'What have you been up to – pretending to be Abbess Eleanor and all?'

'I'll tell you on the way.' Ursula was trying to stand.

'Sir Guy will go with you. Sir Alun and I will stay here to keep an eye on them while you get help.' The Aethling supported Ursula as she hobbled towards the mule.

'This looks like my sort of mount,' she said.

The Aethling helped her up and Agid went to vault on behind her, but Edgar caught him by the scruff and said, 'You walk.'

Sir Guy mounted his horse and they left, yet still Agid could hear no sign of any disturbance from the sleeping thieves. Surely, the rescue had been far too easy. Still, sometimes, thought Agid, you just got lucky.

Chapter Twenty

At St Thomas's Priory, Therese looked around her fellow nuns at vespers. Maude and Mabel were missing as well as Gertrude. She had warned Agnes and tried to warn Hilda about Gertrude's belief of a dangerous event occurring tonight. She wondered how many more knew what would happen and whether those that had already disappeared from the Priory were involved or whether it was those remaining that would be. Her whole body was tense.

Prioress Ethelburga's face was as hard as steel as she said her prayers. Beatrice was out of the Infirmary and she and Sybil were chanting like song birds with the joy of spring in their voices, almost too happy. Leofgyth held her own against the strong tones of the older nuns, Winifred and Aelfgyth – powerful and clever women in their own right. Hilda mumbled, like her heart was broken. Agnes, Therese noted, was watching her watching the others.

She sighed and returned to her prayers.

Eleanor followed Archbishop Lanfranc from vespers. Outside the Church of Christ, the small Italian's face was caught by the light of a taper lit early against a rapidly darkening sky and held by Brother David. Lanfranc's sharp nose pointed at a document the clerk was trying to pass to him.

'It can wait. I will read it in the morning in good light,' he said.

Brother David accompanied him to his door and then left. The Archbishop insisted he did not need light to take himself to his chamber. The residual gloom was quite enough and so the clerk took the taper with him. Lanfranc fumbled with the letter, dropped it and picked it up again. The Archbishop shook his head and opened the door to his chamber. Eleanor rushed up to him. Energy swelled inside her as if she were half her age, and she let go of her caution, but the front of her sandal caught on a flag-stone and caused her to trip, knocking into the Archbishop.

He caught her with his left hand, his right found her head and patted it reassuringly. While he helped her straighten up, his right hand trailed down to her chin, which he nipped slightly. When she was composed he let go of her elbow and gripped her right hand.

'The things I have touched do not make sense,' said the Archbishop. He sounded shocked.

She tried politely to pull her hand away from the holy man's hold.

'Your hands are soft, so is your hair, but you have a tonsure. Your chin is smooth. In the dark you could be a boy, but a boy does not have such a lined face. I do not know you.'

Eleanor snapped, 'If you had agreed to see me on my arrival in Canterbury you would know me well enough. I am Abbess Eleanor of Bayeux. I am here to investigate the difficulties at the Priory of St Thomas the Apostle.'

'But your head, Abbess? And what are these difficulties you speak of?' From the bewilderment in the Archbishop's voice she knew he really didn't know anything of her or even the problems at St Thomas's.

'Has Brother David not told you? I have come to speak with you several times, but he said you were busy,' explained Eleanor.

'I'm sorry to say I have been very busy of late, my beloved daughter.' Eleanor was calmed by his gentle firmness and his spontaneous, kind endearment to someone he had never met. The Archbishop continued, 'Come inside and let us talk there.' He gestured for her to enter his chamber, she thanked him and entered.

At last Eleanor's mind was at rest. She'd pinioned Archbishop Lanfranc with her tight questioning and he'd been generous and curious in equal amounts. After the interview she closed his chamber door behind her and walked out into the cool night air, pulling her cowl up over her head. She would return directly to Saint Augustine's and organise a search for Ursula. With the gatehouse in sight she was aware of horses' feet grinding at the ground in the courtyard behind her.

Several horses were being mounted. They were twisting and turning in excitement. The flapping of full, lined cloaks and the clashing of metals – harness and weapons – filled the air. She fell back against the wall to let the horses and their riders pass. Four sets of hooves pounded so close to her she pulled her feet back.

She did not have to see them to know who they were, so clearly leaving Canterbury while the monks slept: Prince William Rufus and his three guards, Roger, Simon and Ralph.

The gatekeeper was struggling to shut the heavy timber gates behind them so she slipped through when his back was turned. She could have stopped and explained, but this seemed easier somehow. She was just recovering from being nearly trampled when in the gloom she heard another horse. This solitary animal had white skin, and as soon as she saw him she knew the rider was Sir Gilbert. She kept her head covered while she called to him.

'Sir Gilbert, what has happened to Therese? You have not left her on her own!' She tugged at her cowl and cape to keep her monkish garb hidden.

'She insisted, Abbess. I am sorry. She sent me to get you as there is going to be trouble at St Thomas's tonight.'

'We must get help,' said Eleanor looking back at Christ Church Abbey's gates.

'There is not time. I do not know what is going on, but I have been looking for you all evening. At St Augustine's they said you were missing.'

'I should have told you where to find me. I've been so foolish.' She was angry with herself.

'And I think Prince Rufus is heading out of Canterbury in that direction.'

'Pull me up behind you,' commanded Eleanor. 'I don't know what they are about but we must go directly to St Thomas's.'

As they left Canterbury a wind was rising from the south west. The knight's horse made good time despite carrying the two of them and Eleanor thought she saw the movement of horses on the far side of the river. Rufus and his men were only just ahead of them. The returning ferry held the shadowy figures of a mule and two hunched passengers just visible in the light of the ferryman's brazier on the bank. The ferryman was grumbling about so much work so late at night, as he secured the raft to its mooring.

'I'm packing up for the night,' he told Eleanor, leading the mule off the ferry.

'I don't think you are,' replied Eleanor. She called Sir Gilbert over. And as she did so she felt a pull on her skirts from below.

'Abbess.'

She looked down at the present occupants of the ferry who were gathering their strength to disembark. An arm was reaching out and its hand was holding the hem of her habit. 'Ursula?' she asked unable to believe her friend was this crumpled heap so close to her.

'Agid is with me,' said Ursula. The small man rose from beside her.

'We had a guard, Sir Guy – the Aethling's man – but he left us to join Odo and his men,' complained Agid. 'We've had to do the rest of the journey by ourselves.'

'Odon de Bayeux?' asked Eleanor.

'The same,' said Agid. 'That Norman Bishop needed no more help. He is travelling with an enormous number of horsemen already.'

'He was in Dover,' said Eleanor.

'Well he's not now,' retorted Agid.

'I have not seen him,' said Gilbert. 'He did not enter Canterbury on his travels.'

'He didn't come this way either,' said the ferryman. 'I couldn't take that lot across. And the tides have been high and the currents strong today. It would have been difficult for them to swim the horses. They must have travelled the long land route.'

'We need to cross,' Eleanor said to the ferryman. Addressing Gilbert, she said, 'Odon is already in the right direction we only need to alert him and we can go on to St Thomas's.'

'Prioress Ursula is very poorly she cannot ride,' said Agid. He opened his mouth as if he was going to tell a long story but Eleanor interrupted him with,

'Explanations will have to wait.' She looked searchingly at the reluctant ferryman expecting him to offer care. He grumbled and then allowed them to take Ursula to his hut.

Once settled in the ferryman's cot, Ursula looked much more like her old self despite the bruising around her face, which, with the light afforded by a fire in the centre of the hut's only room, Eleanor could now see.

'Do not fear for me,' said Ursula. 'I will be fine now, but the thieves know about the embroidery. I am no martyr, I'm afraid, Abbess. I told them.'

'Hush. You rest. You've been incredibly brave.' Eleanor lingered over her English friend until Sir Gilbert called her away. Outside the hut she told him to stay with them. 'I need you to protect her and keep an eye on Agid. He is not to be trusted. And I will need your horse.'

The ferryman grumbled, 'I don't like taking horses and that's all I've had this evening,' as he fixed on the animal's hobbles to prevent the creature jumping off. 'And this wind doesn't help.'

Odon de Bayeux checked his position. He'd had to split his men. The foot-soldiers could not keep up with the horses so he'd left them to follow on. Speed was the most important thing now. He was at the junction where the Canterbury road, which took the ferry, joined with the landward route. He checked Robert and Edgar's guard, Sir Guy, who'd recently joined them saying he'd left a nun and a beggar at the ferry. He'd even said that it was Prioress Ursula. This must be a lie. Ursula was dead so he didn't trust the man or his tale of thieves and kidnappings. This meant Edgar Aethling and Sir Alun were nearby. Sir Guy could well be part of a plot to draw Odon himself into a trap set by Edgar. Odon placed two of his most trusted men next to Sir Guy, just in case. Even his trust in Robert was tested by the young man's friendship with the Aethling. Now more horsemen approached from the south.

Therese had felt like a guard dog, and although she thought she couldn't rest, sleep must have over-taken her because something had disturbed her and she was now upright as if she had a stake at her back. From the dorter window, Therese saw a light down in the cloister. It was too dark to see who was or was not in their beds, but she had to leave this sanctuary if she were to get to the bottom of the traitors at the priory. She took the stairway from the dorter that came out close to the chapter house. By its door she looked towards the timber stairway which went up to the sewing room. The light was up there, she could just make out a flicker. Whoever was carrying the light must realise the risk they took in being caught. In all her night outings Therese had not risked carrying one, but it was dark tonight, cloud obliterated the stars and moon – if there was any moon. To see anything much, a light would be needed.

Therese felt her way cautiously up the steps, aware that the light was receding from her view. She crouched down below the top and expected the light to turn into the sewing room, but it didn't. It continued along the full length of the corridor and disappeared into the tower at the other end. She rose and checked the corridor for signs of life. It looked bare, with only the one door opening onto it. On the cloister side of the corridor was a line of open arched windows. From these she would clearly be seen from the dorter window so she decided to keep as close to the sewing room side as she could. As she felt her way along the wall she realised that the upper floor walls were timber partitions, plastered and painted, even the secret room.

Just before she entered the stone tower she heard a voice. She knew it instantly. 'Sister Agnes?' called Therese. Therese heard her shush a companion. 'What are you doing, Sister Agnes?' asked Therese. She took the few steps that would bring her just below the hole where she had hidden Eric. And there was Agnes, illuminated by a taper in the holder on the wall. The tall nun had a panel of embroidery wrapping itself about her as it was being fed out through the hole above.

Agnes just looked at her.

There were few people who could fit in that hole. 'Eric?' Therese called out in to the night.

Chapter Twenty One

'Hello, Sister Therese,' said Eric peeping out of the hole. The light from the taper made him look like something from the underworld.

'We're getting the embroidery out of here,' explained Agnes. Therese didn't know whether to trust her. It must have shown. 'For safe keeping,' Agnes added with a hint of exasperation in her voice.

'You knew about it all the time?' asked Therese.

'Prioress Ursula told me before we got her away,' replied Agnes.

'Do any of the other nuns know?'

'They shouldn't. They should all believe that the embroidery has already been taken away. But someone might have worked out where it really was.' Agnes spoke while rolling up a panel of embroidery. 'You can help, or you can go. I don't mind which, but standing right there you're going to be in the way.'

'Of course,' said Therese.

'I think you'd fit through that hole, though you're tall there's nothing to you. The quicker we get those panels out of here the better. Now up you go.' Agnes offered Therese a leg up with her hands clenched together to make a stirrup for her foot.

Inside she found that Eric had pulled down the coverings from the window for some light, but the night afforded little. She went down the steep steps from the timber gallery by the hole and went over to the window and looked out. Surely a better plan would be to drop them directly out of the window? But when she looked out the wind caught at her head covering and she could hear sheep sheltering below. If the panels were not blown away and ripped to pieces in the trees, they would land in filth and be trampled upon.

'Hurry,' said Eric.

'We will be quicker if we can see what we are doing. I think I can see a taper in the holder by the sewing room door. I'll light it from Sister Agnes's one.'

'I can manage in the dark,' Eric muttered.

'Well, I can't,' said Therese. She was proved right as she carefully rolled each panel and carried them individually up the steps with the help of the tiny wavering light on the wall. At the top she handed the rolls to Eric who passed them out through the hole to Agnes.

She was fond of Eric and Agnes and knew she would feel betrayed if they were part of an Anglo-Saxon plot against the Normans. But she could not secure all of the panels without help, and hopefully Sir Gilbert would have raised the alarm by now and others would soon be coming to her aid.

Two horsemen drew up in front of the men lined up as if ready to go into battle.

'It's the Aethling,' confirmed Sir Guy, 'and Sir Alun.' He kicked his horse forward out of line. One of Odon's guards went to draw him back, but Odon waved him away. 'If you don't believe me then you might believe them,' added Sir Guy.

Edgar Aethling introduced himself in his usual courteous manner.

'What are you doing in these parts?' asked Odon.

'Has not my man told you?' asked Edgar.

'I want to hear it from you.'

Edgar's explanation seemed quite unbelievable to Odon, especially the part about Prioress Ursula being alive. But it did coincide identically with what he'd heard from the Aethling's guard. 'There's just one thing that I doubt.'

'And what is that?' asked Edgar.

'You have arrived from the south. According to your man the thieves you were watching are to the north of here.'

'I skirted around your group, Your Grace. I wanted to make sure you were who I thought you were before I made my approach. The darkness tonight is all embracing.'

'These thieves sound as if they require a small Norman lesson. But if this is a trap, Aethling, I will kill you first for you shall ride beside me.'

'You have no need to distrust Edgar or I,' objected Robert.

'Better still, as you two are so friendly towards each other, I will keep you here, Robert, with a small guard as a hostage.'

'That will not be necessary,' insisted Edgar.

'You told me you were on your way to Scotland to see your

sister,' said Odon, 'and yet you are still in Kent.'

'I have been delayed by Prioress Ursula.'

'Prioress Ursula is dead,' Odon felt his temper rising.

'I have seen her with my own eyes, Your Grace.'

'Robert will stay here,' said Odon nodding at the horseman he'd set to guard the King's eldest son.

'Uncle, I am happy to stay as a hostage,' said Robert. 'As you must know you need fear nothing from me.'

Edgar felt his horse shift its weight from front to back as it took great galloping strides towards the thieves' camp. He leapt ditches and fallen tree-trunks. Odon's horse matched his stride for stride and the others followed. Edgar took them into the camp through the widest entrance to the clearing – their swords drawn. Odon's plan was to raid the site while the thieves slept and could offer little resistance. But they weren't there. Edgar had left them sleeping. They must have finally realised Prioress Ursula was gone and moved off. Perhaps they, like him, had become aware of the approach of Odon's men and they'd decided to melt away.

'This had better not be a trap!' declared Odon swinging his sword close to Edgar's head. He sent his men around the scrub and nearby woodland to check for the thieves. They came back with nothing.

'They must have got wind of your presence, Your Grace.'

'You, Edgar Aethling, will remain with me until you leave for Scotland. We will return to Robert directly.'

Edgar was immediately surrounded by Odon's men and escorted from the vacated campsite.

As Odon returned to the small retinue he'd left with Robert he became concerned. More horsemen were approaching from the ferry road.

'Is this your doing?' he asked Edgar. 'Did you intend to split my men in an attempt to weaken me?'

'Your Grace, the group approaching is small. Barely more than were with me.' Edgar sounded reasonable.

Odon still wasn't sure how many men Edgar really had with him. He only knew of two – Sir Guy and Sir Alun, but what of these, so called, thieves? He felt now that he was acting not as Bishop Odon de Bayeux, but that he was back in his role of Earl of Kent. Normandy seemed a long way away. He sighed. Then he recognised the horses that were approaching. His blood chilled. 'My God. It's Rufus.'

Odon's rejoined group bristled around him. On this subject they were all agreed: this man was unsuitable to rule England, and his presence meant trouble whichever way you looked at it. Odon moved forward out of the line of his men, Edgar Aethling, Sir Alun, Sir Guy and Robert de Curthose moved into position behind Odon.

'Halt!' the Earl of Kent demanded of the four horsemen.

They obliged by stopping, but instantly drew their swords. 'Who prevents the passage of Prince William, Son of the Conqueror?' asked the largest one of them flanking the Prince.

'Ah Roger, you feign to not recognise Odon de Bayeux, Earl of Kent. Prince William, my respects to my nephew.' replied Odon with clipped courtesy. 'What business brings you to these parts at this hour?'

'Roger, Simon, Ralph, stay your swords a moment,' said William Rufus reluctantly. 'You may act as king in my father's absence, Uncle, but all this will be mine one day, and there will be no place for you.' There was no mistaking the Prince's flaring temper.

'What are you doing here, brother?' Robert was clearly annoyed by his brother.

'I will not be questioned like this,' snarled Rufus.

Odon detected a movement by Robert's horse. His man had restrained him. Odon could not afford to let these brothers fight, for they would tear each other apart.

'I ask you with great fealty, as an uncle, not to be interested in my activities,' said William Rufus, backing off from the armed force in front of him. 'But I, as the King's son, am interested in yours. You who have treacherous friends. What are you doing here?' Odon watched Rufus scrutinise the line up before him. And Rufus added, 'With all these mighty people?'

Robert surged forward and rushed at his brother. Their swords clashed as they urged their horses against each other.

Odon shouted, 'Order. This is mere quarrelling. Brothers should not fight before their men like this.' But they did not part and Roger, Simon and Ralph started to fight Robert off, so Edgar joined the fight, followed by Sir Alun and Sir Guy. Odon pulled his own men back. He did not want their loyalties to be tested. These two groups of men were evenly matched. Perhaps, once they tired he might be able to break up the fight before any real harm was done.

Chapter Twenty Two

There was just one panel of embroidery left in the secret room at St Thomas's Priory as well as the one left in the sewing room. When Therese had cleaned in there last night she'd noticed that it was already freed from the frame it had been fixed to for the embroidering process.

Therese told Eric to leave, she could manage the last two. He tried to persuade her otherwise, but she had him through the access hole and into the tower with Agnes before he had a chance to think of a way to prevent it. On the stairs, Agnes grasped him firmly by the shoulders.

'Get the embroidery as far away from the building as you can,' instructed Therese.

'We will take it over the kitchen-yard wall,' said Agnes. 'Don't be long, we will wait for you there.'

'Don't wait. Go!' ordered Therese. Her first priority was to get the embroidery safely away. She had to trust Agnes and Eric.

She went directly back to the last panel and started to roll it up when she thought she heard a noise in the next room. It was the scrape of wood upon wood. Someone was in the sewing room moving the carved screen from the door to the secret room. In a moment whoever it was would be in here with Therese. She stood in front of the last panel as the door swung open.

Therese stared at the silhouette of a nun as her eyes adjusted to the unexpected light. Gertrude, Maude and Mabel had left the Priory and she doubted they would return. The figure was too slim for Aelfgyth or Beatrice and not tall enough for Winifred. It could not be Agnes; she would not have had time to unravel herself from Eric and the embroidery. She hoped dearly it was not Leofgyth. Kind, funny Leofgyth.

The sewing room was lit with church candles and tapers. Therese found the flames and the brightness horrifying.

'Sybil?' she called gently. She hadn't wanted a Welsh conspiracy. Michael had charmed her, but it had always been the most clearly indicated of the potential plots. Her doubts rose again about Eric. The silhouette moved a pace towards her and stopped. 'Let your hate for the Normans go. This tapestry is too beautiful to destroy. It goes beyond our differences. It tells the world of our skills and our determination. The story it tells on the face of it is not our story, we know that.'

'I thought it was you in here,' said a voice she could not mistake. It was Hilda's sweet voice, hardened and piercing like the point of a needle.

Therese was completely taken aback. 'So you lied about Prioress Ethelburga,' she said.

'No, she did as I said, but her only need was power.'

'So it was you who stole the key from Prioress Ursula?'

'If only I'd been quicker, I would have finished the job of inking the panel that our little Impostor failed to do, but Ethelburga saw me and organised her little power struggle.'

'And this room?'

'I'm not stupid. You worked it out. Well, so did I.'

'When did you work it out?'

'Only recently. I watched you clean the sewing room remember. You took an unnatural amount of care in doing so, and you could not keep your eyes off that screen. I've come for the rest of the embroidery, I'm sure this is where it's been stored. When you saw me at the ink bottle's hiding place I was fetching it to have another go at the panel. I was going to have another go…'

'You're too late. The embroidery has gone.'

'What do you mean?' asked Hilda rushing forward to look behind Therese.

Therese moved to grab the embroidery. As she did so the single panel was exposed to Hilda's gaze.

'You thief!' The words almost exploded out of Hilda's mouth. In one movement she turned and seized the taper from its fixing by the door.

In the meantime, Therese had picked up the partly rolled panel and was hurrying towards the steps to the gallery and the hole in the tower wall. Hilda was after her. Therese wrestled with the fabric which seemed intent on unravelling itself the more she tried to tuck it up. Hilda was close – too close. The skilled needlewoman seemed intent on destroying her own work. Therese pointed this out, breathless with fear and the task of shifting the panel.

'I don't care. And you needn't give me any of that, "I'm an Anglo-Saxon" stuff. You know too much and this will tidy things up nicely.'

'But your family has not been dispossessed like Sister Sybil's,' reasoned Therese.

'My father died at Hastings. My mother had to marry a Norman so my family could retain their lands. My brother as a land owner himself had to swear fealty to our Norman conqueror. I can hardly swallow with the disgust I feel.'

Therese had reached the top of the gallery steps when Hilda lunged at the embroidery with the taper, her face contorted with hate. The only way she could stop her was by dropping the panel. She did so, but was too late, the corner was burning. At the same time she felt her legs taken from under her by Hilda wrapping her arms about them. She thumped down onto the gallery, winded. She blinked. She could feel heat about her ankles; Hilda had set light to the hem of her habit as well. In her eye line there were a row of pots along the back edge of the gallery wall. She recognised them. Getting up, Therese pushed Hilda back down the steps. There was a crack of skull hitting floor at the bottom and the needle-woman lay still. Therese ran over to the first pot and quenched the flames on her skirt with Eric's urine. The second pot had once contained his food, but he'd clearly had the need to fill that too. This pot went over the burning edge of the panel.

The taper was still clutched in Hilda's hand and its idle flame singed the floorboards, but Therese had to secure the embroidery first so she ran with the panel and dispatched it through the hole. Back next to the unconscious Hilda she trod out the taper's flame. Hilda's hand moved and grabbed her ankle. Therese felt herself being pulled down again as Hilda, her face shaking with anger, regained her feet. Briefly everything went black for Therese.

Eleanor heard the battle well before she could see it as she rode up the hill on the white horse. She'd made good time with the horse now carrying just one rider. But she missed having Sir Gilbert to defend her. She wasn't sure who was fighting whom, but knew she could not afford to be cautious. Therese was in danger.

Bishop Odon must be among them. As she got closer, she realised that most of the large band of mounted men were not fighting. There were just eight and these were no longer on their horses, but slogging it out with swords on the ground. She ordered Sir Gilbert's horse into the centre of the fighting where two men, one with hair the colour of fire the other with red in much softer tones, had discarded their weapons and were mauling, wrestling and punching each other. Their exhaustion was obvious as they staggered at each other with grim determination.

'Stop it!' ordered Eleanor with the full authority of her status as Abbess. 'This is no time for fighting among ourselves.' The two young men separated as did the other fighters. She directed a severe look at Bishop Odon whom she located just beyond the fight in the watching group.

'I heartily agree,' he said. 'I was about to stop it myself.'

'I think, Bishop, you were enjoying the entertainment,' accused Eleanor. 'We must get to the Priory of St Thomas. I have received word that the embroidery is in danger this very night.' She did not say that the word had come from Therese, for she could not tell the Bishop what danger she'd placed his ward in.

The fighters silently gathered their weapons and mounted their horses and, at Odon's command, the whole troop wheeled round and headed towards The Priory of St Thomas.

Coming round Therese felt dizzy. Through a fog, she heard Hilda asking, 'Do you want to save the last panel?' Therese felt herself being dragged into the sewing room. She went to pull away but her hands were tied behind her back. 'Well, you can die in here with it. I will get one panel now and then I'll fetch the others and pile them onto the flames.'

Therese realised that Hilda was crazed. She'd already seen that the panels were gone. She smiled; at least she'd succeeded in saving the embroidery.

'You think I can't get them,' taunted Hilda. 'Did someone help you move them? All the nuns here are Anglo-Saxon. Do you think they would deny me access to the panels, my own countrywomen?'

By this time Hilda had tied her to the leg of the embroidery stand. Therese hoped Agnes and Eric would return the embroidered panels to their rightful owner, Odon de Bayeux, but she could not be sure they would. Therese strained at her bindings. She'd expected to uncover the traitor before any harm was done, but she'd been so gullible. It was as if Hilda had read her mind.

'You can't help being young,' she said.

Indignation filled Therese's lungs with hot air. She felt strength returning to her arms and legs. She grabbed hold of the leg of the embroidery stand she was tied to, gathered her feet up underneath her and heaved it up, pushing it away from her and releasing her bindings from it at the same time. Hilda leapt back out of the way of the crashing wood. She stared at the mess of broken frame; the dust cover was torn, but she thought the embroidery panel would be alright. Therese followed her gaze and her heart sank. She knew she was too late – there were flames licking about the material and almost immediately they were spreading to the linen window screens, the dry rush seating of the needle-women's stools and then the straw in the wattle and daub partitions.

Hilda reached for a candle and rushed at Therese, who still had her hands tied. In return, she charged at Hilda with her head down like a bull. They crashed onto the floor, into the centre of the burning room. Somehow Hilda moved and Therese fell heavily without her arms to break the fall and Hilda pushed her out of the way, heading for the secret room which was still free of the fire, although the screen that had stood in front of it was now aflame. Therese recovered and was soon on her feet. She could not fight effectively with her hands tied. She spotted a jagged nail sticking out of the top of the leg she'd been tied to, where it had come away from the embroidery frame, which had rolled away and was already engulfed by the inferno. The nail was hot and seared through her bindings.

Again she threw herself with all her remaining strength at Hilda. This time she took her down too quickly for her opponent to twist out of it, so Hilda took the brunt of the fall and was knocked out. Therese checked, there was no way out through the sewing room. She started to drag Hilda up to the gallery. They could both still escape from being burnt to death by going down the stone stairway. Hilda stirred. Therese looked round. The fire had already reached the secret room and was rapidly approaching them. Once it took the gallery they would not have a chance. Hilda clearly realised this as she pulled back on Therese, wrapping her arms about her legs.

'We'll die together,' she hissed.

'We will not die. The truth must be known.'

'I know all I need to know,' said Hilda, taking Therese down.

At that moment, the fire reached the top of the timber gallery steps, and the supports, it gave way, taking Hilda with it. Therese found her own body still on the remaining piece of gallery floor but her legs were hanging down into nothing but flame and scorching hot air. She dragged each leg up onto the platform cautiously, reached into the hole and pulled herself through. Her height meant that by dropping down and holding onto the edge of the hole in the stonework the drop onto the stairs was not enough to hurt her. She even missed landing on the panel she'd dropped through not long before. Picking it up, she ran down the winding stairs and was soon out in the kitchen yard. There was no sign of Agnes, Eric or the rest of the panels, but a spark from the sewing room had clearly reached the dry kitchen building and it was already afire. So she turned into the outer court yard. The refectory doors had been opened to make a direct passage into the cloister.

There was a chain of builders with buckets of soil and water trying to douse the flames. Among them were the remaining nuns, sleeves rolled up, covered in sweat and filth. Therese looked along the line until she spotted Agnes.

'Where's Eric?' she asked her.

'He's gone in after you, just now. I tried to stop him.'

'Which way?'

'By the chapter house.' Bands of flame were already reaching into the sky from above the sewing room but the stone cloister was still unaffected. The chapter house was behind the dorter and sewing room and largely constructed of stone. He could have gained some sanctuary there.

Therese took Agnes's bucket and tipped it over herself.

'No, don't go, Sister,' Agnes pleaded. 'I couldn't bear to lose both of you.'

One of the builders took off a cloak, soaked it in water and gave it to her. Therese took it gratefully and went back into the burning building.

Eleanor saw the flames, as did the others when they breasted the hillside by the builders' camp to the north east of the Priory. Fear for Therese struck her like a pain in her heart. Odon had brought his force round by the coast complete with Robert Curthose and Edgar Aethling. The camp was deserted and they could hear the shouts of many men and women trying to fight the fire at the priory, it had clearly not reached the gatehouse or the chapel. Bishop Odon rushed out ahead rapidly followed by Eleanor and the others. Still she dared not utter the name of her charge. Fortunately Odon had been riding hard and had not asked about Therese. At the stream a human chain was formed bucketing water and handing it along to the priory.

Once through the gatehouse she dismounted and ran into the cloister where the most noise was coming from. The sound of crackling and the roar of a hungry fire crowded out normal speech. Everyone was shouting instructions, but it was being done with a stoic orderliness.

'Abbess Eleanor,' called someone from the line.

Eleanor turned and looked. It was a tall nun. She didn't know her well, but she guessed it was probably Sister Agnes. 'Yes, Sister,' she replied.

'Sister Therese is in there,' said Sister Agnes.

'What's that?' said Bishop Odon. He was at Eleanor's shoulder. 'Who's in there?'

Eleanor felt as if the fire itself had rushed through her and torched her mind and body. Her spirit was burnt out. She walked towards the flames but Odon stopped her.

Chapter Twenty Three

Odon was holding onto Abbess Eleanor when he saw Edgar rush towards the burning building. The young warrior ran into the cloister but did not enter the burning building as he was met by the stooped figure of Therese. Her cloak formed a halo of flames above her head. She flung it off, but her habit had also caught fire. Edgar pushed her to the ground and rolled her in the soil of the unplanted garden in the centre of the cloister. He kicked dust over her hem.

The Bishop started to go over to her. At least, he thought, she'd had the good sense to save herself. As he helped her up she opened her arms and a boy rolled out, his whole being blackened by smoke. He ran off like a deer being chased by hounds. Abbess Eleanor was the other side of Therese and the girl collapsed into her arms. Odon felt rage grip him. How dare this boy endanger Therese! 'Arrest the child,' he directed a guard nearby, and the boy was seized by one of Odon's guards and taken away.

A horseman rode through the cloisters and into the central area. 'Your Grace, I have checked the perimeter of the priory and there are panels of embroidery stacked behind the southern wall. The building is well alight, Your Grace. I don't think the Priory can be saved.'

Odon nodded. 'Move the embroidery away to a place of safety – the builders' tents – and get everyone out of here before masonry starts falling.'

Out on the hill above the campsite Odon found Sister Agnes by his side watching the building burn.

'Sisters Maude and Mabel got the animals out, Your Grace,' she said curtseying.

Odon looked at her. She was another of these Anglo-Saxons. He knew he shouldn't have trusted them with such a significant job, but their embroidery skills were renowned across the continent.

'I see you have taken the embroidery to safety, Your Grace.'

'That is none of your business,' snapped Odon.

'But you have arrested little Eric and he helped me save it.'

'You Anglo-Saxons are all in this together. You knew there were thieves coming, you and the boy. And you left the embroidery panels behind the garden wall for them.' Any friendship he'd felt for these people withered away as Sister Agnes cried,

'You are mistaken, Your Grace.'

'Take this one and place her with the boy,' he said to his guard. 'She will be held under arrest with the others. Your thieves did not come, Sister. They heard me and fled.' As the guard dragged her from him he added, 'Ursula, your ex-prioress, will join you in prison, so you won't be alone.'

'Your Grace, please listen,' groaned Sister Agnes.

'You will all have your chance to speak, but not today. I will hold an inquiry into this, and those that have done wrong will be punished.'

As soon as she was awake, Therese had to tell Abbess Eleanor everything. She was comfortable in the Abbess's bed at St Augustine's, she couldn't remember having had cushions before. Her run in with Sister Hilda seemed as if it had been a bad dream and that was how she intended to keep it. The Abbess seemed horrified by her tales, which Therese quite enjoyed too. But when she asked about Ursula and Eric, Abbess Eleanor patted her hand sadly and said,

'Later.' And then continued more brightly, 'The remaining embroidery panels are already on their way to Bayeux.'

'Now I want to hear everything that has happened to you!' Therese realised how forward and disrespectful she'd been almost as soon as the words left her mouth, so she smiled apologetically.

The Abbess took the apology. 'I will tell you everything,' she said. 'Even about an episode I am most ashamed of, where I dressed as a monk.' Therese watched her elder's face redden and then Abbess Eleanor sat for an age on the edge of her bed filling her in on every detail of her investigations. It was lovely just to hear her voice and enjoy the trust of this woman she thought so much of.

As she finished the door burst open and Brother David entered. He was carrying scrolls rolled up under his arm, and he seemed disorientated. His steps wove towards the bed despite the Abbess yelling at him to leave.

'You are at St Augustine's not Christ Church Abbey. This is my room and you have no right to come in.'

He shook his head, and as he turned to go, Therese tweaked the paper at the centre of the loose roll of documents under his arm. While the Abbess took him out of the room she quickly read it. The words made little sense to her, and as the Abbess returned she laid the document on her bed as if it'd just fallen there. This spying would be difficult to get out of, she decided.

'He says he's left a paper,' and under her breath she said, 'he's drunk.' She took the document off the bed and Therese asked her,

'Could I see Ursula or Eric?'

'I'm sorry Therese. They've been arrested along with Sister Agnes.'

'Why?'

'Bishop Odon's got it into his head that they were involved in a plot to steal and destroy the embroidery.'

Therese started to get out of bed.

'No, Sister. There is nothing you can do today. Tomorrow the Bishop holds his inquiry at Christ Church Abbey. I believe Michael the merchant and Alfred will be there also. We will be there. I have Bishop Odon's word on that.'

As Therese entered the inquiry hall, Brother Richard of Caen went past. He nodded politely and she and the Abbess returned the compliment. Therese noticed Abbess Eleanor blush.

'Go in, go in,' urged the Abbess as Therese looked at her curiously. 'I told you that I was posing as a Brother from Caen – where he comes from!' she hissed.

Inside the dignitaries had already arrived and were seated on a platform on one side of the hall. In front of them was a space with just one writing desk, at which a clerk could stand and take notes of the proceedings. Brother David was already stooped over it. She and the Abbess were shown to the other side of the room, where they were seated in the front row facing the podium and barely more than an arm's length from Brother David.

Sitting quietly she observed Bishop Odon opposite her. He had taken the central chair with Rufus on his left and Robert Curthose on his right. Next to him sat Edgar the Aethling. Prioress Ethelburga entered and was shown to a seat next to Abbess Eleanor, while Sir Gilbert filed in with the various groups of bodyguards belonging to the nobility present, who stood behind the nuns. Finally a small group of ragged individuals were brought in. They were bound and their bodies were bent with exhaustion, they were also flanked by militia.

Ursula, Alfred, Sister Agnes, Eric and Michael. They did not look as if they could hurt a soul. Eric spotted Therese and waved; she waved back despite Abbess Eleanor's click of disapproval. They were prisoners. She knew that, but still she felt they were her friends. Yet, from what the Abbess had told her, there seemed so much evidence against them. If they were traitors then they'd deceived her. They hadn't told her lies but they'd concealed the truth. She understood Bishop Odon's need for an inquiry. She too had questions she wanted answers for. If the truth were brought out there might be some way to save their lives, even if she could not free them. How she hoped for their innocence and a way to prove it.

Odon opened the proceedings by pointing out that the prisoners were charged with plotting to steal the embroidery to ensure its destruction, and that they were involved with the earlier attempt to damage it. However he wasn't sure that the matter rested with these individuals and the only way to find out who was at the bottom of all this was to listen to their stories.

Therese wanted to complain that this was presuming their guilt. She almost stood up, but Odon added, 'This is not a court of law, just an inquiry into matters at the Priory of St Thomas and in this respect everyone's co-operation is necessary.'

She sat back and waited as Odon directed Ursula to start. The ex-Prioress explained about finding the Impostor who'd feigned deafness to gain the nuns' confidence, how they'd fought and fallen. Ursula finished with, 'I received no clue as to whom, if anyone, had directed her to do this.'

'Why did you hide?' asked Odon.

'I didn't know who to trust.'

'You could have come to me.' Odon leaned forward.

She bowed her head.

'You mean you didn't trust me? This is diabolical nonsense. What would I be doing trying to destroy a valuable item commissioned by myself?'

'Your Grace, you are a very powerful man. It is not unknown for people to be set up so that it appears they've done wrong, then they can be punished for any number of real reasons – jealousy, spite, political posturing.'

'Are you accusing me of these things?'

'No, Your Grace. I realise now that there must be a more straightforward explanation but I was horrified at the rumours put about, after my apparent death, that I was a traitor. Sister Agnes heard them as I was lying unconscious in the infirmary. When I came round she told me what was being said.'

Therese noticed Prioress Ethelburga twitch, but her tight face gave nothing away.

'That's enough for now.' Odon was clearly impatient. 'Does anyone have anything to say or questions to ask on what has just been said?'

Prioress Ethelburga remained silent.

'Alfred of St Edmundsbury, state your involvement in this matter.'

Alfred stepped forward and claimed that he'd only become involved when Sister Agnes sent word to him at Ursula's funeral. Sister Agnes had told him that his sister was already in hiding at St Augustine's disguised as a kitchen servant. He took the role of her guard until the arrival of Abbess Eleanor and Sister Therese when the three women hatched the plan to put the young novice, Therese, into the Priory of St Thomas the Apostle.

Odon turned to Abbess Eleanor. Therese felt the cold draft of anger flash across from him, Abbess Eleanor rose.

'Your Grace,' she started apologetically.

Therese stood. 'I insisted. It was my idea.'

Odon's face softened as he turned towards her. 'Foolish child,' he said. 'These older women should have known better than to place you in danger.'

The Abbess lowered her head and Ursula lowered hers further.

'I wanted to protect the embroidery,' insisted Therese.

The Abbess touched her arm. 'It does not matter now, Sister Therese.'

Odon's anger had faded to irritation. 'Yes, yes, very well,' he said letting the matter drop. Therese still spotted the frosty look he directed at Abbess Eleanor. 'Sit down both of you,' he said before addressing the row of prisoners: 'Alfred, continue.'

Alfred cleared his throat and spoke without looking at anyone but Odon de Bayeux. 'I was supposed to set up camp beyond the woods on the southern slope facing the priory, but when I got there I met a trader I knew quite well, Michael. I buy wool and he trades in threads. He invited me to stay at his camp, so I did. During the day I waited in the arranged place. I was pleased I'd made the alternative arrangements because there was a freshly dug grave higher up, where I planned to camp. I would not have wished to sleep there.'

Therese decided that she had to agree with him about that place. She would not have wished to spend the night there either.

'On one occasion though, Michael said that I was wanted up at the Priory of St Thomas. I thought perhaps Sister Therese had sent for me, but he said Prioress Ethelburga had directed him to send me to her. I was, of course, concerned as they were not meant to know I was here. I went and I was sent away. There was no such demand from Prioress Ethelburga. I assumed it was some silly joke of Michael's. When he returned to camp I argued with him about it.'

So that was why he wasn't there the day Michael brought her the boy thought Therese. The Welshman must have watched her leave the gatehouse and walk round that side of the Priory before sending Alfred on his fool's errand. Michael had needed to move quickly. That was why Michael's pony was grazing by the wood when he asked her to look after Eric.

'Do you know this child?' asked Odon of Alfred, pointing at Eric.

'He was always in Michael's camp right up until we were all arrested by your men, Your Grace.' Alfred delivered his answers in a respectful manner. 'I did not see him on our march to Dover

Castle so I assumed he'd run away when the soldiers came.'

No wonder her friends looked tired, thought Therese. They'd been marched from prison in Dover for this inquiry. But what concerned her most was that Michael, for whatever reason, seemed to have gone to a lot of trouble to secure Eric a place in the Priory and that must count against them both. Therese brought herself back to the action before her, Odon was already talking to Sister Agnes.

'Before we discuss the boy there is the matter of who lies in the grave of Prioress Ursula.'

'Your Grace, I have done a great wrong. It is Sister Anna who lies there.' Sister Agnes bowed her head. Disgusted whisperings circled the hall.

'Your penance for that sacrilege will be dealt with separately.' There was a great deal of satisfaction in Bishop Odon's voice, thought Therese. 'Now I want to know about the boy,' he continued.

'I found him a home with one of the builder's wives. He only returned on the night of the fire because he wanted to see Sister Therese.'

Therese jumped up again. 'I'd taken him in on the day of the arrests,' she said in defence of Sister Agnes.

'I have heard your story from the Abbess. This Welshman tricked you into taking the boy in, Sister, I can see that.' Odon de Bayeux gestured at Michael. Therese could not deny it. She sat down feeling confused.

'Eric helped to save the embroidery,' said Sister Agnes.

'As I told you on the night of the fire, there were thieves in the area. How do I know that you were not taking it out for them to carry away?' asked Odon.

Agnes shook her head. 'I...'

Eric shouted vehemently, 'We weren't! We weren't! We weren't!' And he stamped his foot. 'I'm not a thief and Sister Agnes is not a thief.'

'Be quiet, boy,' said Odon. The chilling note in his voice brought the child to a halt. 'If you say another word you will be removed.'

Eric slunk back into line.

As she sat listening Therese tried to sift through all the things she'd learnt over the last few weeks. There must be something that would help. She was sure they were just skimming the top of the porridge bowl of information. There was far more to be found, it was just a matter of stirring. She rose to her feet.

'I would like to ask Eric who his father is, Your Grace,' she said. If he was Norman, as Michael had said, then his credibility would be enhanced. But as she posed the question she saw Michael shake his head and cover his face with his hands.

'You may answer,' said Odon.

'My father is Elderic,' came the reply.

There was a shocked gasp from most of those present, though the name meant nothing to Therese.

'Elderic of Wales?' asked Odon through gritted teeth.

The boy nodded. 'Yes, Your Grace.'

From the reaction of the people around her she knew her question had condemned her friends.

'Elderic is responsible for endless raids on the Earls along the Welsh border region,' said Odon. 'He may have once dropped his actions against the Conqueror, but the Welsh have not submitted to the Norman rule. Your blood confirms your guilt and that of your companions.'

Therese sat down and turned to the Abbess. 'I didn't know,' she said, perplexed.

Abbess Eleanor shook her head. 'As Elderic placed his son with Michael, the rebel must respect our merchant friend. So, where does that leave Michael's loyalties?'

'But they are all innocent,' insisted Therese, gesturing to the row of her accused friends.

Chapter Twenty Four

Therese stood up to protest against the summary of justice being handed out to Ursula, Alfred, Sister Agnes, Eric and Michael. But the hall was in chaos, many of the guards, especially the three belonging to Rufus, seemed prepared to take the prisoners to the castle for immediate execution. It wasn't her Anglo-Saxon birth that drove her to rifle through her mind for something that could stir the bottom layer of this porridge of secrets. She realised her only wish now was for the truth, a slight sideways dig could well drag something to the top.

'Your Grace, another matter has recently come to my attention, which may be relevant.' Therese stood her ground and repeated her statement until Odon called for calm. She looked at Brother David and wondered what he would say as she mentioned what she'd seen in one of his documents she'd read in her room. The hall became quiet.

'Your Grace, Bishop Odon de Bayeux, I wish to address Edgar the Aethling.'

She felt a hand on her arm and looked down towards its owner, Abbess Eleanor.

'This is not advisable,' said the Abbess.

'I understand that Edgar Aethling was in this area of Kent for a particular purpose,' explained Therese, trying to remember the details in the letter and trying to ignore the Abbess. It had been sent from the clergy at Winchester and was addressed to Archbishop Lanfranc. The comment about Edgar's visit was made in passing with other news. She could not tell Bishop Odon that she'd been reading the great man's correspondence. Presumably Brother David had been in St Augustine's the day she read the letter because he wanted to discuss its contents with the Aethling who was also staying there, and that was why he'd strayed into her room.

'Yes.' Edgar answered her directly. 'I was here for a reason, but not one that is anybody's business but my own.'

'I think it is all of our business. I understand you went to see your sister at Wilton and she told you about the Priory of St Thomas the Apostle.' The letter mentioned he'd asked about the place.

Brother David stared at her.

Odon turned to her and asked, 'You mean, Sister Therese that Edgar Aethling is somehow involved in all of this?'

'I believe so.'

Next to her Abbess Eleanor muttered the word, 'Scotland.'

Hadn't Abbess Eleanor mentioned something about Edgar Aethling and Scotland when she was talking about her investigations, Therese wondered.

Brother David shifted from one foot to the other. Therese wasn't sure if he was going to accuse her of reading Archbishop Lanfranc's letter, but he clearly decided against it and returned to his work of documenting the proceedings.

But Bishop Odon was shouting at Edgar Aethling, 'The thieves melted away. I knew you'd given them warning. You just created a show as an excuse for being in the area.'

'We rescued Ursula.'

'But she's a traitor too. She worked in the Scottish Court.'

'You've got this all wrong,' said the Aethling. 'I was, indeed, interested in the Priory of St Thomas the Apostle – that is true. I was looking for someone. Back home I received a letter from a distant cousin of yours that their daughter was missing. Her family did not want to alarm anyone in the family as they thought she'd gone to a religious establishment in England. They asked me to make enquiries as they knew my sister, Christina, is in holy orders over here. When I spoke to her, she suggested I tried St Thomas's among others.'

Therese sat down, her mind racing. If this girl went to St Thomas's then, 'The Impostor was a Norman,' she blurted out. 'The Norman Knight who left our ship in the storm and visited the Impostor's grave was not visiting a grave of an Anglo-Saxon lover, but the grave of his Norman love.' She looked at Edgar. 'The girl you were looking for was our Impostor.'

Edgar Aethling looked baffled.

'What is the meaning of this?' asked Bishop Odon of Therese.

'Your Grace, there cannot be a plot to destroy the embroidery and to steal it. If the Anglo-Saxons wanted it destroyed all they had to do was leave it in the fire. Why put it over the back wall?'

'But you told your Abbess that the person setting light to the panels was Sister Hilda, an Anglo-Saxon.'

'I know but listen, Your Grace,' she implored. 'On the last day I cleaned the sewing room on my own. This was my opportunity to see the whole final panel at long last. I lifted the cover and was enchanted by the quality of the work and the brightness of the threads. But it did not take me long to see what it depicted.'

'It showed the coronation of William the Conqueror,' said Odon. 'I commissioned it. So of course I know what is on it!'

'But the coronation was not an auspicious occasion. There was confusion at the combined English and Norman voices hailing the new King. The guards outside reacted and buildings were set on fire.'

'The panel should not have shown that.'

'It didn't. But even I in my convent in Bayeux have heard the story. Everyone would have known the depiction to be a lie.'

'That confirms that the Anglo-Saxons are behind it.'

'No, Your Grace, I think the opposite. I think a fellow Norman, someone loyal to the King. Whoever did it did not wish William the Conqueror to be remembered thus.'

'This is absurd,' said Odon.

'I do believe, Your Grace, that the plot was never more than to destroy this one panel,' said Therese reaching the end of her thread of reasoning with some relief.

Robert de Curthose stood up and addressed the room in a formal manner. 'This, I'm afraid is an unfounded assumption. It does not stand up to examination. For one thing, no-one knew what was on the last panel. Bishop Odon kept the matter a secret.'

'Secrets get out,' said Therese flatly.

'And, anyway,' continued Robert, 'if I felt that the panel design was inappropriate I would simply speak to my uncle and I am sure, as a man of reason, he would make suitable adjustments.'

'You are not being accused of anything Robert,' said Odon.

'The perpetrator is not within Bishop Odon's immediate circle,' said Therese now feeling bold.

'You have not explained away Hilda – the Anglo-Saxon.' Odon was frowning at Therese – his face was thunderous. She felt her knees weaken.

'After the Impostor fell to her death,' she said, 'the conspirators could not place another of their own in danger so they tricked an Anglo-Saxon sympathiser into doing it, Hilda was already involved. The conspirators had arranged for her to attack the embroidery if the Impostor failed on the day of the attempted inking. They did not realise, though, about the secret room which Hilda learnt about at the last minute through my thoughtlessness. I thought, from what Sister Hilda had said, or rather not said, in the burning room that she'd stolen the key for the Impostor. It didn't seem to matter who from. But now I realise she hadn't stolen the key. Someone else had left it for the Impostor.'

'So there is still someone at St Thomas's who was involved?' demanded Odon.

Therese turned to Ursula, 'who did you give the key to, Prioress Ursula?'

'Well, I was going to give it to Sister Winifred, but she wanted to run some errand or other, so I gave it to,' she paused briefly, 'Sister Ethelburga, as she was then. I always assumed it must have been stolen from her. She's always been so reliable, so efficient.'

'So overlooked,' said Prioress Ethelburga rising. She ran for the door.

'Detain her,' said Odon.

A guard caught her by the arm.

'It had to be Prioress Ethelburga,' said Therese. 'She protected Hilda after the inking incident. I suspect she had to stop Hilda inking the panel when Ursula and the Impostor left the sewing room because others were already behind her. It did not take much for Prioress Ethelburga to persuade her to take another opportunity to destroy it, and be rid of me at the same time.'

'Who is behind this?' Odon asked Prioress Ethelburga.

She looked at the King's sons flanking Odon. 'Ask them,' she said.

Therese was aware of Abbess Eleanor rising to her feet next to her. She could see she was trembling slightly.

'I wish to direct a question to Prince William Rufus?' the Abbess asked Odon.

The Bishop nodded.

'On the night of the fire that destroyed the Priory of St Thomas the Apostle, Prince William Rufus and his guards left Christ Church Abbey and headed out in the direction of St Thomas's. I wondered why he went.'

Odon turned to the bright-red-headed man on his left. 'Yes,' he said. 'You never answered me that question. Let us have your answer.'

'You sent me word yourself,' complained Rufus.

'I'm afraid I did not,' said Odon. 'So how was the news relayed to you?'

'My guard told me. Roger!' Rufus pinned a pale, steely stare at the tallest of his guards.

Roger made no movement.

Therese looked around the room. The stirring had worked, but they weren't quite there yet. The porridge was still and settling heavily and without resolution. She wondered how long Bishop Odon would indulge her forwardness, but he would have to, for she still had plenty to say. 'Your Grace, may I ask Prioress Ethelburga how she gets her instructions?'

Odon seemed pleased that the heat seemed to be shifting away from the King's sons seated next to him. 'Carry on,' he said.

So Therese repeated the question to the Prioress but she would not reply. 'It does not matter,' said Therese. 'Because Abbess Eleanor and I have seen the communications taking place. Please, Your Grace, could you bring in Brother Richard of Caen.'

Odon nodded at the guards at the door and Brother Richard was brought in, the militia handled him roughly into the space in front of the Bishop.

'Brother Richard, I believe to be innocent in all of this,' said Therese. 'May I question him?' she asked Odon.

'Carry on,' said Odon, he seemed much calmer now.

'Brother Richard of Caen, you carry letters to and from the various building sites you visit?'

'This is usual practice,' said Brother Richard straightening his tunic over his extended belly.

'Do you bring messages from Prioress Ethelburga to Christ Church Abbey?'

'I do and back again.'

'Who do you hand them to?'

'Brother David deals with all the letters here, but the ones from Prioress Ethelburga are directed to him personally. Does that help?' he asked as the Prioress wriggled against the guard who still gripped her tightly.

'I object,' said Brother David. He dropped his pen and the document he'd been writing slipped to the floor.

'No, this makes sense,' said Abbess Eleanor. 'Brother David went to great lengths to stop me seeing Archbishop Lanfranc. I did get to see him the other night and it was clear that he had not been kept informed of anything that had happened at the Priory of St Thomas. What other reason would Brother David have for keeping these matters secret if he himself was not involved in them?'

'Abbess Eleanor has also seen Brother David in deep conversation with one of Prince William Rufus's guards,' explained Therese. 'Do you recognise which one, Abbess?'

The older nun examined the three of them. They stood haughtily with their faces tilted away from Therese and the Abbess. Abbess Eleanor shook her head. 'I cannot be sure. He was tall, but compared to Brother David they all look tall. I don't think he was fair.'

'I will not tolerate this.' Rufus jumped up. 'I have had nothing to do with this affair. The whole matter would be instantly settled by removing these Anglo-Saxon troublemakers. I can have them put to the sword and that will be the end of it.'

Therese felt her stirring had resulted in the porridge bowl falling and spilling its contents on the floor; this was a disaster. 'Your Grace, I can explain.' She caught his angry gaze and smiled sweetly.

'Sit down and be silent, Prince Rufus. We will get to the bottom of this.' Odon directed his thunderous voice at his nephew. 'Are you women accusing Prince William Rufus of this plot?' Odon was more incredulous than angry as he questioned Therese and the Abbess.

'I don't think he is to blame,' said Therese. 'I think he would tell you if he thought you were doing something wrong – the same as Robert de Curthose would.'

Odon flinched.

Therese paused, and took a deep breath. Courage and foolhardiness sometimes seemed inseparable. 'What, Your Grace, do you think of my behaviour today?'

'It does not befit your station, but I have tolerated it because of your youth.'

'And so many more of my actions have been down to my naivety. I have been impetuous and inclined to do the wrong thing because of a lack of experience. I act almost before I think.'

'So now you are blaming yourself!' Odon laughed.

'There is another prince, a younger one, who might wish to protect his father, if he was ill-advised.'

'Henry? Young Prince Henry!' exclaimed Odon.

Chapter Twenty Five

Therese could see that Bishop Odon's mind was making the same connections as hers. He turned to Prioress Ethelburga and asked, 'Have you been communicating with Brother David?' Ethelburga nodded. 'Brother David,' continued Odon, 'Have you been writing to my nephew, Henry?'

'I have. But I have only been passing on the facts.' Brother David's voice tailed off into a wail.

'Facts can be displayed in whatever manner we please,' said Odon. 'You must have had access to at least one of Prince Henry's guards.'

'He was the one who advised Prince Henry,' complained Brother David scraping his documents together and pointing at Sir Roger.

'Stay where you are, Brother David,' directed Odon. 'All those responsible will be dealt with, but Prince Henry will be protected. Guards, arrest him. All documents pertaining to the case shall be burnt once I have gone through them myself with my own clerk. The last panel will not be remade. The embroidery is already being transported to Bayeux.'

William Rufus stood up his face flushed bristling with anger. 'You were involved in this, Roger. This is just like you.' He did not need to say any more as Ralph and Simon were already holding him.

'I did it for you, Prince William. The little prince is a popular boy. Discrediting him would have done you nothing but good.'

Therese looked at Prince William Rufus, was he really as unknowing as he made out. It was clear no-one was going to challenge him and she had her own agenda. She gripped her hands together. She was nearly there. 'And the prisoners?' Therese asked looking at her friends still raggedly lined up, their heads down. The fact that she'd cleared them of suspicion had not taken away their fear.

'Let the Anglo-Saxons go free. They have been misjudged. But the Welsh are still a danger, they will remain in custody.'

Ursula and Alfred embraced and Sister Agnes squeezed their arms warmly. Prioress Ethelburga and Roger were quickly removed, and once the Royalty had left, the guards removed Brother David and his papers. Therese and the Abbess rushed forwards to hug Ursula, Alfred and Agnes, but while they did so Therese saw Michael and Eric led away. It was too late to plead for them with Odon already gone and her heart sank.

Therese looked out of Dover Castle across the river mouth and harbour. 'I shall miss my friends at St Thomas's,' she said to the Abbess who was standing next to her.

'They are no longer there. They have all gone to different places. Ursula has gone to Scotland with Edgar the Aethling to be with Queen Margaret. But you may see them all again someday, and you will soon be seeing Sister Miriam.'

'Still,' persisted Therese, 'I would like to see some of them again sooner than that!'

'At Christmas the embroidery will be displayed and blessed at Bayeux. I think it would be good for some of the sisters who made it to come across to celebrate its safe completion.'

'That will be wonderful,' said Therese. 'Thank you.' But, after a few minutes, melancholia crept back. 'Abbess I can not sleep at night,' she said. She had given up trying to hide her troubled mind from the Abbess.

'You have done so much, Sister Therese. You have got at the truth. No-one could do more than that.'

'But Eric and Michael are still in prison for something they did not do.'

The Abbess looked down and turned away. 'There is nothing more you can do, let the matter rest. We will soon be back in Bayeux.'

As Therese watched her leave, it felt as if the insides of her chest were burning. She would have to try.

Therese waited for permission to enter Bishop Odon's chamber, and when it came the fire of injustice in her chest seemed to have been put out. She tried to stir the embers by thinking of little Eric in prison. She had courage for them, even if she had none for herself.

'Your Grace, I have come to plead for the freedom of the boy Eric and Michael the merchant,' she said.

Bishop Odon was seated. There were piles of papers about him and he looked tired. 'I have received a letter from the Conqueror, our King. He says that he wants to know why there was such a collection of powerful men at arms within my jurisdiction, and that if he feels I am becoming too powerful I will have to take the consequences. I am not in a position to let traitors go.'

Therese was emboldened by receiving this level of confidence in her. 'Your Grace, because of your constant kindness to me and your patronage I know you are a man of principle and that you will do what you can for them. I am sure you can arrange something that would be to your advantage also.'

He seemed to perk up at this idea. 'Leave it with me,' said Odon, patting her hand.

Odon would do anything for Therese. The Anglo-Saxon girl still clutched at his heart like the baby he held in his arms at Romney all those years ago. He thought of her as a daughter and he'd been so proud of her intelligence and bravery at his inquiry. Even now he knew she was right. He could use this situation to his advantage, with Therese and Abbess Eleanor safely on their way to Bayeux he would interview Michael the merchant.

A guard announced the arrival of the prisoner and Odon braced himself into a stolid position, his legs slightly apart and his hands clasped behind his back. 'Bring him in.'

The man was brought before him, his black hair and ragged clothing wet from the bucket of water someone had thought was a good idea to throw over him. The smell of the prison was not so easily removed.

'Michael, merchant of Montgomery, I have a proposal. I will free the boy, Eric, and yourself on one condition.'

Michael was still arranging himself into a position which was clearly meant to give him some dignity. He cleared his throat. 'What is that, Your Grace?' he asked.

'That you arrange for King William to ride into Wales unopposed; that you make suitable arrangements with the Welsh

Kings. Can you do that?'

'I am just a humble merchant, Your Grace.'

'I think not! You have Elderic's son in your care. He will listen to you and he will make the Welsh Kings listen.'

'In the south it will be easier than in the north, Your Grace.'

'Then do it, and inform me of the most auspicious route for the Conqueror to take.'

'Yes, Your Grace.'

'The boy means a lot to you, then?'

'Yes, Your Grace.'

'When all has been arranged, the boy will be released.'

With that Michael was removed.

At last Therese was able to look at the embroidery, all of it, unhindered. The formalities were over. It adorned Notre Dame Cathedral in Bayeux and she was here for its blessing and exhibition. Abbess Eleanor was at the head of the procession of nuns as they walked past the fabric panels. Therese was towards the back with Miriam, who was clearly trying not to bounce as she took in the visual feast before her.

The royals were here too for the Christmas inauguration. She hadn't seen the Conqueror before and realised how much Prince Rufus was like him. The three princely brothers were already outside enjoying the heat from one of the braziers while their mother was talking to Bishop Odon de Bayeux.

As Therese left the Cathedral she spotted Sisters Leofgyth, Sybil, Beatrice, Winifred and Aelfgyth filing out. She was given permission to go to see them. On reaching them she gave them all a hug except Sybil and Beatrice who greeted her more formerly. After the usual exchanges she soon found herself catching up with events with Leofgyth.

Without warning Leofgyth reached into her pocket and pulled out a familiar container. The little pottery bottle with the narrow neck which had contained the ink. Therese realised they had drifted away from the nuns.

'Leofgyth,' said Therese wistfully. 'I thought it had been destroyed when the fire took hold of the chapel.'

'Did you never wonder why in that week between you finding Sister Hilda's ink bottle and the fire she didn't destroy the panels?' said Leofgyth. 'She'd just worked out about the room from cleaning with you.'

'She started to say something about trying again that night in the fire.'

'I saw you and Sister Hilda in the chapel when you followed her. It's a wonder you didn't wake everyone up.' She gave the last words a little teasing spike. 'Anyway,' she continued, 'when you made her return the bottle to its hiding place, I went down and took it.' She handed the bottle to Therese. 'A memento.'

Therese gingerly turned it over in her hand.

'I washed it,' said Leofgyth.

'Thank you,' said Therese transferring it to her pocket. When she looked up Leofgyth and the English nuns had melted into the crowd.

She moved in the direction she'd left Sister Miriam and soon found herself close to one of the braziers. She couldn't resist the chance to warm her hands so it took a few moments before she realised she was standing next to Edgar the Aethling. She wasn't sure if it was coincidence that brought them together or whether he'd spotted her and now wished to make her uncomfortable for accusing him at Odon de Bayeux's inquiry. Robert de Curthose left his brothers and came over too.

'People give gifts for many reasons,' said Edgar to Therese. 'Being able to create and give such a thing as this embroidery is in itself a show of power. For every great achievement there is always one who looks upon it with jealous eyes.'

'The Bishop deserves his moment of glory,' said Robert.

Their good humour warmed her more than the fire.

'And I have this young lady to thank for removing me from suspicion.'

'She accused you first!' exclaimed Robert.

'But she explained everything,' said Edgar. 'I could not give up the trust I'd given to Judith's family...'

'Judith?' asked Therese. 'Was that her name, the Impostor?'

'Please, don't call her that,' said Edgar. 'Odon de Bayeux was already deeply distrustful of my reasons for being in Kent. I have you to thank for bringing out the truth. Judith's family, however, will never get over it.'

The King was making his way towards the hall.

'The Conqueror is very pleased with the way the year has gone. His march into Wales was a big success,' said Robert.

'South Wales,' corrected Edgar.

'It will keep him happy for a while,' said Robert.

The Queen waved to Robert de Curthose. 'We must take our leave of you,' said Robert.

'If ever you need any help, Sister Therese,' said Edgar, 'please do not hesitate to ask for my assistance.' Edgar Aethling gave a little bow and said, 'Merry Christmas,' before leaving her.

Acknowledgements

The origins of this book go back to a memorable family holiday in Normandy. This resulted in a considerable period of study to bring together all the elements that form the story. Key to this was my tutor Trefor Jones and his solid, almost inexhaustible, supply of information. His enthusiasm and interest in all aspects of the period were invaluable.

The joys and tribulations of writing the first draft were shared with my lovely friends at King's Lynn Writers' Circle, particularly long term members Sue Welfare, Chris Gutteridge, Gina Gutteridge, Maggie, Val and Jim. They listened to each chapter and were always helpful in every way. Sadly Jim and Gina are no longer with us.

When it started to look like a book Alison and Victoria Haines gave their time generously in reading it through and giving their valued comments.

I wish also to thank my work colleagues, Willie, Silke, Spencer, Karen and Ross for their enthusiasm and support for this enterprise.

During the time this book was self-published on the internet a number of people reviewed it. All their feedback has been welcome. Also, my commissioning editor at Pen and Sword, Laura Hirst, has been incredibly efficient and innovative. She has also been amazingly patient with me.

And, the book would not be here without my wonderful family, my husband, Bill, son, Ted, and daughter, Rosie, who are always understanding, encouraging and reassuring.

ALSO AVAILABLE FROM CLAYMORE PRESS...

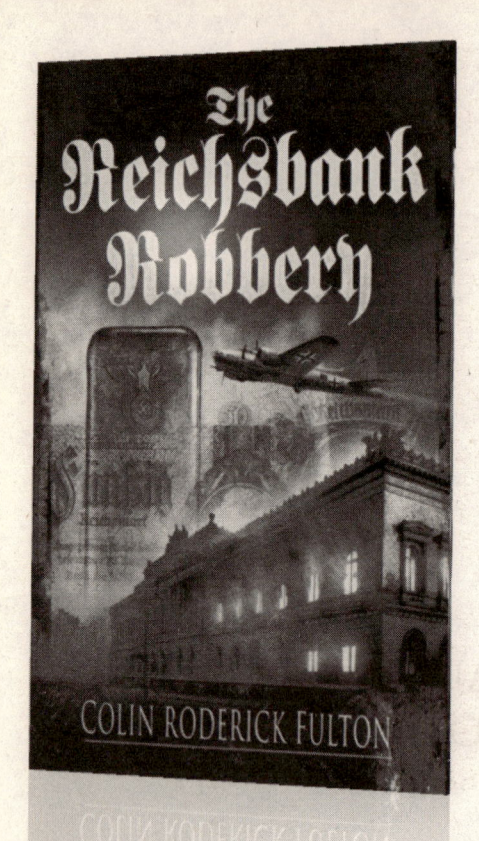

9781781590782 •
336 pages • £8.99

In February 1945 the US Air Force launched the largest day time bombing offensive against Berlin, dropping over 2,250 tons of bombs on the German capital.

The Reichsbank, Germany's state bank, received 21 direct hits. This left the building badly damaged, its vaults unsafe and meant that most of its contents were at risk.

The German authorities made the decision to take most of the Reichsbank's treasure away and hide it for safekeeping. Some $200 million US in gold bars, weighing around 100 tons, plus much of the paper currency reserves, as well as a great deal of foreign currency (approximately $4 million in US currency alone) was sent in trains from Berlin.

All this loot was placed in a salt mine at a place called Merkers. This was captured intact by the US Army. After this disaster, the Germans spent the next six weeks transferring their remaining bullion and currency reserves around what remained of the Reich in armoured trains, an area that included parts of northern Italy, Czechoslovakia, Austria and Germany, looking for somewhere safe.

Much of the treasure actually either ended up back in Berlin, was stolen, disappeared or, was captured, mainly by American troops and the SS.

This novel, by Colin Roderick Fulton, imagines one plot which could have been enacted around this time. The mystery surrounding the locations and ultimate destiny of the liberated treasures provides fertile ground on which to impose such a fiction. Secrecy, intrigue, and fast paced action combine to create a well paced novel, sure to appeal to fans of wartime fiction.

COMING HOME

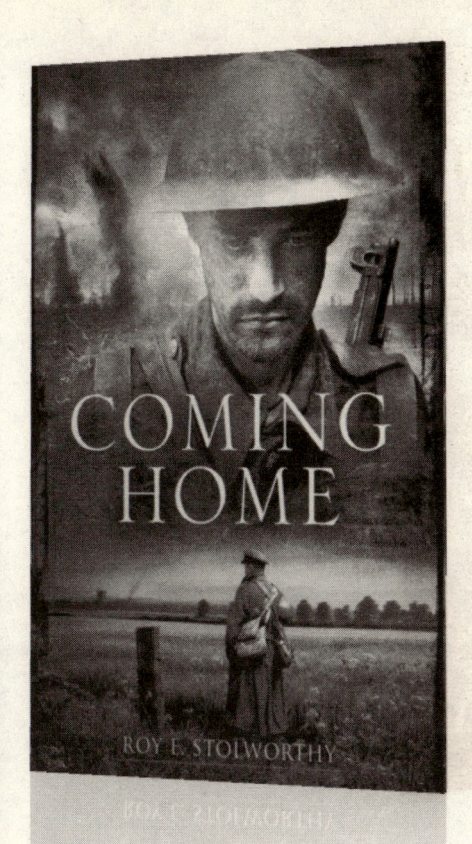

ROY E. STOLWORTHY

9781781590713 •
368 pages • £7.99

A brutally honest portrayal of the realities of war, this novel relays the story of fifteen-year-old Thomas Elkin as he engages in the First World War. A tale of conflict, both global and personal, and of redemption, this is a novel that has the potential to rank alongside the best of retrospective First World War literature. Accepting the blame for the accidental death of his recently conscripted brother, Elkin switches identity with his dead sibling and enters into the fray of the conflict. His burning ambition is to die a glorious death in his brother's name.

Believing that in fully submitting to the reality of war he is atoning for his sins, he faces all the attendant horrors with a steel will and a poignant resignation.

His personal conflict sees itself mirrored in the wider events and soon the two are inextricably linked raising issues of mortality, morality, guilt and faith. This novel enacts the kind of existential crises experienced on the battlefield with the constant threat of the imminent and fatal danger a companion.

Written with deft skill and sensitivity for the subject matter at hand, this is a piece of stylish work that places the reader at the heart of the action. Featuring nuanced characters and vivid action scenes, it works to evoke a real sense of the times as the story unfolds.

BLOCKADE RUNNER

DAVID KENT-LEMON

9781781590645 •
320 pages • £9.99

It is 1861. Tom Wells is in pursuit of a girl from North Carolina. He accepts an offer from his employer to leave the quiet obscurity of his job as an office boy in a London shipping firm to cross the Atlantic to Nassau in the Bahamas. Now he must face the hazards of the Union blockade of the Confederate ports in the American Civil War. Tom's bravado may help him with the dangers of running the blockade, but how will he cope with the conflicting issues of love, loyalty and morality as he becomes entangled with a lady of easy virtue in Nassau?

Tom's adventures take him through the perilous triangle between Nassau, Charleston and Wilmington NC, where he must smuggle arms and munitions through a gauntlet of Union warships to the Southern ports, bringing cotton and tobacco back to Nassau.

David Kent-Lemon presents us here with a fast paced and dynamic narrative, exploring a fascinating, dramatic and less well known corner of that extraordinary conflict – the American Civil War. The characters are finely drawn, with the balance between deceit and morality offset by courage and humour. The realism and historical accuracy of the background complete the picture.

As the Civil War reaches its climax, so does the drama in Tom's life, heightened by the historical events within which he is embroiled.

ROBERT SOUTHWORTH

SPARTACUS
TALONS OF AN EMPIRE

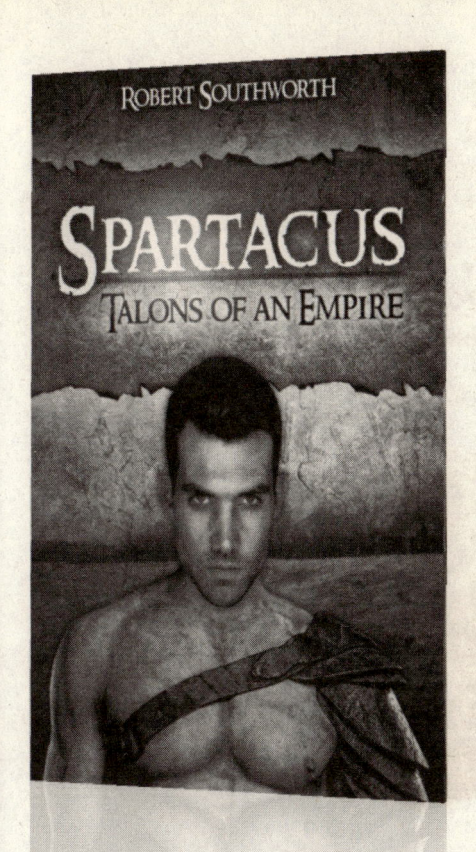

9781781590843 •
208 pages • £8.99

This enthralling piece of work by first-time novelist Robert Southworth explores the avenue history could have run down if Spartacus had survived the slave rebellion in 73BC, an uprising whose aftermath didn't deliver the remains of the famous slave leader. The brute force of this famous figure of Roman history is relayed, and the events of the period re-imagined to great effect. The work is sure to appeal to fans of Roman history, as well as those enamored by stories of action and adventure. Whilst the figure of Spartacus continues to hold massive appeal for contemporary audiences, this work offers a fresh vision of the Roman era; a dark and brutal reenactment of high gladiatorial drama.

**9781781592403 •
320 pages • £9.99**

When Germany's leading tank ace meets the Steppe Fox it's a fight to the death. Faced with overwhelming odds Kampfgruppe von Schroif needs a better tank and fast; but the new Tiger tank is still on the drawing board and von Schroif must overcome bureaucracy, espionage and relentless Allied bombing to get the Tiger into battle in time to meet the ultimate challenge.

Based on a true story of combat on the Russian Front, this powerful new novel is written by Emmy™ Award winning writer Bob Carruthers and newcomer Sinclair McLay. It tells the gripping saga of how the Tiger tank was born and a legend was forged in the heat of combat. Gritty, intense and breath-taking in its detail, this sprawling epic captures the reality of the lives and deaths of the tank crews fighting for survival on the Eastern Front, a remarkable novel worthy of comparison with 'Das Boot'.

THE TRIANGLE TRADE
GEOFF WOODLAND

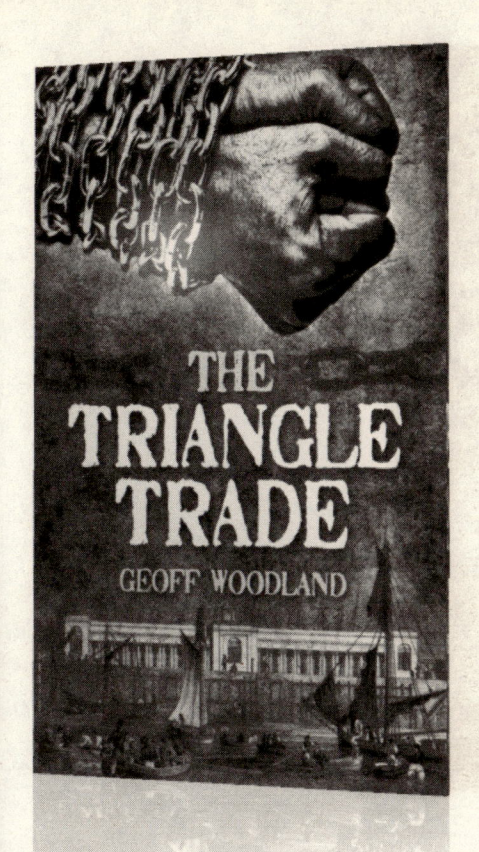

9781781591741 •
272 pages • £9.99

In 1804, Liverpool was the largest slave trading port in Great Britain, yet her influential traders felt threatened by the success, in Parliament, of the anti-slavery movement. Few, in Liverpool, condemned the 'Trade'. William King, son of a Liverpool slave trader, sickened by what he experienced aboard a Spanish slaver, was one of the few who did speak out. This epic, set during the dying days of this despicable practice, weaves themes of generational change, moral wickedness, greed, romance, and the fortunes of war as they impact upon the lives of a father and son caught up in the turmoil that preceded the implementation of the British Trade Act of 1807, which would end Britain's involvement in the slave trade.

The city of Liverpool is one still scarred by its past involvement with the morally contemptible Triangle Trade. Indeed, the cities prosperity was built on the profits of slavery, and the reverberations of this inheritance continue to impact on the city today. This novel roots the reader firmly in a city on the brink of change, evoking a real sense of the struggles at play, and informing our understanding of the realities of slavery, those who fueled its continuation and those who brought about its eventual cessation, as well as the legacy inherited by the City of Liverpool and the wider world.

9781781591734 •
256 pages • £9.99

Peenemünde: windswept corner of the Third Reich and birthplace of the space age. Otto Fischer, a severely wounded Luftwaffe officer and former criminal investigator, is summoned to solve a seemingly incomprehensible case: the murder of a leading rocket engineer during a devastating air-raid. With only days until the SS assume control of the production of a remarkable new weapon, Fischer must find a motive and perpetrator from among several thousand scientists, technicians, soldiers and forced labourers. As he struggles to get the measure of a secretive, brilliant world in which imagination moves far beyond the limits of technology, what at first appears to be a solitary crime draws him into a labyrinth of conspiracy, betrayal and treason.

McDermott brings skills previously honed whilst producing well-researched history books to the discipline of writing fiction, creating work that is both historically accurate and evocative as well as stylish in a literary sense.

If you would like to read some of these fantastic new fiction titles you can order your copies direct from
PEN & SWORD BOOKS

Please call 01226 734222

Or order online via our website:
www.pen-and-sword.co.uk